STAYING HOME IS A KILLER

"If you like cozy mysteries that have plenty of action and lots of suspects and clues, *Staying Home Is a Killer* will be a fun romp through murder and mayhem. This is a mystery with a 'mommy lit' flavor. . . . A fun read."
  —*Armchair Interviews*

"Thoroughly entertaining. The author's smooth, succinct writing style enables the plot to flow effortlessly until its captivating conclusion."
  —*Romantic Times Book Reviews* (four stars)

"A satisfying, well-executed cozy . . . The author inclues practical tips for organizing closets, but the novel's most valuable insight is its window into women's lives on a military base."
  —*Publishers Weekly*

MOVING IS MURDER

"A fun debut for an appealing young heroine."
  —Carolyn Hart, author of the Death on Demand mystery series

"Armed with her baby and her wits, new mom and military spouse Ellie Avery battles to unmask a wily killer in this exciting debut mystery. A squadron of suspects, a unique setting, and a twisted plot will keep you turning pages!"
  —Nancy J. Cohen, author of the Bad Hair Day mystery series

"Everyone should snap to attention and salute this fresh new voice. Interesting characters, a tight plot, and an insider peek at the life of a military wife make this a terrific read."
  —Denise Swanson, nationally bestselling author of the Scumble River mystery series

"An absorbing read that combines sharp writing and tight plotting with a fascinating peek into the world of military wives. Jump in!"
—Cynthia Baxter, author of the Reigning Cats & Dogs mystery series

"Reading Sara Rosett's *Moving is Murder* is like making a new friend—I can't wait to brew a pot of tea and read all about sleuth Ellie Avery's next adventure!"
—Leslie Meier, author of the Lucy Stone mystery series

"Mayhem, murder, and the military! Sara Rosett's debut crackles with intrigue. Set in a very realistic community of military spouses, *Moving Is Murder* keeps you turning pages through intricate plot twists and turns. Rosett is an author to watch."
—Alesia Holliday, author of the December Vaughn mystery series

"A cozy debut that'll help you get organized and provide entertainment in your newfound spare time."
—*Kirkus Reviews*

"Packed with helpful moving tips, Rosett's cute cozy debut introduces perky Ellie Avery . . . an appealing heroine, an intriguing insider peek into air force life."
—*Publishers Weekly*

"Ellie's intelligent investigation highlights this mystery. There are plenty of red herrings along her path to solving the murderous puzzle—along with expert tips on organizing a move. The stunning conclusion should delight readers."
—*Romantic Times*

Magnolias, Moonlight, and Murder

Sara Rosett

KENSINGTON BOOKS
http://www.kensingtonbooks.com

KENSINGTON BOOKS are published by

Kensington Publishing Corp.
119 West 40th Street
New York, NY 10018

All Kensington titles, imprints, and distributed lines are
available at special quantity discounts for bulk purchases for sales promotion, premiums, fund-raising, educational, or institutional use.

Special book excerpts or customized printings can also
be created to fit specific needs. For details, write or phone
the office of the Kensington Special Sales Manager: Attn.
Special Sales Department. Kensington Publishing Corp.,
119 West 40th Street, New York, NY 10018. Phone: 1-800-
221-2647.

ISBN-13: 978-0-7582-2682-2
ISBN-10: 0-7582-2682-9

First Hardcover Printing: April 2009
First Mass Market Paperback Printing: March 2010

10 9 8 7 6 5 4 3 2 1

Printed in the United States of America

Chapter One

One hour. Just give it one hour, I told myself. That's the advice I give my organizing clients when clutter overwhelms them. Break up the large jobs into smaller tasks. It's what I told Livvy when her attempts to write her name nearly drove her to tears. One letter at a time. One chunk of clutter at a time.

Of course it's easier to give advice than to follow it yourself, I decided as I folded the flaps back on a box that contained our tax returns from the last five years. It was the same box I'd opened almost an hour ago, but life, in the form of dirty diapers, lost socks, and a spider in the bathroom sink had whittled away at my time.

Mitch stuck his head around the door frame of the spare bedroom and said, "Wow, doesn't look like you've gotten much done."

His tone was matter-of-fact, but I was aggravated. "That's because I haven't." I surveyed the room and decided we were in denial. The bed frame and mattresses were propped against the wall so we could fit stacks of boxes into the rest of the space. "This isn't a spare bedroom. This is a storage room."

"There's nothing wrong with having a storage room," Mitch said in the same reasonable tone.

"There is if you're a professional organizer. I should have

had these boxes unpacked months ago. We've lived here for *ten* months. I always unpack all our boxes right away."

"It's a well-known fact that professional organizers who have a three-year-old and a toddler get an exemption from perfection. Let's tackle it this weekend. I'll help."

"No. That's okay," I said quickly. "I'll try to get in another hour tomorrow." It was sweet of him to offer, but if I let Mitch unpack these boxes I'd probably never find the tax records again. He'd put them anywhere there was an open space. They could end up under a bed or in the laundry room. I clambered over two boxes to get to the door. "Sorry I'm so crabby, but knowing we have all this stuff crammed in here is like an annoying gnat that keeps buzzing around my head."

"You'll get it done," Mitch said, and rubbed the back of my neck as we walked down the hall. "How about a relaxing game of Galaga after we get the kids in bed?"

I'd found a game system with Mitch's favorite classic arcade games for his birthday. "Yeah, that'll help," I said dryly. I had to be the worst player ever. "Let me get in a walk first before it gets dark."

"Great idea. I'll get the stroller." Mitch had already gone for his run, but he was always up for any type of workout.

"No, I meant a walk by myself." The words popped out before I had time to check them.

"Oh." I could tell from his subdued tone that I'd hurt his feelings.

"Mitch, I'm sorry, but I need some time alone."

He leaned back on his side of the hall and crossed his arms. "Why don't you want to spend time together, just us? Every night, it's like you can't wait to sprint out the door for your walk. You're already by yourself all day."

I gaped at him. "How can you say that?" I usually get tongue-tied when I'm in a heated discussion, but not this time. "No, I'm not. I have two kids and a dog with me *all the time*. That's not being alone." I braced myself on the other side of the hall. "While you're talking to adults, going to lunch with the guys, and working out, I'm making peanut butter and jelly sandwiches and changing dirty diapers. I load and unload that dishwasher so much I feel like I run a restaurant and I know every word to 'There's a Hole in My Bucket,' which has to be the most annoying song in the world."

I blew out a breath, trying to calm down. I hated it when we argued. "Look, I want some couple time for us, too, but I feel like I'm being pulled in a million directions. The kids are so . . . labor-intensive right now. A twenty-minute walk is a sanity break."

"My job isn't all fun and games either," he said quietly. Mitch never raised his voice. He just got quieter and more still.

"I know that. I know being in the squadron is stressful, too." How could I explain? "Imagine if you never left the squadron. You were *always* at work. That's how it is for me."

Arms extended straight in front of her, Livvy "flew" between us, the pillowcase I'd pinned to her shoulders flapping out behind her. "I'm Super Livvy," she shouted. Nathan "cruised" behind her, stumbling along on his pudgy legs as he transferred his grip from one piece of furniture to another to help him keep his balance. He gripped my knees for a second as he passed, then inched his way down the hall with one hand on the wall.

We stared at each other for a few seconds; then Mitch cracked a small smile. "Reminds me of my office. 'There's a Hole in My Bucket,' huh?"

My shoulders relaxed and I smiled, too. "As sung by Goofy, but don't say it too loud or Livvy will break into song."

Mitch stepped away from the wall. "You go on. I'll get Super Livvy and her sidekick in their pajamas."

I slid my arm around his waist and kissed him. "Thanks."

A few minutes later, I punched in the remote code to close the garage door and then let out the leash as our Rottweiler, Rex, ran down our long driveway. He'd been waiting for me at the door, ears perked and an air of barely suppressed expectation nearly vibrating off him. With two weeks of almost constant rain, his walks had been severely curtailed. I rotated my shoulders and tried to put our spat out of my mind and enjoy being outdoors.

It was still slightly muggy, but the humidity was so much lower than it had been during the summer. After our move to Georgia in January, we'd enjoyed two months of ideal weather and I now understood snowbirds. A winter without snow tires was such a welcome break after our last assignment in Washington State, where it would already be cold by now and there might possibly be snow. Here in middle Georgia, the only signs of fall were pumpkins dotting the wide porches. Even though we were barely halfway down the block, a fine layer of sweat beaded my hairline and my shirt plastered itself to my shoulder blades.

I wondered what my old neighbors, Mabel and Ed Parsons, would think of our new neighborhood. We'd gone from an arts and crafts bungalow that could verifiably be called an antique to a house built three years ago. Only one occupant before us. We had all the bells and whistles now: remote garage door opener, garbage disposal, security system, and those clever windows that fold down inside so you can clean the outside of them without leaving the house. Although I didn't see much window cleaning in my immediate future. In fact, my days seemed to consist only of keeping the basic necessities of our life clean: the clothes, the dishes, and (sometimes) the house.

Our new subdivision, Magnolia Estates, certainly lived up to its name with magnolia trees dotting almost every yard. Tonight, the scent of jasmine hung in the still air. Set back from the road, new brick houses in a traditional style kept up the southern theme: rooflines soared above Palladian windows and wraparound porches. A few homes had white rocking chairs on their porches.

I paced down the street as it curved around the edge of a large drainage pond to the end of the street. A silver Cadillac coasted to a stop at the curb behind me and Coleman May leveraged himself out of the car. As always, he wore a golf shirt—today's was yellow—and khaki pants. A visor shaded his eyes, but left his mostly bald head bare to the sun. Surely his few strands of comb-over hair didn't protect his head from sunburn during all the hours he spent on the course?

He popped the trunk and pulled out a black garbage bag. "Evenin'," he said as he tore a garage sale sign from the corner light post and crumpled it, then picked up some litter.

"Mr. May," I said, and reeled the leash in, then bent to help him with the bright flyers and posters that clogged near the drain. The rains had softened the paper and made the ink a runny mess.

"Can you see this light post from your house?" he asked.

"I suppose so."

"If you see anyone putting up signs, flyers, or posters, give me a call. I'll come down and take care of it. The only one who's authorized to put anything up is Gerald Lockworth," Coleman said as I picked up a flimsy water-soaked paper. "He's filled out the permit with the homeowners' association." Even though it was smeared, I recognized the flyer.

It looked like hundreds of other flyers taped in business windows all over North Dawkins. FIND JODI read the bold letters above the picture of a smiling young woman in her twenties. Straight blond hair framed a pretty face. Her smile was wide and showed her even, white teeth. It was hard to reconcile the open face with the word below the picture, MISSING.

I wasn't about to become the neighborhood tattletale, so I said, "You know, I don't really notice things like that. Too busy with my kids."

"You should notice. It's everyone's responsibility to maintain the standards of Magnolia Estates."

It sounded like a line from the monthly homeowners' association newsletter that Coleman wrote and delivered each month in his role as HOA president. It probably *was* a line from the newsletter, but I couldn't really say for sure, since I never read the thing. For all I knew, Mitch and I were in violation of several obscure HOA regulations.

Coleman said, "I've made a special exception for Gerald because Jodi lived here."

I looked at the blurry photograph again before I put it in the trash bag. "Really?"

"You didn't know that?" He yanked the ties on the trash bag closed, then held it against the bulge of his potbelly. His gaze flickered to my house again and I had the feeling he was about to say more, but stopped himself.

"How long has she been missing?" I asked.

He put the trash bag in his trunk and walked around to the driver's door. "Let's see, it was right about the first of the year, so that would be around ten months. Keep an eye out for those illegal flyers," he called before he shut his door and drove away.

Rex pulled on the leash. I turned and followed the street's blacktop, which extended a few feet. Then the road switched to a gravel track that had been an entrance for the construction crews during the building of the first phase of Magnolia Estates. It would eventually be paved and lined with homes, but now between building phases the road was quiet and used mostly as a jogging and walking path.

I let Rex off the leash and he hurtled down the path. The missing woman, Jodi, had lived in Magnolia Estates. How weird was that? I'd seen her picture around town, but knowing that she lived here, drove the same streets, might have even walked this same path gave me a strange, eerie feeling. I picked up my pace.

A few scraggly rays of sun angled through the dense growth of trees, bushes, and vines. The path was the only swath of openness. The thick foliage made me feel like I was miles from civilization, but I reminded myself that the path curved around the far side of the pond, then ran parallel to our street, creating a perfect walking loop.

I looked up. Directly overhead, a strip of sky was still light blue with one tiny paisley-shaped cloud tinged pink. I took a deep breath and drank in the beauty of the blush-colored cloud.

I noticed Rex hadn't trotted back to me in a while. I called him, but the gloomy path was empty. I jogged to the bend in the path and called again. I saw a flicker of dark movement up on the left. I hurried over. "Rex, come down." He was nosing around the small cemetery plot that was set back off the path at a slightly higher elevation.

"Rex," I said in my firmest voice, and his head swung toward me. "Come."

Reluctantly, he trotted to me and I clipped the leash back on him. I glanced back up at the cemetery, thinking that it was slightly odd that the place didn't creep me out. I'd walked past it for weeks without seeing it since it was higher than the path and the black wrought-iron that had once enclosed the rectangle of land now tilted at a crazy angle and trailed a skirt of kudzu that camouflaged it.

I had noticed it one day when I spotted a pale yellow stone marker, an obelisk, poking through the curtain of leaves and bushes. I'd taken a few steps up the embankment and stopped there to study the worn markers. No poison ivy for me, thank you. It hadn't made me feel the least bit scared, only a little sad to see the graves so abandoned.

Rex pulled on the leash, ready to move on, but I paused, frowning. "Now, that's not right," I said. In the fading light, I saw a white Halloween mask, a skull. It sat under a bush outside the kudzu-draped fence, contrasting sharply against the dirt and dark leaves.

"Kids," I muttered as I climbed two steps up the embankment and angled my foot to kick the mask clear of the greenery. It looked like the Halloween pranks were starting early this year.

I hesitated and leaned down. It looked so realistic.

Correction. Not realistic. Real.

Chapter
Two

Even though I've watched those TV forensic shows and seen bones and human remains in all their grisliness recreated on the small screen, nothing had prepared me for the real thing. I think that was what freaked me out the most. I knew the skull was real. I didn't have to touch it or move it to understand that. I just *knew*.

I stepped back and slipped. My arm splatted down into the soft mud. Thankfully, I didn't land on the skull, since I'd stepped back, but I didn't want to be on eye-level with it either. I righted myself, holding my left arm away from my body.

All I could think of was the bleary picture of the missing woman. I swallowed and looked at the skull. Was that Jodi? My heartbeat ramped up.

I wanted to sprint away, but my jerky movements made my feet skid again. I hadn't noticed on my quick climb up the embankment that the earth was still soaked from the rain, but now, as I took a few deep breaths to calm down, my feet shifted slightly in the sludgy earth. My heart hammered like it did when I actually got around to doing my kickboxing video.

My gaze followed the trail of mud that had cascaded down

from the cemetery. Rex's paw prints dotted the mud slide. At the top, I could see a piece of the kudzu-covered wrought-iron fence that had surrounded the plot of land, broken away and dangling. A few kudzu vines threaded through the piece of fence and were stretched taut, which had kept it from slipping down with the rest of the mud.

The back corner of the cemetery plot had sheared away, leaving a casket exposed. Its sides had collapsed, creating a gaping darkness under the lid that had tumbled sideways and was wedged in the earth, half covering the other pieces of the casket.

I thought I saw another skull-like shape.

Surely not. In the fading light it was hard to make out the details in the mix of dark mud and shadows, but it did look like another one, another skull. I squinted, then forced myself to take one more step up the embankment. As much as I didn't want to believe what I was seeing, I had to admit that even to my untrained eye, it was another skull. It was half buried in the mud near the splayed casket, but the curved dome of the skull and the empty eye sockets were impossible to mistake.

I stayed as clear of the mud slide as I could and picked my way directly up the rise of land and circled around to the back of the cemetery. I didn't realize that Rex had been trotting along beside me until he rubbed against my leg. I transferred the leash to my muddy left hand and rubbed his head as I studied the cemetery. The rest of it was intact and undamaged. Well, undamaged was probably not a good word choice. The rest of the cemetery looked the same as it always did, abandoned and disheveled. There were no more exposed graves. I looked back at the two skulls and got that ice-cube-down-the-spine feeling. One of them could be her. I stood on the rise, considering what I should do. Call 911 was the obvious answer, but I didn't have my phone with me.

I looked up and down the path. I couldn't see back around

the bend, the direction I'd come, but I could see several feet down the path in the direction I'd been walking. Not a soul in sight. It was late. The color was draining from the sky, leaving it icy blue. The cloud was now tangerine and the darkness around the trees was thicker. I doubted anyone else would walk this path again until tomorrow morning. I did my best to shake the uneasy feeling.

I carefully sidestepped down the embankment, going out of my way to avoid going too near the washed-out portion of earth. I went slower on the way down. I didn't want to get any muddier than I already was. Once back on the path, I thought about cutting through the trees. It would be the quickest way since I was past the pond. The path mirrored our street, and our house was directly above the curve in the road. I could cut through and go in our back gate.

Rex trotted off in the direction we'd originally been headed, and after a few seconds I followed him. The woods were too dark and I wasn't feeling that brave, especially after seeing two skulls. I stuck to the path and jogged home.

The garage door clattered and began to rise as I walked up the driveway. With a lithe movement, Mitch ducked under the door when it was halfway up. He was carrying a garbage bag in one hand and didn't see me right away.

"Mitch," I called as Rex bounded up the driveway.

He turned and reached down to rub Rex's ears, then glanced up at me and froze. "What's wrong? Are you okay?" he asked, his face concerned.

"The little cemetery on the gravel path—" I had to stop, catch my breath.

He took in my muddy side, dropped the garbage bag, and gripped my upper arms, steadying me. "Take your time."

The garage door stopped with a final rattle. My ragged breathing was the only sound in the sudden quiet. Another deep breath and I realized my legs felt quivery. "The cemetery?" Mitch prompted.

I nodded. Mitch knew the path as well as I did from his jogs. "Part of it's washed away. There's an open grave and bones."

His grip eased a bit. "It's probably been there for at least a century, Ellie. It's not surprising—"

"Mitch." My sharp tone cut him off. In the twilight, his dark eyes looked almost black. "There's one open grave and two skulls." We stared at each other for a moment. "The missing woman—the posters. We have to call the police," I said.

He nodded, reluctantly. This wasn't the first time we'd had to call the police. "Look, I wish I hadn't seen it. I don't want to call them either." I knew there would be an endless round of questions and a very late night after that phone call. "But we have to."

"I know." His voice was quiet, restrained. "Were they . . . recent?"

"I don't think so. I mean, there was no . . . skin or anything. That's why I think it might be her . . . Jodi. She's been missing for almost a year. If her body's been in the woods that long . . ." I couldn't bring myself to talk about a human body decomposing. "I thought it was a Halloween mask. It wasn't gross, just . . ." I searched for the right word. "Eerie. The path was so still and deserted."

He released my arms, picked up the garbage bag with one hand, and circled my shoulders with his other arm. "Let's go inside. I'll call. You can go wash the mud off before they get here."

Two hours later, I sat on the curb near the stop sign where I'd talked to Coleman May. I felt a bit of mud still stuck to my arm and rubbed it away. The sky and woods were dark, but the path was full of light and movement. Bars of light sliced through the trees and hurt my eyes when I glanced from the pale moonlight that bathed the rest of the street to the glaring lights.

I checked my watch and figured Mitch would be here in a few minutes. We'd decided that he would stay and get the kids in bed, then call our neighbor Dorthea to come sit with them while he met me at the path. We figured it would be best to keep the kids on their schedule and not disrupt their routine. No need for the whole family to be freaked out.

It wasn't the police, but the sheriff's department that responded to the call. I'd forgotten that our subdivision was in an unincorporated area of the county and the sheriff had jurisdiction here. The man who arrived first was unfailingly courteous, but his good manners barely coated his skepticism when I told him what I'd seen.

By the time I walked down the path with the officer, I'd begun to doubt my story, too. But his strong flashlight picked up the unmistakable human remains and cracked casket.

The officer had escorted me back to the neighborhood street and cordoned off the whole path. Then the parade began—cars, vans, SUVs, all with official logos on their doors, disgorging their official people. I watched the show with a strange feeling of detachment. When the neighbors began to emerge from their houses, I'd shrunk back, not wanting to talk to anyone. I planted myself on the curb where the dark night and the front tire of a sheriff car shielded me from curious looks.

I watched a young man stride quickly toward me. He had a badge clipped to his belt and was dressed in chinos and a navy polo shirt with the words *Dawkins County Criminal Investigation Division* stitched on it. I stood up.

"Mrs. Avery?" he asked, extending his hand. "I'm Detective Dave Waraday. You found the remains?"

As I shook his hand, another officer trotted up to us and hovered. Waraday said, "Excuse me, ma'am," and stepped over to the officer. When we first moved here, I might have been slightly offended to be categorized as a "ma'am," but now I knew it was just ordinary courtesy. Southerners took politeness to a new level and sprinkled "ma'am" and "sir" throughout their conversations.

The second officer said, "The GBI is on the way."

"Good." Waraday nodded. "Let me know when they get here. And move those people back," he said, glancing at a cluster of people beside the yellow tape. "I don't want anyone slipping past us through the trees to the site."

"Yes, sir." The officer nodded and raised his voice. "Okay, step back, please. Y'all can head on home."

I studied Waraday as he turned back to me. This was the boss? The other man had certainly spoken to him with a deferential tone and looked to him for instruction, but Waraday looked more like a high school quarterback than a crime scene investigator. How long had this guy been investigating crimes? Was he even old enough to rent a car?

I couldn't see a wrinkle anywhere on his face. My path had crossed with a few law-enforcement types, and from what I'd seen, time had certainly left its mark on them: wrinkles, gray hairs—or no hair—and a weary manner marked most of them, well, except for Thistlewait, a military investigator I'd met at our last assignment. He'd actually had a full head of nongray hair, but he'd been in his thirties.

Waraday tilted his notepad toward the light and jotted down my pertinent information, then said, "Do you walk this path often?"

"Yes. Lots of people in the neighborhood take it when they're walking or jogging."

"When was the last time you walked it, before tonight?"

"I'm not sure." I looked over his shoulder at the beginning of the path. "I'd have to look at a calendar, but I think it was last Saturday. It's been raining nonstop for at least a week, so it wouldn't have been this week."

"And you didn't notice anything out of place with the Chauncey Cemetery last time?"

I shook my head. "No. But it's not like I check it every time I walk by it. For weeks, I didn't even notice it. Chauncey? That doesn't sound familiar," I said.

"The Chauncey family died out a couple of generations back. They owned everything south of the railroad depot. You know that white house on Scranton Road right before the turn-in to Magnolia Estates? That was theirs. It was the only house for miles and the cemetery was their family plot."

"I'd wondered why no one kept it up. It's not surprising it's in such bad shape." Waraday went back to writing in his notepad. I was surprised he'd shared that bit of local history with me. In my run-ins with the police, I'd found they were fond of asking questions and never too keen to give answers.

Maybe I should stop right here and clarify. I've never been arrested. Although it's been close. I wondered how Waraday would feel about me once he found out that I'd been involved in murder investigations. Would he be as chatty? Maybe his friendliness was a southern thing.

I rotated my shoulders to relax them. No need for me to worry about getting mixed up in this investigation. I'd sworn that off after last time. And there was no way I could be considered a suspect *this* time. Those bones had obviously been there a long time, and since I'd never set foot in Georgia, much less Dawkins County, until ten months ago, I was in the clear.

"Did you touch anything?"

"No. I thought the first one was a Halloween mask, but when I got closer, I knew it wasn't a costume. I did go to the top of the little rise beside the cemetery to see if any more graves were open. I tried to stay away from the mud."

He'd been writing, but his gaze snapped up to mine. "And why did you do that?"

"Because if there were other graves open, then two skulls wouldn't be that strange. It would be bad, don't get me wrong, but it wouldn't cause this." I looked around at the jam of cars and milling people.

He had me walk down the path with him again and show him exactly where I'd walked and describe what I'd done after I found the bones, then thanked me and turned away.

I slipped under the tape and breathed a sigh of relief. Most of the neighbors had retreated to their houses, and the few that were still hugging the tape didn't see me as I circled around behind them. I trudged up the street, punched the garage door button, and padded through the house. The clean towels still overflowed the basket in the laundry room, but the dryer was clicking away. The kitchen, dining room, and living room were dark, so I went back to the bedroom, walking carefully since toys on the floor seemed to be the staple of our interior decorating theme these days.

When I stepped into the bedroom, Mitch had the phone to his ear. "Oh, wait. She just walked in. Looks like we'll be fine. Okay. Sure." He punched a button on the phone and tossed it down on the duvet beside him.

"Kids go down okay?" I asked as I softly shut the door.

"Yeah. Well, Livvy had to have two drinks of water and she just couldn't get her eyes to close."

"I've heard that one before." I smiled and dropped onto the bed. "I'm so glad to be out of there." I looked down at my hands. In the soft light from the lamps, I could see dirt encrusted in my cuticles.

"What happened?"

"They asked the basic questions." I focused on my hand, rubbing at the dirt. "Waraday looks like he's slightly older than Opie Taylor on *The Andy Griffith Show*. He told me the cemetery belonged to a family named Chauncey and they used to own all this land. Then I got out of there."

His hand covered mine. "Ellie," he said, and then his voice trailed off.

I knew what he was going to say. I gripped his hand. "It's okay. I'm not going to get caught up in this." It came out in a rush. "After what happened last time." I closed my eyes and swallowed. "I can't."

An Everything In Its Place Tip for an Organized Party

Cost-cutting Tips
- Use computer software to create your own invitations.
- The easiest way to cut costs for large events, like wedding receptions, is to limit the number of guests.
- The more casual the event, the easier it is to reduce costs. A buffet is less expensive than a formal dinner. A children's birthday party at a local park will cost less than a party for the same number of kids at a popular children's party venue.
- Keep decorations simple. To save money, look around your house or scour dollar stores for ideas. Use what you have before purchasing a centerpiece. Flowers from your garden can be just as lovely as store-bought bouquets. If you're serving Mexican food, a sombrero could be the perfect centerpiece.
- Party trays are easy to assemble. If you have the time, you can save money by doing it yourself. Purchase fresh vegetables and cut them yourself for veggie trays. Cold cuts, cheeses, and croissants, with condiments on the side, make a great sandwich bar.
- Purchase in bulk. Warehouse stores are your best bet for finding large quantities of everything from napkins to food and drinks.
- Borrow from friends and family instead of renting.

Chapter
Three

The next morning I was in what I'd begun to think of as the box room—I refused to call it a storage room. I'd worked my way through two boxes and was taking a break to change Nathan's diaper when the doorbell rang.

It was too early in the morning for Geneva, Livvy's playmate from down the street. Geneva's mom, Bridget, had a strict schedule for her daughters. I knew Geneva was listening to Mozart until ten o'clock; then they were off to Gymboree.

A petite woman of about fifty with short, curly blond hair stood on the porch. I opened the door and pushed the heavy glass screen door open a few inches.

The woman said, "I'm Nita Lockworth. I'd like to talk to you about what you found last night."

She wore a sweatshirt embroidered with pumpkins, neat jeans, and Keds tennis shoes. I glanced over her shoulder at the end of the street. The gridlock of official cars had cleared out. Only one sheriff's car remained. I couldn't see the entrance to the path, but I could see the taut line of yellow tape tied to the stop sign.

She waited with her hands clasped together at her waist and her head tilted slightly, her dark eyes on me. She reminded me of a bird as she stared patiently. I fumbled for a reply. Waraday hadn't specifically asked me not to say anything, but he probably wouldn't want me to talk about what I'd seen. And there hadn't been anything in the paper this morning about the discovery. How had she found out about it?

Sensing my hesitation, she tilted her head to the other side and said, "Dorthea told me you'd found the bones. I've already been to the sheriff's department, but they're not telling me anything until all the official tests are done."

"Well, I'm afraid that I'm not going to know anything more. I don't know anything about bones or skeletons."

"But you saw them and you're as close as I can get right now." She said it calmly, but there was an underlying persistence that indicated she wasn't going to leave my porch any time soon. Nathan wiggled in my arms and I shifted him to my other hip.

"You don't recognize my name, do you?"

"No, I'm afraid not."

"I'm Nita Lockworth. Jodi's mother." She pulled her practical brown purse forward so that I could see the small button with a picture clipped to the strap. The same picture dotted the town on billboards and flyers. I'd completely missed her last name when she introduced herself earlier.

Nathan squirmed again, pulled his thumb out of his mouth, and let out that whiny whimper that meant he wanted down. I twisted the screen door handle. She was wondering if the remains I saw last night were her daughter. Even though I wouldn't be able to tell her anything, I couldn't turn her away. With Nathan's pudgy body shifting impatiently in my arms, I thought how horrific it would be for your child to disappear, even if that child was an adult.

I pushed the door open and said, "Come in. I need to change a diaper. Then I can talk." I gestured at the dining room table and said, "Why don't you have a seat and I'll be right back?"

I glanced down the hall as I went into Nathan's room. She'd pulled out a chair and was sitting primly with her hands in her lap. The pile of clean clothes at the other end of the table almost hid her diminutive frame. I'm pretty speedy when it comes to changing diapers, so I was done and back out of Nathan's room in under a minute, with him again riding my hip, but much happier now.

Livvy met me in the hall. "Can I finger-paint?"

Ah, finger-painting, the ultimate messy activity. "Not right now, but I'll let you and Nathan watch *Tom and Jerry*."

Her eyebrows shot up. "Really?"

I normally didn't let the kids watch television in the morning. I saved it for the afternoon or evening when everything always seemed to fall to pieces. Typically, it was right around the time I was trying to cook dinner, so that's when I usually parked the kids in front of the TV for thirty minutes, but they didn't need to hear the conversation I was going to have with Nita Lockworth.

I arranged them in the living room, clicked on the show, and put a stack of plastic blocks and books beside them. Our house had an open floor plan. No walls separated the living room, dining room, and kitchen, so I'd be able to keep an eye on them.

I went to the dining room and paused with my hands on the back of a chair. "Can I get you something to drink? Iced tea? Water? I could make some coffee." I didn't drink it, but my friend Abby did and I kept a supply for her.

"That's kind of you, but no."

"All right."

I sat down and tried to think how to begin, but before I could gather my thoughts she said, "The house looks very nice. Thank you for taking such good care of it."

"Excuse me?" I asked. Why was she talking about the house? Wasn't she here about her missing daughter?

She smiled and the fine skin around her dark eyes crinkled. "I'd forgotten, you wouldn't know because we used a rental agency. This was Jodi's house. My husband's a builder, and for some reason, we couldn't get this one to sell. It's a bit smaller than the others in the neighborhood. Maybe that's why. Anyway, after a year on the market he convinced Jodi to move in. She was going to buy a house, but why should she do that when we had a perfectly good house sitting vacant?"

"Oh." I sat back. Jodi Lockworth lived *here*? That news explained Coleman's rather strange hesitation when I asked about Jodi. Why hadn't I heard about this? Dorthea hadn't mentioned it. There weren't a lot of homes on the market when we moved to North Dawkins. Christmas isn't that big of a selling season, so we'd rented the house through a property management company, which was also where we sent our rent each month and called if we had any problems. Dorthea and I had never talked about the missing woman. But still, you'd think it would be something that would be mentioned, even in passing.

"I didn't realize," I said. "I can see why you'd wonder about the . . . what I found."

"Yes, the bones. What can you tell me? What did you see?"

I glanced at the kids, but they were enthralled with the TV. That's the thing about not letting them watch it all day; when I turn it on, it's like they're in a trance.

"Well, I was on a walk. Lots of people in the neighborhood walk that path," I said slowly, not sure how she'd handle what I was saying.

She nodded briskly. "Yes, Jodi often jogged that trail."

Apparently, she wasn't going to break down and cry, so I described seeing the skull, then my discovery of the second one and the open grave. She nodded as I spoke, then pulled a small handheld computer from her purse. "Do you mind if I make a few notes? I'm afraid my memory isn't what it used to be."

I said, "No, of course not." But I was thinking, what kind of person analytically takes notes when it's possible her missing daughter's body has been found?

Mrs. Lockworth spent a few moments tapping away at her palm-sized device and I picked up a T-shirt and folded it.

She paused with the stylus in the air. "Did you see anything that would help identify the bones? Any clothing? Jewelry? Anything at all?"

"No." I put the shirt in a pile and picked up another. "I'm sorry. I wasn't looking for anything in particular. It was almost dark and I'm not an expert. I'm sure the sheriff's department will have more information than I do."

She tucked the computer back into her purse and picked up one of Nathan's shirts. She folded it, smoothing the fabric slowly under her fingers.

"The sheriff's department has called in some experts, and contrary to what you see on television, the tests they run take time. There may not be any definitive answers for weeks or months."

"Oh. I see."

I couldn't imagine how difficult it would be to wait, not knowing anything. Yet she seemed closed off from any emotion. Maybe it was a defense mechanism she used to deal with the stress and uncertainty.

She pulled several miniature socks toward her and matched them up. A smile turned up the corners of her lips. "So small," she said. She worked slowly, caressing each sock and matching it with its mate. It was quite a contrast to my usual slapdash manner. I just wanted to get everything sorted out and put away.

I thought back to Waraday's young face. "Do you have concerns with the investigation? Is that why you're asking your own questions?"

She pushed the stack of neatly folded socks back to the center of the table and looked me square in the face. "Davey is a good investigator. I know he's doing everything he can to find out what happened to my daughter."

"Davey?" I asked. "As in Detective Waraday?"

"Yes. I've known his family for fifty years. His mother was one of my best friends growing up. We played hide-and-seek together and climbed trees, until we realized that boys were so much more interesting than games and trees."

Despite her words of praise, wouldn't it be hard for Mrs. Lockworth to see "Davey" as anything but a kid? She'd probably wiped his snotty nose and scolded him when he got in trouble.

"I've had cancer, Ellie."

The abrupt subject change threw me. Weren't we talking about Waraday? How had we gotten onto cancer? I glanced quickly at the kids. Had I misjudged her? Maybe I shouldn't have let her inside.

"Cancer changes everything. I learned that no matter how kind and helpful the doctors were, no one had more interest in my treatment than me. I was my best advocate. I learned to ask questions and keep asking until I understood everything. I learned to be persistent. I've been cancer free for fifteen years and part of that is because of the questions I asked and the decisions I made.

"It's the same thing with Jodi. Waraday is a good investigator. He'll do his best, but he's got other cases. To the state forensic team, those bones are another set of remains to be processed. Don't get me wrong. I know everyone cares and wants to find the answers, but I'm her *mother*. No one cares more than me."

"I can understand that."

She looked at Livvy and Nathan. "I'm sure you can. Thank you for talking to me. I've taken up enough of your time."

"Not at all. You've helped me fold laundry, which you didn't have to do at all. I'm sorry I couldn't help any more."

"It's nice to do something so normal." She shouldered her purse and pushed in the chair.

"We have a meeting once a month for the community. We go over strategies and leads to help find Jodi. If you're interested, we'd love to have you." She pulled a business card out of her purse along with a silver pen. She jotted a date and time on the back and handed it to me. "We normally meet on the third Tuesday of the month, but this week we're having a special meeting on Friday."

The card had the familiar picture of Jodi. "Thank you. I'll think about it." I walked her to the door and held it open. "Do you mind if I ask you why you decided to rent out this house?" It was a question that I couldn't get out of my mind.

She paused on the front porch, her gaze running over the wicker chairs and potted flowers. "After she'd been gone three weeks it became obvious that Jodi wasn't going to come home or be found quickly. The investigation stalled. They'd followed all the leads they could and there didn't seem to be anything else to do. The national media gave the story some attention early on. When they did stories on Jodi, tips flowed in. It seemed like a good idea to consolidate our resources and use everything we could to keep her picture in the public eye." She smiled and said apologetically, "The billboards and the flyers, those cost quite a bit. Then there's the eight-hundred number and the Web site. The rent on this house helps to pay for some of that. We have all of Jodi's things waiting for her." Her gaze suddenly flew back to me. "But don't worry, when Jodi comes home you won't be without a place to live. This is your house for as long as you need it."

A cry sounded from the living room. I knew it wasn't an emergency. It was Nathan's "I'm not getting enough attention" cry. Nita said, "I know you're busy. Thanks again for talking to me."

I closed the door and dropped the card onto the kitchen desk before going back to pick up Nathan and get the next load of laundry.

Chapter
Four

"What's that?" I asked Livvy. "A flower?" Livvy and I were drawing with chalk on the driveway while Nathan pushed his bubble mower across the lawn.

Intent on filling in her shape with pink strokes, she didn't look up. "It's a whale."

I stood up to stretch my cramped legs and watched Nathan turn at the magnolia tree at the end of our yard and begin his long trek back. A breeze had chased the last of the humidity from the air as it whipped the limbs of the loblolly pines and made the glossy cottonwood leaves dance. Today actually felt like a fall day, crisp and a little on the cool side. Since most of the summer had been so hot and muggy when you stepped outside that it felt like you'd entered a sauna, I figured we'd better make the most of the lovely weather.

"Hello, there!" a voice called, and I turned to see our neighbor Dorthea making her methodical way down the street. She walked half a mile every day no matter what the temperature or humidity. The only thing that stopped her was rain.

Livvy waved. "Hi, Mrs. Dorthea."

That was how she introduced herself to me and Livvy on the day we'd moved in. "Just call me Mrs. Dorthea, sweet pea," she'd said to Livvy. Livvy had looked slightly confused at this combination of words.

"I brought you some Oreos," she'd said as she placed a paper plate in my hand. "Don't do much baking anymore, but I live two doors down toward the pond, so if ya'll ever need anything, give me a holler." *Haller* is how it sounded with her southern accent.

A widow, she lived alone in the spacious new house she'd bought after she sold the only other house she'd ever owned, an old rancher on Scranton Road. We'd learned all these details and more during our first chat on the front porch, before she had placed one blue-lined hand on the brick wall to steady herself as she went down our three porch steps and made her labored way back across the street.

Livvy had looked at me and whispered, "Her name is Mrs. Dorthea *Sweet Pea*?"

I'd explained that sweet pea was an endearment and she wanted Livvy to call her by her first name, Dorthea, but with the added courtesy title of "Mrs." I'd discovered that here in the South it was a common way for children to address adults.

"She walks like a turtle, hunched over and slow," Livvy had said as we watched her unsteady progress. "Do you think she'll be okay?"

There hadn't been a trace of self-pity or sadness in Dorthea's bright hazel eyes, only cheerful delight. "I think so."

I walked to the end of the driveway.

"We've certainly had some excitement, haven't we?" Dorthea said.

"Yes. You sent Mrs. Lockworth over to see me?"

She nodded and adjusted her wide-brimmed hat. "Were you able to tell Nita anything?"

I shook my head. "No. I don't know anything about bones and there wasn't anything there to help identify them."

Dorthea sighed. "So sad for her. She's such a dear, so staunch and persevering, but you know it has to be tearing her up inside. I hoped you'd be able to help her."

"Why didn't you mention Jodi lived here?"

"There never seemed a good time to talk about a woman

who'd disappeared." Dorthea rested a hand on our brick mail-box and flicked her gaze at Livvy, who was curled up over her chalk drawing. "The young ones were always around and I didn't want to scare them. There's so much fear in their lives today anyway."

"In theirs and ours, too," I said as I thought of the conversations we'd already had with Livvy about how she had to stay with us in stores because someone might want to "take" her. Even in our front yard, I never let the kids out of my sight. I'd seen too many news stories about kidnappings.

Nathan made another turn and set off diagonally across the lawn, and Livvy added waves with blue chalk. "They're both out of earshot now. What happened with Jodi?"

"She moved in summer before last. The house had been vacant for quite a while. I think because it was smaller than most of the others."

I nodded. "No loft over the garage."

Dorthea continued. "Jodi told me she was going to live there until the market picked up. Her daddy's a builder. He was going to build her a house over near the base, close to her work, but since this house was one of his and it was vacant she moved in here."

"Lockworth Homes?" I asked. I'd seen that sign around the neighborhood.

"Right. I'd say he probably built a third of the houses in here. From what Nita says, they're building all over the county, which is a real blessing. All that stuff they're doing to find Jodi isn't cheap, you know."

"Oh, I know." I'd looked into the price of advertising for my organizing business when we first arrived and I knew even an ad in the paper would set you back a few hundred dollars. "So Jodi worked at the base?"

"Yes. Something to do with the children's sports teams. I didn't really understand it."

I ran through possible programs in my mind. "The Youth Center, maybe?"

"Yes. That was it. She was very sporty. I'd see her running every evening. And she had all sorts of fancy equipment. She was always toting around golf clubs and tennis rackets. My, she was active. Tired me out, just watching her. She did articles for the paper, too, but that was only part-time. Her main job was at the base, coordinating all the teams."

I kept my gaze on Nathan. He'd abandoned the mower and now squatted over the flower bed by the front door. He wasn't digging up anything or putting things in his mouth, so I decided to leave him for now.

"So she just disappeared? What happened? It sounds like she had a great life." Free housing, a civil service job, and all the sports she could play.

Dorthea put her hand over her lips briefly. Her hazel eyes watered and I patted her shoulder. "You don't have to talk about it, if it bothers you."

"No." She blinked and patted her lips, then pulled her hand away. "No. That's another reason I haven't mentioned it to you. I get misty when I talk about it. I was the last person who saw her. She'd gone for her run, up the path. That was the route she ran every day."

I swallowed. No wonder Nita Lockworth had been on my doorstep this morning.

"I saw her leave her house for her run about six o'clock that night. She waved to me. Later, about eight, I was closing my blinds and I saw her sitting at her computer, typing away." Dorthea pointed to one of the windows on the front of our house. "Her blinds were open and it was dark enough that I could see her."

I glanced across the street from Dorthea's house to the window of the room that we also used as an office. Dorthea would have had an unobstructed view, no bushes or leafy trees to block the sight.

"It took them until Monday to figure out she was gone because it was a Friday night. She didn't have any of her teams playing that weekend. The holiday, you know. It was after

New Year's. No one saw her on Saturday and Nita thought she'd skipped church."

"No sign of foul play?"

"Oh no. Everything was neat as a pin, like always."

Sounded like my housekeeping standards weren't quite up to Jodi's standards. Nita must have been being polite in her comments about how good the house looked this morning. "What about her car?" I asked.

"Still in the garage. No luggage missing, just her purse and keys. She sent Nita an e-mail, saying she'd be out of town for a few days, but Nita always did think that was strange because Jodi was conscientious. It wasn't like her to leave without planning for it at work. She hadn't requested any days off."

"Did she have a boyfriend?" Where were these questions coming from? It wasn't like I was interested. Oh, who was I kidding? Of course I was interested. Who wouldn't be, especially after learning I lived in the same house she'd lived in before she'd gone AWOL? And even though I told Mitch I wouldn't get involved . . . a girl could ask questions, couldn't she?

"No. I don't think so," Dorthea said. "I never saw her with any boyfriends and Nita says she wasn't dating anyone seriously."

Livvy marched up and said, "Mom, can we wrap Geneva's present *now*?"

"In a few minutes."

Dorthea said, "Let's see if I have something in my pocket."

She made a big production of digging deep into the pocket of her stretchy elastic-waist jeans, then pulled her hand out and opened it with the flair of a magician. A shiny new quarter caught the sun. "It was so bright and new I thought I'd save it for Livvy, if that's all right."

"Of course. Oh, I'd better go," I said. "It looks like Nathan is pulling up our gardenias."

Chapter
Five

I was dashing into the Base Exchange to pick up a bag of dog food before I met Mitch for lunch when the name Topaz Simoniti caught my eye.

I pushed the stroller over to the cash register for a closer look at the sign that read MAKE CHECKS PAYABLE TO TOPAZ SIMONITI.

The woman running the kiosk was turned away from me, helping a customer. She had brown hair and was shorter than me. *It could be her.*

I checked the sign again. *Come on, who else could it be with a name like that?* Memories of Mrs. Daniel's ninth grade history class—the last, endless class of the day—came rushing back: the smell of Corey Tate's stinky shoes, the ping of the metal high bar clattering to the ground through the open windows in the spring when one someone missed their jump, Mrs. Daniel's boxy-heeled shoes clomping along the aisles as she passed out papers, the chain connected to the frame of her half-glasses swinging back and forth with each step. You knew you were in trouble when Mrs. Daniel stopped at your desk and pulled those glasses down to the tip of her nose and looked over them at you.

Thankfully, I was hardly ever on the receiving end of her

glare. Topaz, on the other hand, had endured the glare often, but it didn't bother her.

"Mom, where's Dad?" A tug on my sleeve and Livvy's voice brought me back to the present and I glanced around the mall area of the Base Exchange. To call it a mall was stretching it. Minimall or lobby would be more accurate. The wide high-ceilinged hallway stretched the length of the Base Exchange, which was a department store located on Taylor Air Force Base. The minimall had a small food court at one end and shops—a florist, the uniform shop, a barbershop, and a dry cleaner—lined the rest of the space. Kiosks of independent vendors filled the middle aisle.

You never knew what vendors would be in the minimall. I'd seen rugs, paintings, cookware, clothing, military memorabilia, and books. Topaz's booth was divided in half. One side displayed home decor items made from metal. Candlesticks, metal-framed mirrors, napkin rings, and flower buckets ranged along the shelves. Each featured delicate twists of metal threaded with sparkly beads or interesting meshwork. The other side of the booth displayed a range of jewelry from chunky metal designs to fragile shells.

I glanced around again before I answered Livvy. "He'll be here in a minute," I said. "Why don't you go get a drink from the water fountain?" She skipped a few feet over to the water fountain and pulled a step stool into place. I could tell by the way she moved she felt grown-up. Getting to go to the water fountain alone was a big deal at three. Of course, she would point out that she was "almost three *and a half.*"

"Were you looking for something in particular?" The woman had finished with the other customer.

I swiveled slightly, so I could keep Livvy in sight as I said, "No. I mean, everything is lovely, but I wanted to talk to you. You're Topaz Simoniti?" She'd put on a little weight, but then again, hadn't we all? Her eyes, her namesake, were the same light golden brown. She'd once said, "They're brown, your basic brown. Boring. Trust my mom to go from 'brown' to 'topaz.' I guess it could be worse. I could be named coffee or something."

She thought her eyes were boring, but everything else I remembered about her was interesting. Even as a sophomore she'd been eccentric. Because I sat behind her, I'd spent a lot of time looking at the back of her head during American history and even that hadn't been boring. At the beginning of the year she'd had long straight brown hair. Each day was a different style—braids, ponytail, slicked back with gel, crimped. You named a style and Topaz had done it to her hair. After Christmas break, she came back with jet-black hair and clothes to match the goth look. By spring, she'd shifted to white blond and red lipstick. I wasn't sure if she was doing a retro–Marilyn Monroe thing or an ironic take on Madonna. Then she cycled through looks, chameleon-like, as styles changed.

Today her hair was back to brown, but streaked with bold blond highlights at half-inch intervals. The asymmetrical cut was shorter on the left than the right and exposed a dangly chandelier-type earring of different size keys on one side. Her hair curved longer on the other side, hiding all but the tip of the other earring. Her round face and padded cheeks looked the same, if a little more plump. Her porcelain skin was still flawless. She'd never had a zit and I'd told her once it was a crime to cover up her great skin with all that white makeup during her goth phase. She'd laughed it off and said she'd rather have my tiny hips than perfect skin. Well, my hips weren't so tiny anymore and Topaz still had her great skin.

"I'm Ellie Avery—I mean Ellie Westby. That was my maiden name."

She blinked a couple of times, a puzzled look still on her face. "From high school," I added. "Mrs. Daniel's class. Remember the awful Saints and Sinners quizzes?" Her eyebrows scrunched together as she tilted her head slightly toward me like she was having trouble hearing me. This was getting embarrassing. "You probably don't remember. I had the Rachel haircut and sat behind you in sixth-period American history at Llano Estacado High."

Her face cleared and she broke into a grin. "Ellie! Of course I remember you. And how could anyone ever forget those Saints and Sinners quizzes? So, how are you?"

"Good." How do you sum up your life in a couple of sentences? "I'm married now, obviously. New name and all. My husband's a pilot in the Air Force and we were transferred here last winter. I'm a professional organizer."

"And a mom, too," Topaz said as she leaned over to look in the stroller.

"I always think that's kind of apparent," I said, grinning as I pulled back the stroller's visor. "This is Nathan, our youngest. He's eleven months old."

"Mom, can I get another drink?" Livvy said, pulling on my arm.

"No. Not right now. This is a friend of mine from school." I introduced Livvy and she suddenly became shy, clinging to my hand and hiding her face against my leg, her standard operating procedure with new adults.

"You do not look old enough to have two kids!" Topaz exclaimed. "You look great. How do you do it?"

I shrugged a shoulder. "Must be all that chasing after the kids—keeps me in shape, at least a little bit. So, tell me about what you've been doing for the last—what would it be—ten years? Are you here at the BX a lot?"

"Some. I hit the bases' exchanges in the fall and winter. I spend the spring and summer on the road at craft fairs and visiting shops. I have a lot of merchandise on consignment at little boutique-type places. North Dawkins is home base for me now. It's a good central location."

"How did you get started?" I picked up a candlestick holder. The base was weighty and solid. Several fine wires twisted around it and swirled up to encase the taper candles. A couple of glass beads were spaced irregularly along the wire. The candlesticks were good quality and the twisty wires added a quirky flair to them.

I wasn't much of a shopper. In fact, I'd designated Abby as my personal shopper. The only retail section that interested me was the designer purse section. I liked browsing the handbags at department stores, but what got my pulse racing was looking for purses at thrift shops and on Internet auction sites. On the topic of Kate Spade versus Louis Vuitton, I knew what I was talking about. All other types of shopping bored me silly and I left those up to Abby. She had a knack for putting things together and making a room or an outfit look spectacular. I thought she'd approve of the candlesticks.

"Oh, you know." Topaz shrugged. "I liked to make stuff. I tried the college thing, but it didn't work out. Business classes, well, any classes really, just bore me, you know? I was always making something and one day a woman offered me twenty bucks for a belt I'd woven from leather strips. *Twenty bucks!* I was amazed, but then it dawned on me that I could make some money from basically nothing. I got a booth and started selling my stuff."

I picked up one of her business cards from a smooth wooden holder, a four-inch section of a tree branch with the bark removed and the wood sanded to a silky finish. "Found Objects," I read.

"It's a fancy name," she said. "Basically, I take stuff people don't want—what they throw away or what nature leaves lying around—and make it into things, then sell them."

"How long will you be here at the BX?" I asked.

"Through the end of the week and then I'm not sure where I'm off to. There are a couple of stores I need to visit on the coast . . . but I don't know. I might hang here for a little while. Depends on what I feel like."

I set the candlestick holders down by the register. "These are beautiful. I'll take them," I said.

There were other customers lining up behind me, so I paid for the candlesticks, then gave her one of my cards for Everything In Its Place, my organizing business. I had to dig pretty deep into my purse to get one. I hadn't exactly had people clamoring for help organizing their life since we'd moved to Georgia. Starting a business was hard. I'd had a fairly good stream of clients while we were stationed at our last assignment in Vernon, Washington. But I'd discovered that starting *over* in a new city was even harder than the initial business start-up.

I bought the dog food, then went on to the food court, where I spotted Mitch in line. I grabbed a table and waved him over. He set down a tray with several slices of pizza and before I could tell him about Nita Lockworth's visit or running into Topaz, he said, "The list came out today."

He didn't have to explain which list. We'd been waiting for the major promotion list for weeks.

"And?" I stopped cutting pizza into bites for Livvy.

"I'll have to buy new rank."

"Mitch, that's great." Buying new rank meant changing the pins and patches on his uniforms to reflect his promotion. We'd been hoping for the promotion to major. Mitch was a year under the zone, which was complicated to explain. There was a time frame, a group of years, when Mitch could be selected to be promoted. "Under the zone" meant he'd been picked before most of the people in his time frame. The others could still make it, but it would be next year or the year after. "We can celebrate it when we go on our date on Sunday." We'd been trying to go on a date for weeks, but so far either our sitter had canceled or the kids had gotten sick.

"You know what pinning on new rank means," he said.

"Um . . . it doesn't mean we're moving sooner, right?"

"No, we're here for at least a couple more years. It means a party—a promotion party."

"Oh. How could I forget?" It was kind of strange, like a lot of things in the Air Force, actually. You got the promotion and then you threw your own party and invited the whole squadron. Sounds selfish, I know, but that's how it was done. Tradition. I didn't understand it and—most of the time—I didn't try.

I caught my cup as Nathan knocked it over. "So, did anyone else get promoted?" There was another tradition associated with promotion. If more than one person got promoted, they usually pitched in and hosted the promotion party together. Since an event like that could run several hundred dollars, it was nice to split it several ways.

"Nope. I'm it. I'm thinking a cookout in two weeks on Friday."

I pulled out my organizer and flipped to the calendar. I'd be lost without it. "That would work. Nathan's birthday party is the week before and Halloween is the weekend after."

He picked up on the reluctance in my tone because he said, "Don't stress. A cookout will be simple. Just burgers, chips, and some beer."

Somehow I didn't think it would stay that simple. And a cookout would mean making sure the house *and* the yard looked great. We'd be hosting fifty people, at least. Probably more. My stomach clenched. I was a nervous wreck when we entertained. Lists. I was going to need lots of lists. "Okay, I'm writing it down on the calendar. About what time should we tell people? Six o'clock, you think?"

Mitch whistled. "On the calendar. You know what this means—no turning back now. It's official."

"Stop it," I said, but I was smiling. "It's in pencil, not ink."

"Oh," he said with mock seriousness. "Just pencil, well, that's different. Yeah, six sounds good. What's the date again? I'll start to get the word out."

"Hmm . . . you need the date?" I couldn't resist teasing him. "Good thing I've got it written down, isn't it?"

I mentally shifted gears back to my news. I knew if I focused on the party I'd drive myself crazy worrying. I was really good at worrying. Plenty of time for that later.

"Okay, I'm not going to think about that right now, be-cause—well, you know me, so you know why. I have some news, too."

I told him about Topaz and he asked, "Was she a good friend? I don't remember you mentioning her."

"No, more of an acquaintance. I don't think she had any really close friends. She was one of those unique kids—to-tally herself and completely confident. I always had the feel-ing she was too exotic, too unconventional to fit into any group." Our high school had been a strange blend of *The Breakfast Club* and an Edward Hopper painting. Topaz seemed to have walked out of a Salvador Dali world. She didn't quite fit, but it didn't bother her at all.

"Are you going to get together and catch up?"

"I don't know. I'd like to, but it sounds like she travels quite a bit. And that's not all that's happened. We had a visit from a friend of Dorthea's today." I explained about Nita Lockworth's visit. "Can you believe Jodi lived in our house before she disappeared? Isn't that weird?"

"Yeah, really interesting and quite a coincidence, too."

"Mitch, I *did not* know anything about this. There's no way anyone could know, unless they lived in the neighborhood when Jodi lived here, since the house was listed through a property agent."

Nathan started to fuss, so Mitch transferred him out of the high chair and into his lap. "I know, I know. *You're* inter-ested, I can tell. You've got that spark in your voice." His phone rang and he had to take the call. I finished off my pizza, wiped the kids' faces and hands, and began to pack up toys. Mitch hung up. "I have to get back."

"That's okay. I need to go, too," I said. "I want to work on those brochures during nap time." Mitch transferred Nathan to the stroller and I dumped our trash.

As we walked to the parking lot, Mitch said, "Ellie, have you thought about shutting down Everything In Its Place?"

"Why would I do that?"

"You're pouring tons of time and money into it and nothing's happening with it. It's not like we need the money."

I stopped the stroller at the Jeep, got the kids strapped in, and spun back to him. "It's slow right now. It takes time to rebuild a business."

"It's almost been a year," he said gently.

I bristled and collapsed the stroller a little more forcefully than was necessary. "Mitch, you don't get it, do you? I'm not doing it just for the money. It's something I'm good at and it's something that's completely mine. You've got this whole other work life. Sometimes I feel like my identity is being gobbled up in being a wife and a mom. I need something that's all me."

Mitch sighed and said, "I'm only saying that you always have a lot going on, and like you reminded me the other day, your days are pretty full. The spare bedroom is driving you crazy and if you weren't doing all the work for your organizing business you might feel better. You're investing a lot of your time and energy in it and not getting much return. It's a business. Don't get too emotional. You've got to make a business decision. That's all I'm saying. Is it a business or a hobby? I know you're probably mad, so I'm getting out of here now." He gave me a quick kiss and headed to his car.

I managed not to stomp over to the driver's side of the car, but I was only able to restrain myself because I knew Livvy and Nathan were watching. *A losing venture! Make a business decision. Don't get too emotional.* Easy for him to say. It wasn't his project he wanted me to walk away from.

As soon as everyone was down for nap time, I hit the computer with a renewed sense of energy and purpose. I clicked over to our e-mail and was delighted to see some new e-mails, but then I realized it was on our personal account. I pulled out the calendar and flipped through the last few months. I'd bought it in January, right after we'd moved in. I'd expected that my business would be slow. It would take a while to build up a new client base. But ten months was a little long to wait for *one* client. I'd tried advertising, but that hadn't drawn much interest.

Most of the date squares in the winter and spring months were pristine white, except for playdates, pediatrician appointments, and library story times. The pattern didn't change in the summer. I'd cooled down a bit and, objectively, I had to admit that Mitch was right. Everything In Its Place wasn't going anywhere.

I blew out a breath that sent my bangs flying off my forehead. A feeling of frustration mixed with depression swept over me. I couldn't give up. Not yet. I'd give it until the end of the year. That would be one full year and if I didn't have some organizing clients by then, well, then I'd reassess.

I squared my shoulders. I thought of the advice from Organizers Online, an e-mail discussion group that I belonged to. Networking was the key, they said.

Okay, network.

Chamber of commerce meetings—check. I'd been attending those since May. I'd had a few nibbles, but nothing that turned into a job. I had the Magnolia Estates Homeowners' Association monthly meeting on the calendar, too. I frowned. *What else could I do?* I shifted around in the chair and my jeans caught on the drawer that didn't close completely. I shoved it closed and began sorting though the debris that accumulated on the desktop each week. Sometimes tidying things helped me think. Other times, it did absolutely nothing for my mental organization, but at least I'd have a clean desktop when I was done.

I put the notepad and pen back by the phone, clipped Livvy's crayon drawing to the refrigerator, and shredded two offers from credit card companies. The last thing, Nita Lockworth's business card, was stuck under the keyboard. I pulled it out and tapped it against my chin as I thought about an idea that might help me get the word out on Everything In Its Place and help a few other people, too.

An Everything In Its Place Tip for an Organized Party

Cleaning
- Before the party: don't kill yourself doing a "military clean" of your home. Most of your guests will be so busy enjoying the company and the food, they won't notice your floorboards. Place trash containers in the kitchen and near any buffet lines. Place several plastic bag liners in the bottom of each trash can. If you're serving food outdoors, make sure your trash cans have secure lids to minimize bugs. A "bug zapper" near the trash area is also a good idea for outdoor parties.
- After the party: use paper plates and cups to minimize cleanup time. If your party is more formal, make sure your dishwasher is empty so you can get the dirty dishes out of sight quickly. Or, if your guests are dying to help out, put them to work drying dishes. Nothing makes people feel more at home than helping in the kitchen.

Chapter
Six

I pulled to the curb when I saw the glittery LITTLE PRINCESS TEA PARTY sign.

Livvy bounced in the backseat. "Are we there?"

"Yes. I think so," I said as I climbed out. Livvy unbuckled and clambered out without my help. Nathan was at home with Mitch. They were having a boys' night with pizza and SportsCenter.

We climbed the steps of the house's wide front porch and a little girl about Livvy's age with a long braid down her back opened the screen and grabbed Livvy's hand. "Over here! They've got hats and gloves and feathers!"

I followed the sound of giggles and squeals and found ten little girls gathered around a kitchen table. If it was pink, purple, glittered, sparkled, or had feathers, it was on that table. Livvy dug in, her eyes shining like the rhinestone tiara that she was jamming on her head.

"Hi, I'm Kay," said a woman about my age, decked out in a wide-brimmed straw hat decorated with silk flowers. She was wearing a dress and white gloves that reached to her elbows. "Welcome to the Princess Tea Party."

"Thanks. Looks like I'm a bit underdressed," I said, gesturing to my jeans, white T-shirt, and cranberry zippered fleece.

"Oh no. You're fine. You're welcome to stay and play

dress-up, but I like to give the moms a break, too, so you can pick your daughter up around seven, if you'd rather. I've got two capable assistants." Kay nodded to two teenage girls who were sitting with the kids. I left my cell phone number with Kay and said good-bye to Livvy. Ensconced with her friends, she didn't mind me leaving.

I took the state highway that paralleled the base and headed toward North Dawkins, which spread out between the base and the north-south interstate highway five miles away. Once a stop on the railroad surrounded by farmland, North Dawkins was now booming, sprouting big box stores and chain restaurants along the three major roads that connected the state highway to the interstate like rungs on a ladder.

This part of Georgia was an interesting mix of rural areas interspersed with suburbia. I was surprised at how much I liked it. The one drawback was the muggy, buggy summer. Of course, there were still some things I didn't quite understand, like the roadside boiled peanut stands. Those just didn't sound good to me, but peach ice cream was another story.

Development hadn't reached the road I was on and I cruised through the flat green land. In the distance, I could see the thick bank of farmed pine trees that grew straight as arrows. I passed a small graveyard and felt a frisson of unease as I thought of the skulls in the Chauncey plot. I'd never look at the small cemeteries again without remembering the skulls and those gaping eye sockets. Tall grass and weeds were engulfing this cemetery and kudzu, the creeping green vine of the South that was almost impossible to eradicate, covered the nearby field and draped over a telephone pole. Unless someone did some cutting back, it wouldn't be long before wide leaves swallowed the cemetery.

I knew I'd pass at least two more small family plots before I got into North Dawkins. I'd never seen so many cemeteries in my life. They dotted the Georgia landscape and popped up in the most unexpected places. Small, forgotten patches of solemnity being reclaimed by the earth. Except for my quick glance at the Chauncey plot when I'd found the bones, I'd never looked at any of the family plots closely, but I assumed some of them probably dated from the late 1700s, since Georgia was one of the original colonies, something I tended to forget since the first things I associated with Georgia were peaches, the Civil War, and *Gone With the Wind*.

There wasn't much reminiscent of the old South in North Dawkins since it hadn't really grown until the base was located here at the beginning of World War II. It didn't have the classic small southern town look. There were plenty of towns within driving distance that had the redbrick courthouse, the town square with the statue of the Civil War soldier on horseback, quaint shops, and antebellum homes lining the streets under live oaks draped with Spanish moss.

North Dawkins did have live oaks, but that was about it for the quaint department. No Spanish moss, no gracious antebellum homes, no courthouse square. I passed the front gate to Taylor Air Force Base and turned into the older section of North Dawkins, which had several antiquated strip malls that had been in their heyday about 1950, but were looking a bit seedy and tired now. Neighborhoods in this part of town had small bungalows and mature landscaping. The farther I drove away from the base, the newer the structures became. It was a bit like driving through a time warp from 1950 to present day.

I suppose the trade-off of not having a picture postcard town square was that North Dawkins had used the tax dollars that flowed in with its most recent growth boom to construct a modern county government complex. City hall, the sheriff's department, the courthouse, and the library were all built around a central concrete courtyard with a huge fountain and curved benches. What would be shade trees in fifty years were now barely taller than me. I turned into the library parking lot and went to find Meeting Room B.

Light and airy with soaring ceilings, the library had every

up-to-the-minute detail—wireless Internet, a coffee cart, racks of books on tape, and self-checkout kiosks. Oh, and books. Sometimes I wondered if the books were getting lost in the shuffle of all the newfangled gadgets and gizmos. But it looked like the books themselves were pretty popular since the aisles were crowded with people browsing the titles, even on a Friday night.

I found the meeting room in the back. It was crowded, too, with about thirty people pressed into the small room. I took a seat about halfway to the front. Nita Lockworth was at the front, setting up a map on an easel. A tall, solid man who was probably in his fifties stood near her, situating the feet of the easel so it didn't wobble. He had a fair complexion and one of those awkward tufts of hair at the forehead and a thinning spot on the top of his head. And I thought I had bad hair days. At least I didn't have to deal with bald spots and tufts of hair.

There was something about the way Nita and the man moved, a sort of nonverbal communication, glances and gestures, that made me think they were married. He adjusted the map on the easel; then she patted his arm and nodded toward a stack of boxes lining the wall. He moved them to the table. If he was Nita's husband, then he was the one Dorthea had said built homes. He certainly looked the part in his work boots, jeans, and slightly worn plaid shirt. The sunburn and creases on the back of his neck indicated he spent many of his hours in the sun.

A young woman with short hair dressed in a white oxford shirt and black pants sat down beside me. She held an iced coffee in one hand and was sipping from it as she sent a text message. I went back to watching the room.

More people flowed in, greeting each other. Most people made their way to the front and talked to Nita. One woman, a statuesque black woman in a lime-green shirt and brightly patterned pants, sailed into the room and broke through the crowd around Nita. The two women embraced.

The woman beside me put her phone away and I heard her say something under her breath that sounded like ". . . the only one who really understands."

She noticed me glancing her way and said, "Sorry to be talking to myself. I didn't realize I was doing that." She pushed her frizzy mustard-colored hair behind her ear and said, "Seems I do that a lot, talk to myself, I mean. Hi." She stuck out her hand. "I'm Colleen Otway."

After I'd shaken her hand and introduced myself, she said, "Have you been here before? I don't remember you, but then I'm terrible with faces. And names, too, actually."

"No, I haven't been here before. I'm new. Well, fairly new. We moved to North Dawkins in January. I met Nita Lockworth the other day." I'd been about to say, "after I discovered the bones in the old graveyard," but I stopped myself in time. Better to just leave it at that, I decided.

"Military?" Colleen asked, like it was an inevitable conclusion.

"Yes. My husband is a pilot at Taylor. You don't sound surprised."

"Practically everyone who lives here is connected with the base in some way. Even me, I teach seventh-grade science, but my dad's a contractor at Taylor."

"It's the most military community I've ever lived in, and that's saying something because we've moved around a little bit."

We sat for a few moments in silence and watched more people enter the room; then Colleen tilted her head to the front of the room and said, "I worry about Mrs. Nita. Even though she hardly ever shows it, all of this has to be taking a toll on her and Mr. Gerald."

"Is that her husband?" I asked, looking at the man in the plaid shirt steadily moving boxes to the table.

"Yes, that's Jodi's dad, Gerald," Colleen said. "He's a great big bear of a man. He used to scare me when I was a kid. He's so tall and has such a deep, rough voice. It took me a while to figure out he's actually a teddy bear." The smile left her face when Gerald opened one of the boxes. You could see the familiar Find Jodi flyers stacked to the brim of the box.

Colleen sighed. "With all this rain, so much is going to have to be redone. Any flyers that were out in the open aren't readable now, even if they're still there." We both looked back at the two women at the front of the room. They'd stepped apart and Nita was running her fingertip gently below her eyes. The other woman handed her a tissue.

Colleen said, "We're going to have to blanket the whole town again. And last time it was kind of haphazard. Some parts of town had five flyers tacked to the same telephone pole, and other parts of town didn't have anything. There were even letters to the editor in the paper complaining about litter." Her tone turned indignant on the last word.

"A system might help. If you divided the town into sections, then assigned different people to each section, you could cover the whole town pretty quickly. Another option might be to only focus on businesses. If you posted the flyers in the windows of businesses, you wouldn't have to worry about the rain anymore."

"That's a great idea. You should mention it during the meeting." Colleen's gaze drifted around the room and she shook her head. "I can't believe we're still doing this. It's been almost a year. I know the first anniversary will be a good way to get her name back in the news, but it's so discouraging. I can't believe she's been gone this long."

"So you knew Jodi?"

She grinned. "Yeah. You could say that. She's been my best friend since she rescued me in fifth grade from the snotty girls." She gave a mock shudder. "Fifth grade was awful, so cliquey, you know, and I was the new kid, which made everything ten times worse. My dad had just gotten the job at Taylor, so there I was—the geeky, short kid with the frizzy hair. At the end of my first day at school, Jodi caught up with me and asked me if I wanted to go to the mall with her that weekend. We got our ears pierced. BFF ever since."

I had to smile at the acronym for "best friends forever." Funny how acronyms were becoming more and more a part of our daily lives. I was used to deciphering them when it came to Mitch's job—the military had an acronym for everything—but now with text messaging and e-mail short-hand we had more acronyms in our conversations than ever.

"She sounds like she was a really nice person."

"She *is*," Colleen replied with a slight emphasis on the present tense.

"My neighbor, Dorthea, knew her and said she was very athletic, that she worked with the youth center on base."

"Yes, we made quite a pair back in school. I'm a klutz. Zero athletic ability, but Jodi—she can do anything she tries."

It struck me as a bit odd that Colleen talked about Jodi in the present tense, since the possibility was very high that I'd found Jodi's remains just a few days earlier. Surely, Colleen knew about that? Remembering the sight of the bones, I felt a shiver creep down my spine. It sounded like Jodi was a nice, kind person. Why did she go missing and, possibly, end up in an abandoned graveyard?

"You know, normally she's the type of person you'd hate, or at least be inclined to be jealous of," Colleen continued. "She's beautiful and smart and talented. And it's not just sports she's good at. She's an excellent writer. She was work-ing as a part-time reporter for the *North Dawkins Standard* and even as a stringer for the *AJC*."

"That's an interesting combination," I said.

"When we were kids we watched that movie, *His Girl Friday*, during a sleepover. Mrs. Nita had all these rules about what Jodi could watch and what she couldn't. Old movies were okay, so we watched it and Jodi thought the whole re-porter bit was too cool. She wanted to be Hildy, ace reporter. Her parents thought it was a phase, that she'd grow out of it after she edited the school newspaper, but she just wanted more after that. Jodi got the job at the Youth Center for the pay and benefits, but if she could get a solid job at a newspaper that's what she'd do full-time."

I was a bit surprised that Colleen was telling me so much about Jodi. It reminded me of how people talked about their loved ones at funerals. There seems to be this compulsive urge to vocalize what the person was like, and relive memories. I supposed when someone is missing, people experience some of those same feelings, the urge to keep the missing alive, if only in their words.

A man slipped into the chair on my other side, smoothing down his yellow tie. Colleen looked at him and stiffened. Like a sheet of vellum paper that was worn and crinkled, he had a slightly rumpled air. He was young, probably in his mid-twenties, with wavy black hair that drooped over the collar of his wrinkled suit jacket. Black-rimmed eyeglasses framed gray eyes. His conservative suit and tasseled loafers were at odds with the longish hair and his subtle citrus scent.

The young man leaned across me and said, "Hi, Colleen."

Colleen immediately grabbed her messenger bag, muttering, "I can't believe you continue to show up here." To me she said, "I'm going to let Mrs. Nita know about your ideas for the flyers." She left as fast as she could, but her progress was pretty slow since she had to step over people's knees and purses to get to the aisle.

"I think she likes me," the man said to me as he pulled a pack of gum out of an inside pocket of his jacket. He tilted it toward me. "Gum?"

"Sure. Thanks. If she likes you, she sure has a unique way of showing it," I said.

"It's a misunderstanding. I'm Scott Ezell. You must be new," he said.

What was this? Did I have a sticker on my head that read *Visitor*? "You're the second person who's said that to me tonight. Is it that obvious?"

"With the military component, we're a pretty tight group here in North Dawkins. It's kind of like a rotating carousel. People get off, others get on, but it doesn't take long to recognize the regular riders."

"I'm a new rider, I guess," I said, and introduced myself.

I heard my name called and turned to see Colleen standing beside Nita and beckoning to me. "Ah, excuse me," I said, and made my way up to the front of the room.

Nita said, "Your idea for organizing the flyers is terrific. Would you be interesting in coordinating it?"

I sensed I was talking to an expert in delegation. She would have to be to keep the Find Jodi campaign running this long. "Actually, I wanted to talk to you about something along those lines. I'm a professional organizer and I'd like to donate some of my time to help you out, if you're interested. I wouldn't charge you. It could work out nicely for both of us. I can help you with the flyers and it would give me a reference in North Dawkins and some publicity." I pulled my information packet from my purse and handed it to her. "This tells a bit about me."

Nita looked through the packet quickly and then smiled at me. "Thank you. That would be wonderful. What do you need to help with the flyers?"

"Just a map and some highlighters," I said, and felt as if a tightly coiled spring inside me had relaxed. It might not be paid work, but I had an organizing job. It was a start.

"Terrific," Nita said, and dispatched someone for the items. "You two sit right here. I'm going to introduce you, Ellie. That should help get the word out." She ushered us to front-row seats and stepped behind the table.

Nita raised her voice and the murmuring around the room faded as she said, "Thank you all for coming out tonight. As you know, this is a special meeting time for us. Because of recent . . . developments . . ." Her voice faltered and she swallowed.

Gerald had been leaning against the wall, but as Nita struggled to control her wobbly voice, he quickly crossed to the table and placed his arm around her shoulders.

He scanned the crowd and I got the sense that he'd rather be anywhere but speaking to fifty or so people, but he cleared his throat and said, "We appreciate y'all and want to say thank you for supporting us. We couldn't have made it this long without our friends. We know there's lots of questions and speculation about Jodi right now. That's one reason for this meeting. We've always been honest and open and shared what we know with you. Right now we don't have any definite news about the remains that were found." He paused and I thought he was about to get choked up, too, but instead his deep voice boomed out again and he said, "I won't lie to you. It's been a tough week for us. But Nita and I decided that we can't quit now. We've got to keep going, keep Jodi's picture out there, keep up the searches."

He looked down at Nita. She gave him a reassuring smile and a small nod. I heard the distinctive sound of a digitized camera shutter and looked over my shoulder. A photographer stood at the back of the room. Two local television station photographers were beside him. They were rolling, getting every minute of the scene between Nita and Gerald.

Gerald squeezed Nita's shoulder, then stepped back to let her have center stage again. That scene hadn't been staged, had it? Surely not. It had seemed authentic to me.

"Gerald is right," Nita said, her voice strong and calm again. Despite her small size, her voice filled the room. "We have to press on. Because of the discovery earlier this week, there is a renewed interest in Jodi," she said, acknowledging the reporters and photographers in the back, "and we have to take advantage of it. This may be the week that someone sees Jodi's picture on the news and recognizes her. Or it may be a flyer that sparks someone's memory."

Nita picked up a flyer from one of the open boxes and held it up. "The rain has washed away most of our work, so

we need to post flyers again. We have a professional organizer, Ellie Avery, who lives here in North Dawkins and has
volunteered her time to coordinate the flyer distribution."
Nita waved her arm at me and I felt a bit like a contestant on
The Price Is Right. I gave a little wave to the room.

"Before Ellie tells us how we're going to organize the
flyer distribution, I want to remind everyone about the search
Saturday in Magnolia Estates. The sheriff's office can't guar-
antee that they will be finished, but we're planning a search
for that morning. If they're not finished, we'll postpone the
search until the next Saturday."

I was only half listening to Nita's words because her
statement that I'd be talking to the group had thrown me. I
wasn't fond of public speaking. Well, that's an understatement.
Honestly, I'd have to say that I'd rather host a party for two
hundred people at my house than speak to this group—or
any group of more than ten people—but it looked like I was
going to have to speak. I'd keep it short. Really, what was there
to say? Just a few sentences should do it. Then why was my
heart beating like I'd just had a near miss on the freeway?

A familiar voice brought me back to the meeting. I turned
and saw Coleman May, standing. "You can't search Magnolia Estates."

Chapter
Seven

"There's procedures, Nita. You can't call for a search in Magnolia Estates," Coleman repeated.

"I'm sure we can work it out, Coleman," Nita said, but he didn't sit back down.

He continued. "Magnolia Estates is private property. We can't have a couple hundred people tramping over lawns and through flower beds."

"The search will be of the undeveloped area. Gerald will have a map and show you the area. We'll contact the home-owners' association with all the details," Nita said. She was still smiling, but her smile was a bit strained.

"That's even worse." Coleman's tone was belligerent. "There's all sorts of wildlife out there and poison ivy. Who's liable if there's an injury?"

"Coleman." Nita's voice was patient. She'd obviously dealt with him before. "I promise you, everything will be taken care of to the satisfaction of the Magnolia Estates HOA. Now, we can't get derailed on this one point."

I *so* admired a person who actually ran a meeting, as opposed to letting people wander off-topic. I glanced at my watch and realized I still had thirty minutes before I had to leave to pick up Livvy from the party. With Nita in charge I thought I'd make it.

Colleen nudged me and I realized Nita was motioning me to come up to the table beside her. My heart rate, which had calmed down during Coleman's little speech, kicked up into high gear again and my palms went sweaty.

I took my place beside Nita, who handed me a map and several highlighters. I explained how the system would work and asked people to highlight the area of the map they were going to cover. I colored in Magnolia Estates as I said, "I'll take my neighborhood." I saw Coleman getting to his feet again and I hurriedly added, "Because Gerald has a permit for flyers in Magnolia Estates, I know that will be fine, but check with the neighborhood associations before you post flyers."

Coleman sat back down and I said, "We'll have a sign-up sheet here at the front for people volunteering to do areas that aren't picked tonight." I flipped one of the flyers over and scrawled, *Flyer Volunteer Sign-up* across the top. Nothing like organizing on the fly.

Even though my pulse was still pounding like I'd run half a mile—I'm not a big runner (obviously)—I didn't think I was doing too bad. Then I noticed the photographer slipping out of the room and the guys operating the video cameras turning off the spotlights and moving to the back corner. Well, there you go. I wasn't even important enough for the newspeople to keep their cameras rolling. Clearly, I could relax.

I finished my little impromptu speech with an encouragement for people to try to get the flyers in the windows of businesses so the weather would be less of a factor. I nodded at Nita and she thanked everyone for coming out, then said, "Now, y'all come on up and pick up your flyers."

I was surprised to see Topaz was first in line. I hadn't noticed she was in the room. How could I have overlooked her stripy angled bob, not to mention her red top with billowy sleeves paired with jeans, a turquoise and leather belt, and aqua boots?

"I'll take my neighborhood." She leaned over the map

and a trio of necklaces swung away from her neck as she highlighted a square in the older part of North Dawkins near the base. "I've got time before I leave for a fair on the coast." She stood and the necklaces fell back against her skin above the V-neck of her shirt. I bet she made those necklaces, a mixture of tiny shells and beads with a twisty chunk of metal that dangled from the longest necklace like a medallion.

"Thanks. How's everything going?" I asked.

She shrugged, pulled a handful of flyers out of the boxes, and moved around the edge of the table to make room for the next person in line. "Same old thing."

"So, where are you off to?"

"Tybee Island, first. Then I might stop for a few days with a friend in Savannah. It's been a while since I've been there. Seems a good time of year to do the whole scary cemetery thing, right?"

"Oh, is that the one from *Midnight in the Garden of Good and Evil?*" I'd never been to Savannah, but I knew of its most famous cemetery.

"That's it. Bonaventure Cemetery." She shrugged again. "I'm not sure, though. I might drive up the coast and see what I can find up there."

"I can't imagine traveling like that. Without a plan or hotel reservations. We'd have practically a U-Haul full of luggage."

"Well, you have kids. You have to take the kitchen sink, right?"

Right. I felt a twinge of jealousy at Topaz's breezy travel itinerary. It wasn't that I wanted to go see Savannah's cemeteries—I'd had my fill of cemeteries—but I wouldn't mind seeing Savannah and I knew for us, it would be a major production and sightseeing would have to be planned around nap time.

The chime of a cell phone sounded. "Oops. That's me. Just a second." Topaz pulled her phone out of her back pocket and turned away from me.

I gave myself a mental shake and told myself to stop comparing myself to Topaz. We were different. We'd taken different routes in life. I might not be able to flit off to a city on a whim, but I had it pretty good.

I checked the table. People were still highlighting the map and grabbing flyers. The system seemed to be working. Scott Ezell had already been through the line and stood alone at one side of the room, holding a stack of flyers. Several people walked by him without speaking and I saw Colleen change direction and go to the other side of the room when she spotted him.

Topaz finished her conversation and I said, "Is this a normal-size turnout?"

"Maybe a little high because of the news, but we usually have around forty people."

"What about him?" I looked toward Scott Ezell. "Is he usually here?"

"Yes, the pariah shows up faithfully. Although I can't understand why he puts himself through it."

Before I could ask what she meant, Nita joined us. She gave Topaz a hug and said, "Now, here's one of our best volunteers. I don't think Topaz has ever missed a meeting."

Topaz hugged her back and said, "That's what happens when you're an artist. You're broke, but you've got time. I've got to run." She waved her flyers and called out, "See you Saturday."

I checked my watch. "I have to go, too. I'll take the map and the volunteer sign-up with me and contact people for the areas that aren't covered."

"Wonderful." She pulled out her handheld computer, tapped in my e-mail address, then said, "So nice to have you on board, Ellie. I know you'll make a real difference for us."

"Some jerk keyed my car while I was at the Find Jodi meeting," I said to Mitch when I got home. He followed me out to the garage and we examined the damage together. "Do you think it's worth filing a claim?" I asked doubtfully.

"Nah. Not with our deductible. We might as well wait and put our money into a new car for you." Mitch slapped his hand down on the hood as we walked back inside. "It's about time to put The Ancient One out to pasture."

"Maybe. It's only a scratch. It still drives fine." Despite its age, I liked my old clunker, a Jeep Cherokee, which I'd kept because it had four-wheel drive and that was a great thing when you lived in Washington State, but now that we were in the heart of the South, it might be time to upgrade to something with power locks and windows.

After I'd tucked in the kids, I told Mitch about the organizing work I'd volunteered for. "It's pro bono, but at least it's a start."

"That's good."

I could tell from his tepid response that he wasn't nearly as excited as I was. "I did think about what you said about Everything In Its Place being a business. I decided to give it until the end of the year. If I don't have a paying client"—I blew out a sigh—"I'll *consider* closing it down or possibly putting it on hold until the kids are older."

Mitch nodded. "Sounds reasonable."

"Yeah, I know. Sometimes I hate being reasonable," I said as I pulled my hair back to wash my face.

He asked, "Anything else happen at the meeting?"

I told him about the plans for the search, then said, "It doesn't make sense." I paused before I splashed water on my face, but I didn't hear a reply from Mitch, who was still in our bedroom. I rinsed the makeup from my face, then grabbed a towel and dabbed the water away. I walked into our bedroom and leaned on the closet door frame. Mitch was moving patches from one flight suit to another.

"What doesn't make sense?" he asked over the sound of Velcro ripping apart.

"The whole situation with Jodi. I don't understand it. There doesn't seem to be any reason for her to run away. She had a loving family, a good job, two jobs if you count her part-time work for the paper, and a huge house to live in rent free. What's to run away from? And it's not like she had anyone to run *to* either. No boyfriend in the picture, according to Dorthea."

Mitch transferred the last patch, then balled up his dirty flight suit. "Maybe everything wasn't so great in her life. Appearances can be deceiving. You know that, better than most people," he said with a smile as he dumped his flight suit in the hamper.

He was right. I'd run across people who gave one appearance to the world, but inside, they were completely different. I went back into the bathroom, pulled out moisturizer, and slathered it on my face. "You could be right, but I didn't get the feeling that her parents were hiding anything and everyone seemed so genuinely upset that she'd disappeared. So if everything was fine in her life and she didn't have a reason to leave, then that leaves the other option, someone either kidnapped her or killed her."

"Or both," Mitch inserted, his voice floating out of the closet. He tossed his gym bag on the bed, and then his workout clothes landed by the bag.

"But that doesn't make sense either." I went into the bedroom and sat on the bed. "No one disliked her. Apparently, she was a kind person. Why would anyone want to hurt her?"

Mitch packed his gym bag and zipped it up. "There may not ever be an answer," he said, his voice serious. "Her parents don't think it was her remains in the cemetery?"

I traced a finger along the stitching on the duvet. "I think they're afraid that it is her, but they're going ahead with their plans for a search, hoping that it's not her." I looked up. "If it is her, then why kill her and leave her so close to her house? Why not bury her miles away?"

"I'm sure it's not the easiest thing to move a dead body," Mitch said. "The gravel path is fairly deserted and there's not much activity."

I swallowed, thinking that if what Mitch was saying was true, then Jodi would probably have been killed close to that area. Maybe even in our house. I felt the hairs rise on my arms as I mentally ran through the rooms of the house; then I told myself to calm down. The police had been over this house, they'd searched here. If she'd died here they would have found evidence.

I thought back to the path. It was usually pretty quiet. And the graveyard was abandoned. No one would be up there, looking around. Really, it was a brilliant solution to the question of where to dispose of a dead body. What better place was there than a grave in a forgotten cemetery?

I nearly jumped off the bed when a knock sounded on our door. Even though I knew that knock, my heart was still fluttering when I opened it. Livvy stood there in her pajamas with her hair damp around her face. "I had a bad dream."

I picked her up and she wrapped her arms and legs around me as I carried her back to bed. "I'm sorry," I said.

I tucked her back in and smoothed down her hair. We said a prayer to chase the bad dream away and then I stroked her back until I felt her body relax and her breathing slow down. She'd wanted to sleep in her tiara and gloves, her party favors along with a huge bag of candy and a real china teacup. I'd managed to convince her to leave her tiara on her nightstand. Her gloves were spread out beside her bed on the floor and I carefully stepped over them before I walked down the hall to check on Nathan.

Now, there was a boy who loved his sleep. Livvy hadn't been a baby who liked to sleep, but Nathan was the opposite. He always settled down to sleep with hardly a whimper and I'd wondered if something was wrong in those first few weeks after he was born. It was just one of the first things that I discovered that was different about my two kids. I peered into his room and could barely make out the soft fuzz of his hair from the hall's night-light. His tiny snore made me smile.

I went into the kitchen and turned on the computer. I didn't want to go to bed right away in case Livvy woke up again, and I had too many thoughts and questions in my mind to sleep right now.

I went to the Web site for the *North Dawkins Standard* to do a search for articles by Jodi Lockworth. The page loaded with a headline that read REMAINS IDENTIFIED. I leaned forward and scanned the article.

> *The remains of two bodies found in an open grave last week have been identified. Sources with the Dawkins County Sheriff's Office confirmed that one body was that of Albert Clarence Chauncey, who died in 1919. The other remains are William James Nash. Nash, a resident of North Dawkins, has been missing since 1955.*

I'd been reading so fast to get to the names of the people that I had to go back and read the first lines of the story again. Then I leaned back in the chair. Two men? The bodies were two *men?* I couldn't imagine how Nita felt about this news. I knew I'd been hoping the remains didn't belong to Jodi because that would mean she was possibly still alive, but at the same time, the news would also mean that Nita and Gerald didn't have any more answers this morning than they had before I'd stumbled across the open grave.

I ran the name Nash through my mind, but I couldn't come up with anyone I knew with that last name. Who was he? There hadn't been anything in the news about him. There were two pictures with the story, one of a white man and another of a black man. Both were young, probably in their late teens or early twenties. The caption under the white man read Albert Clarence Chauncey. His dark hair was parted down the middle of his head and pressed flat. He wore a suit and tie and a serious expression. Even with the formal clothes and the solemn face, he looked so young. There seemed to be a tentativeness in his gaze.

The name under the photo of the black man was William James Nash. He was also dressed in a suit and tie, but he was smiling, one arm flung out along the roof of an old car with wide white-sidewall tires and generous sloping curves along the wheel wells. I read the rest of the article. William Nash was born in North Dawkins in 1937. He lived with his widowed mother and worked in the paper factory. He disappeared in 1955 when he was eighteen years old. I scanned the article, then went back and studied the pictures again. He was last seen during his shift at the paper factory.

I shook my head. I guess it had been a bit foolish to assume that Jodi was the only missing person in the history of Dawkins County.

The article went on to describe Albert Chauncey's short life. He was raised in North Dawkins and left in 1918 to fight in World War I. He contracted tuberculosis, was discharged, and returned home. He died a year later and was buried in the family cemetery. A firsthand account of his return and subsequent death could be found in his sister's diary, which was located in the North Dawkins Museum.

I frowned over the last paragraphs of the article. The sheriff urged people to remain calm while the Nash case was investigated. *Why would the sheriff say that?*

I looked at the stack of flyers I'd picked up earlier with Jodi's smiling face. She was still missing. The person everyone seemed to like and who didn't have any serious troubles in her life. It didn't fit. Since no one seemed to be the least bit upset with Jodi personally, maybe she made some enemies with her reporting. I typed her name in the paper's search bar.

The first articles that popped up in the search were the most recent ones and they weren't articles she had written, but articles about her disappearance. I read through a few of them because I didn't remember the news coverage. I'd been so busy with our move and taking care of a newborn that I hadn't been paying attention.

The stories covered the fact that Jodi was a hometown girl who ran the youth sports program at Taylor. They also mentioned she was employed part-time at the newspaper. One article under a picture of our house ringed in yellow crime scene tape focused on the neighbors and their reactions. Of course, everyone was shocked and worried. The official search had turned up nothing and after a few weeks the articles shifted focus to Jodi's parents and the formation of the Find Jodi campaign.

I ran another search, this time using the search terms "Jodi Lockworth" and "reporter" with an older date range, which brought up a list of stories with her name in the byline. I printed her articles and then went to the Web site for the Atlanta paper and did the same search. Only three articles came up and a quick scan of those showed they were regional local interest pieces on fall festivals, the peach harvest, and day trips for antique lovers. I couldn't see how any of those articles could make someone mad.

Mitch came into the kitchen, opened the fridge, and pulled out a bag of baby carrots. "Working on organizing stuff?"

"No. I'm looking up Jodi's articles. The newspaper Web site is reporting that neither one of the sets of remains were hers. They were two men, a local guy who served in World War I and a man who disappeared back in 1955. Isn't that weird?"

"Odd." Mitch's response was guarded. "That's good news for Jodi's family, I guess."

"Yes, it is."

"Carrot?" Mitch sat down on a bar stool and held the bag out.

"No, thanks, not unless you've got a vat of ranch dressing for me to dip it in." I joined Mitch in some of his healthy snacks like popcorn, but I drew the line at raw carrots. I said, "Looks like those remains had nothing to do with Jodi."

An Everything In Its Place Tip for an Organized Party

Keep in mind special requests your guests might have as you plan menus. Do any of your guests have food allergies or special diets? Don't forget to include nonalcoholic drink choices and vegetarian options.

Chapter Eight

I picked up the empty pan and took it to the sink. Funny how we never had leftovers when I made cinnamon rolls. Okay, I didn't really make them. I pried the tube open, arranged them in a pan, and popped it in the oven. That was about the limit of my baking skills right now. Leftovers were a different story when I made lasagna or broccoli. Plenty of leftovers then.

I felt the familiar pressure on the back of my knees and looked over my shoulder. Nathan grinned up at me, swaying as he gripped my jeans. I was his favorite stationary object. His expression seemed to say, "I caught you!"

"You did get me, but I'm one up on you. I've already cleared the table so I don't have to move." I rinsed and stashed the dishes in the dishwasher. I could hear the muted roar as Mitch powered the riding lawn mower around our huge yard.

Nathan held on until I finished. Then I picked him up and transitioned him to the kid-size table and chairs. I pulled out a set of stacking blocks and a muffin tin and he quickly forgot that he'd rather be clinging to my jeans. Livvy was playing with a floor puzzle, so I had a few minutes of quiet.

I put away the list of phone numbers with checkmarks down the side. This morning I'd called the volunteers who signed up to put out additional Find Jodi flyers, figuring Saturday morning was as good a time as any to find people home. The response had been good and all areas of North Dawkins were covered.

I pulled out the articles I'd printed the night before. I'd made it halfway through the stack and hadn't found anything that looked like it would cause any sort of controversy. I found six months' worth of articles. Jodi had written her articles starting in July of the previous year and there was a pattern. She covered two community events, like the Fourth of July parade, did one human interest story, usually of a prominent county resident, and rounded it out with a profile of a local business.

So far, I'd read about colorful local characters like Topaz and the junk dealer named Crooner who ran what he called an antique shop down by the hardware store, but it looked more like a flea market to me. I'd also learned there was a new boutique in town and had brushed up on my Halloween safety tips.

A photo of Scott Ezell caught my eye. The headline beside the photo read STAND NAMES NEW DIRECTOR. STAND was short for Save Taylor And North Dawkins. Since the economy of North Dawkins depended almost solely on Taylor Air Force Base, the community had set up STAND, a nonprofit community lobbying group, to help ensure that the community and the base worked together to keep Taylor off any base closure lists. If Taylor closed, then North Dawkins would shut down, too.

I studied the picture of Scott. He looked more polished than he had the other night. No wrinkled clothes and his hair was shorter. I scanned the article until I found this sentence. "The executive director position has been vacant since the retirement of Lena Stallings eight months earlier." I'd met Lena Stallings last spring during a trip to Washington, D.C. I wasn't surprised she wasn't with STAND. I bet that after certain details of her personal life came to light last spring she retired and moved out of town. The chances of running into her at the gas station or grocery store were pretty slim.

I skimmed through the rest of the article that highlighted Scott's background. Jodi emphasized that he grew up in a military family, moving from coast to coast since his dad was in the Navy. Then he went to college at the University of Georgia on an athletic scholarship. That surprised me. I would have pegged him as a business major and member of the chess club. I skimmed a bit more and found out he was a long-distance runner and had gone on to get his MBA.

I heard a thud, then Nathan's cry. It wasn't his "I'm really hurt" wail, but a hiccupy "I'm not hurt that bad, but I scared myself" kind of cry.

"He hit the drawer when he slipped," Livvy informed me.

I gathered him up in my arms, checking for injuries. He had one small scrape on his arm. I kissed it and said, "All better. You don't even need a Band-Aid." I sat him down at the table and restacked the blocks.

There was a block on the floor near my built-in desk. He must have slipped when he tried to pick it up. He still wasn't too steady on his feet, so it wasn't surprising that he'd fallen. Spills were part of life at eleven months.

I couldn't do anything about how often Nathan fell, but I could fix the drawer. It couldn't be that hard. With Mitch's unpredictable schedule, I'd had plenty of experience in minor household repairs.

I pulled out the drawer and set it on the desktop. The metal slides that were mounted inside the cabinet looked fine. I grabbed a flashlight, sat down on the floor, and shone the light in the cabinet. There was nothing that I could see that would make the drawer stick.

"What are you doing?" Livvy asked, leaning on my shoulder and breathing heavily onto the back of my ear.

"Trying to figure out why the drawer sticks and won't close."

"Oh." She shoved herself in front of me, completely blocking the opening. "What's that?" she asked, pointing.

"I don't know. I can't see because you're in the way." She moved and I had to lean down even farther to see what Livvy saw. Nathan grabbed my shoulders and shouted, "Horsey. Horsey game."

"No, not the horsey game. Mom's trying to work here." I set Nathan back on the floor, then angled the flashlight at the back corner. An envelope was taped to the top of the cabinet. One piece of tape still held the envelope partially in place, but another piece had come loose and half of the envelope hung in the air. When I pushed in the drawer it must have folded the envelope back on itself. I reached in and pulled the envelope down. The tape gave easily and I set it on the desk.

I tried the drawer again and it closed, the front stopping flush with the other drawers. Nathan pulled the drawer out and closed it again. The drawer game was one he could play for quite a while. "Mom, what can I do now?" Livvy asked.

"Here." I handed her the flashlight. "I bet if you go in the hall closet it'll be really bright."

She was off in a flash.

I had a weird feeling about the envelope. It's not something you find every day, an envelope taped to the underside of a cabinet. I knew we were only the second people to live in this house and I knew *we* didn't put it up there. That only left two possibilities—the cabinet installer had left it or Jodi had put it there. A long, narrow notebook about four inches across and about eight inches long with a spiral binding at the top slid out of the envelope when I tilted it.

The front was plain white and blank. I picked up one of Livvy's fat pencils and used the tip to flick the cover back.

I frowned. The first page was filled with a . . . code of some sort? A few recognizable letters and numbers were sprinkled among random dashes and loops. At least, it looked like random gibberish to me. It wasn't anything I could understand. I flicked through a few pages. More of the same.

I opened another drawer, a lower one, and pulled out my business card holder, looking for Nita's business card. I found it, but it didn't have her number on it. Of course it wouldn't. It only had the eight-hundred number for tips and the Find Jodi Web site.

Dorthea would have it. After a quick call to Dorthea, I dialed Nita's number. The phone rang and rang. Just when I was trying to think of a coherent message to leave on her answering machine, she picked up.

"Hi, Mrs. Lockworth. This is Ellie Avery. Dorthea gave me your home phone number. I have a question that you might think is kind of strange, but . . . well, it's hard to explain."

"Please call me Nita. What's your question, Ellie?" She wasn't sharp or irritated. In fact, her voice was calm, almost serene. "I've gotten some very strange questions in the last year. I don't think you're going to surprise me."

Best to just come out with it, then. "Did Jodi know shorthand?" I asked.

There was a long pause; then she said, "Yes. Yes, she did." Now her voice wasn't so composed; there was a bit of excitement and also wariness, too, in her tone.

"Okay." I took a deep breath. "I think I'd better call the police. I mean the sheriff. You should probably see this, too. I think I found Jodi's reporter's notebook."

Chapter
Nine

"I don't think you should touch it," I said, reluctantly. Nita's hand hovered over the pages for an instant. She'd been about to pick up the notebook.

"They'll probably want to examine it. Fingerprints, all that," I said.

She withdrew her hand and clasped both hands behind her back. "I suppose you're right." She leaned over, bringing her face close to the notepad. She looked like she was smelling a flower, soaking up every wrinkle in the paper and stroke of writing. "No need to irritate Davey," she said mildly.

"Have a seat," I said, indicating the desk chair. She pulled it out and sat down, her gaze still locked on the notebook.

"So, you do think it belonged to Jodi?" I asked.

"There's no question. This was Jodi's notebook. I've got several exactly like this one that I packed when we decided to put the house up for rent. They're in a box at my house. And I recognize her shorthand. I taught her some basic words when she was in middle school. Even then, she knew she wanted to be a reporter. Hardly any universities teach shorthand in journalism schools, but I learned it in my first round of secretarial courses. I worked in a law firm before I had Jodi." She looked up at me briefly and smiled. "Shorthand doesn't get used that much nowadays, but it's a valuable skill for a reporter."

Out of the corner of my eye, I saw a car with the distinctive markings of the sheriff's office pull up to the curb in front of our house. I hurried to the door. I didn't want anyone to ring the doorbell since I had Nathan down for his nap. Livvy was back in her room, too. She was reading—or supposed to be reading. She was too big for a nap, but nap time was as much for mommies as it was for kids. I wasn't sure who they would send to pick up the notebook, but I recognized Detective Waraday striding across our lawn. Looked like he was taking the call seriously.

I opened the door as he stepped onto the porch. "Please be as quiet as you can. It's nap time."

He looked a little surprised and I thought it was probably the first time he'd been asked to keep it down since a kid was sleeping. "Yes, ma'am," he said, and stepped inside.

I led the way into the kitchen and Nita stood up.

"Mrs. Nita." He smiled at her. "I can't say I'm surprised to see you here."

I jumped in and said, "I called her to make sure the notebook belonged to Jodi. I didn't want to bother you if it wasn't hers."

Waraday gave me a long look, then turned to Nita. "I assume, since I am here, that this was Jodi's?"

"Yes," Nita said, her gaze fixed on the notebook again. "It's Jodi's." She explained how she recognized the notebook itself and the shorthand inside it.

"So, we'll need to get in someone who knows shorthand," Waraday said, speaking to himself more than to us.

"I'm afraid that might be difficult. I taught Jodi shorthand when she was a teenager. She worked on the middle school newspaper and was complaining about how long it took to write everything down. Over time, she developed her own style, her own shortcuts. Essentially, her own version."

"No one will be able to read this except Jodi," Waraday said, exasperated.

"No. I'm sure you'd be able to figure out parts of it eventually. See here"—Nita pointed to a page at random—"that says 'safety tips' and here's the word 'flashlight.' Of course, there's quite a bit that I don't recognize."

"Oh, I bet that's from her article about Halloween." I grabbed the stack of papers I'd been going through earlier and found the article. "Here." I handed it to them. "Safety First for Trick-or-Treaters."

This time Waraday leveled a long look at me as Nita scanned the article and compared it to the page in the notebook. I shrugged. "I was curious about her. I found out she lived in this house and I wanted to know more about her."

"I see," Waraday said, but his usually smooth forehead was creased with wrinkles as he turned back to Nita, who was nodding.

"Ellie's right. I've found several words that are the same as her notes. This can be translated, but it will take time."

"Right." Waraday reluctantly pulled out a bag and slid the notebook into it.

Nita looked bereft. He saw her face and said, "First, we have to analyze it. Then, I'd like to get an outside expert to look at it. I'd also like to make a copy and have you translate as much as you can, Mrs. Nita. Would you mind?"

It was clear Nita was eager to try and decipher those words, so the question was more a formality than anything else. "Of course," Nita said. "Anything you need."

"Now." Waraday turned to me. "Where did you find this?"

With the notebook out of sight, Nita turned her curious dark eyes on me, too. She tilted her head, again reminding me of a bird. "Yes, I didn't even think to ask. Where *did* you find it? The crime scene folks searched everywhere after we realized she was gone."

I pulled out the drawer. "This drawer never quite closed

and today I pulled it out to see why. I found the notebook taped to the underside of the counter." I released the levers and slid the drawer all the way out and set it on the floor. "You can see where one of the pieces of tape came off and it folded over, preventing the drawer from closing."

Waraday knelt down and peered into the dark space. Nita bobbed behind him, trying to look, too. "Now, why would she put that one in there?" she asked.

Waraday twisted around and looked at her. She explained about the other notebooks she had at her house.

"I'll send someone out to pick those up." Waraday stood and turned to me. "How long have you lived here, Mrs. Avery?"

"Since January."

"Ten months. You waited almost a year to see why this drawer didn't work?"

I laughed. "I've got a preschooler and a toddler. Some days I don't even get to bring in the mail, much less open it. That drawer wasn't a priority. Nathan scratched his arm on it today and I decided I'd take care of it, so that's why I found it now."

"We'll have to check the rest of the cabinets." Waraday's mouth quirked down and I could tell from his tone he wasn't happy. I couldn't tell if he wasn't happy that the notebook had been missed in the original search or if he wasn't happy to have the new evidence. I was surprised at his reaction. You'd think he'd be excited to find something a missing woman had hidden in her house. It *had* to be important. Why else would she hide it, and not her other notebooks?

The door to the garage opened and Mitch stepped inside, sweaty and covered with bits of grass.

I hastily performed the introductions and said, "I found a notebook that belonged to Jodi taped under one of the cabinets. Detective Waraday is calling in a team to look at the rest of the cabinets again."

Mitch paused a moment, shook his head, and said, "Figures." Then he headed to our bedroom. "I'll be in the shower. Ask them to save the master bath for last."

He took that much better than I thought he would. I noticed Waraday watching Mitch's receding back with a funny expression. I'm sure most husbands wouldn't be so blasé if their house was about to be searched.

I smiled brightly. I wasn't about to tell Waraday that this wasn't the first time our house had been searched. "Mitch is so easygoing. Nothing fazes him. Could you wait until after nap time to call your people in?"

"You're going where?"

"The homeowners' meeting. Networking opportunity, remember? For Everything In Its Place. If you'll stay home with the kids tonight, I'll go and network. Unless you want to go, too. I can call Anna—"

"Are you kidding? Saturday Night Football is on. You go network your heart out and I'll hold down the fort here."

Sports trumped the HOA meeting for Mitch and if I wasn't looking for paying organizing clients I'd probably have stayed home, too, because we were renters, not homeowners, but I shrugged into my denim jacket and walked a block to Coleman's house.

I'd never been to a homeowners' association meeting before, but I discovered that they were very much like the spouse club meetings—old business, new business, food, and chatting.

I tried to focus on Coleman, who was wearing his usual golf casual attire minus the visor. He stood in front of the fireplace with a sheaf of papers. If those papers were the agenda for tonight, I was in trouble. I wouldn't make it home until after midnight.

We'd gone around the room and introduced ourselves, said where we lived and what we did, so I'd been able to mention Everything In Its Place at least once, so that was good. Coleman finished talking about the need to bag leaves so they wouldn't clog the drains. He straightened the papers and said, "Now, let me again reiterate the importance of getting permits for any, *any*, type of flyer or notice that you want to post in the neighborhood." He held up the stack of paper and fanned through it. "I pulled these flyers down in the last two days. The covenants are what keep Magnolia Estates . . ."

The flyer thing again. It was kind of pathetic, really. He probably spent several hours a week pulling down garage sale and lost dog notices. I shifted around on the bar stool, my concentration drifting again. I was surprised to see Nita Lockworth seated on the couch, her back straight and head tilted to one side, her bright eyes fixed on Coleman. I knew she didn't live in Magnolia Estates and figured she must be here in case Coleman tried to shut down the search. Even though the bones didn't belong to Jodi, the search was still on. Nita wanted to capitalize on the renewed interest in Jodi. Nita had stayed at our house until Waraday's search was complete. The technicians hadn't turned up anything else and since they'd confined themselves to the cabinets and closets, they'd finished pretty quickly.

I felt a tap on my shoulder and turned. It was the woman I'd sat beside at the Find Jodi meeting. She jerked her head in the direction of the kitchen, which caused her frizzy mustard-colored hair to dance. "Want to help me with the food?" she asked quietly.

"Sure." I slid off the bar stool and followed her around the corner into the kitchen, trying to remember her name. I wished Abby was with me. She was a people person and could remember the name of practically every person she'd ever met. But there was no way she was going to come to an HOA meeting. She lived on-base.

"You remember me, right? From the Find Jodi meeting?"

"Yes, of course, except I've forgotten your name," I admitted.

"Colleen. Colleen Otway," she said as she opened the refrigerator and pulled out a tray of fruit. "You looked like you were about to fall asleep in there."

"I was. Thanks for the escape. What can I do?"

"Just take the plastic off these and help me set out the cups."

We worked quietly for a few seconds as Coleman's voice droned on in the next room. When we had the food and drinks set up on the island I asked, "So, is he almost done?"

"Oh no. He could go on for hours. He was a politician, so he can talk endlessly and never say a thing."

"He was in politics? I didn't know that."

"City politics. He was the mayor for years and years. Ever since I was a kid. He's retired."

She went to the door and nodded to someone, then came back into the kitchen. "Nita will cut in when he gets to the new business and tell him the food is ready. Everyone will stampede in here and that will end the meeting."

"Good plan. I didn't realize you lived in Magnolia Estates."

"I don't. I live in an apartment complex out near the interstate. Nita and I crashed the party. We brought food, which no one can turn down. We both know we have to be here to make sure we can do the search." She went still, listening. "There's Mrs. Nita's voice."

We both went to the door. ". . . so you can see that it's in the best interest of the homeowners of Magnolia Estates to have the search. The area of the search will be restricted to the tracts of undeveloped land and the group will be instructed not to search around homes."

Coleman pointed the stack of papers at Nita. "You've already had searches in the neighborhood. We can't have a horde of people swarming over undeveloped land. The liability—"

A commanding voice from the back of the room interrupted Coleman. "I own one of the undeveloped lots in Phase Two."

Beside me, I felt Colleen tense as she saw the speaker was Scott Ezell. I hadn't finished reading Jodi's profile on him and I made a mental note to find that article. Colleen took a deep breath and was about to speak, but Scott continued in his reasonable and confident tone. "I have no problem with a search. In fact, I think it's a good idea. It will help all of us feel more comfortable about the lots we've purchased and settle any questions there might be about whether investing in the next phase in Magnolia Estates is a smart move or not."

Coleman was at a loss for words. I could tell the idea that someone might not want to move to Magnolia Estates had never entered his thoughts. I glanced at Colleen. She had a perplexed look on her face as she stared at Scott.

Dorthea jumped in. "I think a search is a good idea, too. I move we vote on a search of the undeveloped land."

"I second the motion," Scott said quickly.

Coleman looked frustrated as he asked for a show of hands in favor of the search and almost every hand in the room went up.

"Wonderful." Nita sprang up from the sofa and patted Coleman on the back. "It'll work out fine, I'm sure. I think I saw some delicious refreshments in the kitchen."

I moved out of the doorway as people began to file into the kitchen. I shifted over to the table with the drinks and checked my watch as I grabbed a can of Diet Coke. Another meeting wrapped up neatly, but this time it was thanks to Scott and Dorthea. I'd make it home in time to tell Livvy good night. She might be in bed at seven-thirty, but that didn't mean she was asleep. She stayed awake as long as she could to prove to us that she wasn't sleepy and her bedtime was way too early.

I moved across the room to greet Dorthea. "Did you and Scott have that planned? The call for a vote?"

"Oh no, honey. I just thought the timing was good. Better

to get an actual vote taken and get it over with." Colleen joined our group and Dorthea said, "How have you been? Haven't seen you in an age."

"Fine," Colleen said shortly, her narrow gaze fixed on Scott, who was piling his plate with food from the trays. "I'm amazed Scott said he wanted a search. Why would he say that?"

"Why wouldn't he want a search?" Dorthea asked.

"I don't know. He was so helpful and it makes me mad he keeps showing up. He's always at the Find Jodi meetings and everyone knows he couldn't stand her. Why is he so concerned now?"

This was something new. I raised my eyebrows at Dorthea and she gave a minimal shrug, so I asked, "He and Jodi didn't get along?"

Colleen said, "He hated her."

An Everything In Its Place Tip for an Organized Party

Lists are essential when it comes to party planning. Keep everything together, either in your handheld computer or in a binder or folder. Here are some lists that will help you stay on-task:

- Guest List with space to note RSVP. Generally, about half the number of people you invite will attend your party.
- Menu. Make a detailed list of food and drink you're planning to serve, then use recipes to make shopping lists.
- Shopping Lists. Make at least two lists. One for nonperishable items like decorations, favors, and paper items that can be picked up one to two weeks before the party. Make a second list of perishable items, like food, ice, fresh flowers, and balloons. It's also helpful to have a separate shopping list for each store.

- To-do List. Jot down items like clean house, mow yard, weed flower bed, remove breakable knick-knacks from the fireplace mantel, etc.
- Returns List—to keep track of rented and borrowed items.
- Thank-you Note List.

Chapter
Ten

"That didn't come across in the profile Jodi wrote about Scott for the newspaper," I said.

"That was before the whole Jackson Hollow issue."

"Jackson Hollow?" I'd heard that name somewhere, but couldn't place it.

"The old development near the base," Colleen clarified.

"Oh, that's right," I said. "We looked at a couple of houses there when we first came here." Actually, a drive through the neighborhood was all it took for us to decide we needed to keep looking. The houses in Jackson Hollow were tiny postwar bungalows that needed some major sprucing up.

"Scott wants the city to condemn the houses and turn the property over to the base."

Dorthea added, "They're practically at the end of the runway."

Before we moved to North Dawkins, I'd heard about the space issues—encroachment was the term the military used—around Taylor. Every couple of years the military had a commission assess the military installations and recommend which ones needed to be expanded and which ones needed to be closed. Encroachment was one of the factors the commission considered.

"You said Scott wants the property condemned. Is it Scott or the group he works for, STAND?"

"Of course, he's the director of STAND," Colleen snapped, "and he says he's doing it for the good of the community, but *he* wants those houses gone."

"So what happened? Jodi didn't agree with him?"

"Jodi covered the city commission meeting where Scott made the proposal. She reported exactly what Scott wanted. Then she did what any good reporter would do. She went out and got the other side of the story. She interviewed several people who lived there. Scott hated that. Letters poured into the newspaper and most of them were on the side of the Jackson Hollow people."

Dorthea shook her head and said, "I'd forgotten all about that dustup. The city commission, cowards that they are, decided they needed a study to evaluate whether or not they should condemn the land. It took them until this summer to decide which consultant to hire. The report isn't due until January. Such a waste of money, if you ask me."

"So that must have calmed things down," I said.

"Hardly," Colleen said. "The commission didn't decide to hire a consultant until after their next meeting, which was where Scott and Jodi got into it."

"Got into it?"

"He accused her of slanted reporting, playing up the sympathy angle."

"This was during the meeting?" I asked.

"During the comment time. After the meeting they had a shouting match in the parking lot."

"Wow," I said. "That doesn't sound like the Jodi I've heard described so often."

Colleen took a deep breath. "She did get a bit carried away. She was passionate about doing her job and doing it right. Saying she wasn't fair . . . that was low. Scott deserved to be shouted at. Jodi *had* reported both sides of the issue. Scott didn't like it that the interviews with the Jackson Hollow neighborhood put him in such a bad light. That's why it doesn't make sense that he's so involved now."

"So what happened after the shouting match?" I asked.

"Jodi wrote her article about the commission meeting and she followed up with the Jackson Hollow people."

"She went right back and wrote another article? Scott wouldn't have been happy about that." I looked across the room at him, devouring a plate of food. Now that he wasn't speaking in that self-assured tone, he didn't look like a threat to anyone. Instead, he looked like the IT guy you'd call at work when your computer refused to boot up.

"Does Detective Waraday know about their disagreement?"

"Oh, he knows about it, all right," Colleen said. "Has he done anything about it? No."

"Nothing?"

"He interviewed Scott. He interviewed everyone who knew Jodi, but nothing's come of it."

"Seems odd, though," I said. "Scott's the first person I've heard of who had any disagreement with Jodi . . ."

"I know." Colleen pounced on my words. "I think he had something to do with her disappearance. That's why he's always around, hanging out at the meetings. He wants to keep track of what's going on. Oh, here's Mrs. Nita. Tell Ellie what Detective Waraday said when we told him about Scott."

Nita pursed her lips. "Yes, that was a bit disheartening. Detective Waraday sees their argument as a small contretemps. As he's told me, there's nothing else there to investigate, no indication that he was ever near Jodi or had any contact with her except at those two city council meetings. There's no physical evidence, and physical evidence is what counts with Davey. He's very methodical and since he's eliminated Scott, I think you can, too, Colleen."

"Eliminated him?" Colleen said, her voice squeaking. "He's not a suspect at all?"

"Apparently he has an alibi. He was out of town the weekend when Jodi disappeared."

"Where?" Colleen demanded.

"Washington, D.C."

Colleen still looked disbelieving and made a move in Scott's direction, but Nita put a hand on her arm. "Fortunately, we have some new physical evidence, thanks to Ellie." She described the notebook, then turned to me. "I wanted to thank you for calling me today and then allowing me to stay at your house until the search was over."

"It wasn't a problem at all." Hey, it was her house—technically—so it seemed like the least I could do. "I'm just glad we found her notebook. Have you been able to transcribe any of it?"

"Yes, several pages. I've e-mailed them to Davey." She shook her head slightly. "I don't know if the notes will be that helpful to the investigation. The first pages are more details about the Halloween story she was working on. I'm afraid Davey wasn't as enthralled with her notes as I am, which is completely understandable."

"Well, I'm interested and I'm just a . . . bystander. Otherwise, why hide it? It must be important."

"My thoughts as well. And I know Davey will get to it. He requested someone to transcribe it, but I think it will take a while. He was preoccupied when I talked to him this afternoon. He does have other issues besides Jodi."

"Of course. At least you're on it."

"Yes, I am," she said firmly, then tilted her head and blinked her dark eyes as she studied me. What had been a conversation shifted to something else that felt a bit awkward. As she examined me, I felt as if I were under a microscope. She was assessing me. "Ellie, you've shown an interest in finding Jodi. I truly do appreciate all your help with the flyers."

"I'm glad I could help." It did feel good to know that my organizational skills could contribute to finding Jodi, even in a small way.

"Would you be interested in helping in another area?"

"Yes." Sometimes I got myself a bit, well, let's say over-extended, because I didn't like to tell people no. It was the hardest word in the English language for me to utter, but at the moment, I didn't have a lot going on. "I'd love to help."

"What I'm thinking of wouldn't be directly for the Find Jodi search. Coordinating the Find Jodi campaign does take quite a bit of my time. What I need help with is the note-book. If I e-mail my transcription to you, would you match it with the articles she wrote? Since it would be to help me stay organized, I'd pay your going rate for organizing."

"Yes, I can do that, but you don't need to pay me."

"Nonsense. It will help me out tremendously and give me some peace of mind. I know Davey will get to the notebook, but I'd like to pull all the information out of it as soon as possible. You never know what can make a difference. I don't want to overlook anything."

"I've already printed most of her articles, so I'll just match them up with her notebook entries."

"Yes, I noticed you'd been doing some research. That made me think you might be interested in helping me."

"I'm curious. She lived in our house and . . ." I trailed off, not wanting to talk about the bones I'd found.

"You don't have to explain to me," Nita said. "I've learned that some people care. You're one of those people. That's why I asked you."

Nita looked over my shoulder and her face switched into neutral. "Scott. How are you?"

"Fine. Fine. How are you, Mrs. Lockworth?"

"Good. How is everything at STAND?" Nita asked, clearly making an effort to be nice to him, but I could tell from her stilted speech that she really didn't want to talk with him.

"Busy." Scott transferred his small plate from one hand to another and then pushed his dark-framed glasses up the bridge of his nose. "Actually, that's why I came over. I wanted to talk with Ellie about some organizing help at the office."

"Well, I'll leave you two. I can tell you that Ellie is a wonderful organizer. Consider me a reference. She's whipped the flyer program at Find Jodi into shape."

"What did you have in mind?" I'd never had a corporate client before, so I wasn't sure what to expect, but inside I was giving myself a high five. My business might survive the transition to North Dawkins after all.

"We have stacks of boxes we need sorted, a whole storage room of them. The papers keep piling up and we can't get to them. Would you take a look and give me an estimate of what it would take to get it organized?"

"Yes, I could do that."

"Great. How about Tuesday?"

I did a quick mental scan of my schedule, which was wide open, except for taking care of Livvy and Nathan. I knew Mitch was scheduled for a weeklong trip beginning Monday, so I wouldn't be able to count on him to back me up with the kids.

"Could we meet in the afternoon around four?" I was sure I could call Anna, a teenager who lived in the neighborhood, to watch the kids for an hour.

"That should work," Scott said. I confirmed that STAND's office was in the new business office park near the interstate; then I said good-bye to my neighbors, who were still chatting. I pulled the front door closed and set a brisk pace down the driveway.

The sky was inky except for a sliver of moon. The air was perfectly still. I peeled off my denim jacket, which I'd needed at the meeting. Most houses and businesses had their thermometers set to the "freezer" temperature to combat the muggy heat that had come back after our too-brief taste of cool temperatures. A dog barked at me as I hurried past dark clumps, the brick mailboxes that loomed at the end of each driveway. I almost wished I had driven. Or at least waited for Dorthea.

Headlights spotlighted the road beside me as a car approached behind me. I moved over as far as I could to the side of the road, glad I was wearing a white T-shirt. At least I was visible to the driver.

The car hung back, slightly behind me. I kicked my pace up a notch and rushed along, ducking under the waxy leaves of a magnolia tree.

The car hovered behind me. I glanced over my shoulder quickly, but I couldn't see anything except the blazing headlights.

Great. Why didn't the driver pass me? It wasn't like I was taking up the road. There was plenty of room to get around me, but the car continued to linger. I didn't have a good feeling about this. Was this what happened to Jodi? Had she raced along, unable to see into the blackness past the headlights?

I bit my lip and scanned the houses on my side of the road, fleetingly thinking of turning up one of the driveways and ringing the doorbell. I didn't know anyone who lived on this street and every house near me had the buttoned-up, we're-not-home look. The houses' windows were dark and I wasn't even sure where the driveway ended at the closest one because trees shrouded the lawn.

The car veered closer and the headlights angled toward me. *Not good*. I broke into a jog as I hopped onto a lawn and dodged around the nearest mailbox.

The engine accelerated behind me.

I sprinted, my feet thudding through the grass. Since I didn't jog and I *never* sprinted, I knew I couldn't keep up the pace long. *Almost to the corner*. If I angled across the lawn at the corner, I'd be on our street, almost home.

I flew across the corner yard, my breath choppy. I glanced over my shoulder and saw the car pause at the stop sign, then roar into the turn, cutting off my path.

I wasn't going to make it to my street. I froze for a second, then reversed and headed back the way I'd come. Better to get back where there were plenty of people. Why hadn't I done that first?

I ran, breath heaving now. Instead of going on, the car reversed, curving back around the corner. I heard a honk and a shout.

Was that . . . my name?

Another honk and, yes, that was definitely the driver calling my name.

I stopped sprinting and turned. Now that I was behind the headlights, I could make out the car, a small hybrid, but I didn't recognize it. The passenger window slid down. "Ellie! It's me, Colleen."

The car backed up even with me and I walked over on wobbly legs. I braced one hand on my knee as I bent down to look in the window. "Colleen? What were you doing? You scared me to death."

"I'm sorry. I wasn't sure if it was you. That's why I was going so slow. I thought you were wearing blue, not white, so I wasn't sure."

I was still panting, so I held up my denim jacket I had clutched in one hand.

"Oh, sorry. I'm really sorry. Do you want to sit down for a minute?"

The cool air blasted out of the vents in her dash and I angled one toward my face. "No, that's okay. I need to get home."

"Come on, let me drop you at home. It's the least I can do."

"Okay," I said, and collapsed into the seat. "Turn at the corner and about halfway down."

"Right. Look, I'm really sorry. Nita told me Scott wants to hire you for an organizing job and I wanted to tell you to be careful."

"Got it. You don't like him. Don't trust him." I pointed at the mailbox. "This is mine."

Colleen pulled into the driveway, then stomped on the brakes. "You don't get it, do you? Scott could be very dangerous. He may have gotten away with . . ." She closed her eyes and reluctantly said, "Murder. At the very least, kidnapping."

"Colleen, of course, I'll be careful, but if the sheriff's investigated and Scott has an alibi—"

She tossed her head back and her wiry hair trembled as she said, "I don't even want to talk about the sheriff's office. They are so stuck on her 'boyfriend' they can't see anything else."

"She had a boyfriend?" I asked, surprised.

"No," Colleen said derisively.

"Sorry," I said. "It's just that Dorthea said she wasn't dating anyone."

"She wasn't." Colleen's tone had lost its sharpness. "She met this guy—Peter Yannis—at one of the online dating sites. They e-mailed a few times and talked on the phone. Jodi said he seemed nice. He was a physical therapist who lived in Florida. After a couple of weeks, he mentioned he was driving up to a conference in Atlanta and they decided to meet for dinner since he'd be practically driving through North Dawkins to get to Atlanta."

"So what happened?"

"They met for dinner, they talked, and he went on to Atlanta, but he didn't stop again on the way back home to Florida. Jodi said he was extremely enthusiastic."

"Enthusiastic about meeting her face-to-face?"

"Yes, she said he was excited about that, but apparently, he was like that with everything, his work, his hobby. What did she say it was? Oh yeah, deep-sea fishing. I think he came on too strong. Jodi is"—Colleen waved her hand in the air and shrugged slightly as she searched for the right word—"self-contained. No, that's not a good description. Reserved. Self-sufficient?" Colleen tried out the words, testing them. "That sounds very lonerish, doesn't it? Jodi doesn't need a lot of noise and flash to be happy, and I got the feeling that Peter was very extroverted and overpowered her. Anyway, whatever happened, one date doesn't make a relationship. I wish I could make Waraday understand that."

"So Waraday knows about this Peter—what was his last name?" I reached for the door handle and tucked my jacket over my arm.

"Yannis. Yes, Waraday knows about him. That's all Waraday wanted to cover when he questioned me. He's stuck on Peter Yannis. I don't know why. Maybe it's that thing about 'it's usually the husband who's guilty when something happens to the wife.' Since Jodi isn't married, that only leaves a boyfriend and Peter Yannis is the closest thing Waraday can find to a boyfriend."

"So, what does Peter Yannis say about all this? Does he have an alibi like Scott?"

Colleen frowned. "That's the problem. Waraday hasn't been able to find Peter."

Chapter
Eleven

I released the door handle and twisted around to face Colleen. "You mean he's disappeared, too?" This story got stranger and stranger.

She held up her hand, fingers splayed. "I know, I know. On the surface it looks like there might be a connection, but she wasn't attracted to him. She wouldn't run off to see him and not tell anyone. She's not like that. She'd never worry her family like that."

"You have to admit that it does sound like more than a co-incidence."

"I know, but I know Jodi. She'd never do that, no matter what showed up on her credit card. That stupid charge combined with Peter's disappearance have derailed the whole investigation," Colleen said, frustration vibrating through her tone. "The night she disappeared, she charged some bottled water, an energy bar, and a map of Florida at a convenience store on the interstate. Waraday's focused on that trivial charge and assumed she headed off to Florida to meet Peter Yannis, but that's not logical. Not for Jodi. She doesn't do things on the spur of the minute and she's considerate of other people. She'd never go off like that."

"Why wasn't there anything about that in the newspaper, I wonder?"

"They kept it out of the news and I only know about it because Mrs. Nita told me. I was so frustrated with Waraday and how he wouldn't do anything else about Scott." Colleen leaned back against the headrest and blew out a deep breath. "She wanted to help me see why the investigation was focused on Peter Yannis. Sorry I get so worked up about this, but it's important. You do need to be really careful around Scott."

"I will be. Thanks for the lift home," I said as I stepped out of the car. I shoved the door closed and gave a quick wave.

I went through the automatic motions of punching in the code on the keypad, but I hardly noticed the rumble of the garage door as it rose. So Jodi had a conflict with Scott and she'd met a guy through an online dating service. Neither bit of info was that exceptional. People had arguments all the time and online dating was downright common, but combining those factors with her disappearance put them in a new light. I couldn't really blame Waraday for his interest in Peter Yannis, especially since he couldn't locate the guy. And Colleen's fixation on Scott as a suspect, that was a bit excessive. I shook my head, mentally telling myself it wasn't my problem and it didn't have anything to do with me.

Well, except for the fact that I was going to help Nita match up the notes to Jodi's articles. That was all I was going to do. I stepped into the house, expecting everything to be dark and quiet, but I heard giggles coming from the kitchen. I found Mitch and Livvy huddled over bowls of ice cream, playing High Ho! Cherry-O.

Livvy put a finger to her lips and said, "Shh. Nathan's sleeping. We don't want to wake him up."

"I bet you don't," I said, and reached for a bowl.

I dropped onto the overstuffed chair and propped my feet up on the huge ottoman, listening for a moment to make sure the house was going to stay quiet. Nathan was sleeping—of course. There was no doubt he was deep in dreamland, but I was sure my little night owl, Livvy, was still awake. As long as she stayed in her bed, she could stay awake as long as she liked. Rex collapsed on the floor beside me with a gusty sigh and I said, "I hear you, boy. I'm exhausted, too." My shoulder muscles ached from carrying Nathan, who seemed to be putting on a couple of pounds every week. It felt so good to sit down. I flexed my feet back, stretching my calf muscles. I'd never been so worn out in my life. The sheer physical exhaustion I felt after a day of chasing two kids and running a house surprised me. No workout I'd ever done in the past had the effect of basically turning me into a puddle. Mitch had left this afternoon for his weeklong trip and I was on my own.

It had been a crazy day. Sometimes I thought Sundays were the most stressful day of the week. The morning had been a mad dash to get everyone dressed and out the door for church. We'd gone to the park after lunch and exhausted everyone, including Rex. Then, I'd squeezed in another hour in the box room between washing laundry so Mitch could pack. His trip had been moved up and he had to leave this afternoon, which meant we had to cancel our date.

A chime sounded from my computer. I checked the new e-mail and could tell from the address it had been sent through the Find Jodi Web site and was from Nita. She wrote:

Hello, Ellie.

I've attached the first set of transcriptions from Jodi's notebook. It was slow going, but after a few pages it began to flow more quickly. If you could match these up with her articles, that would be terrific.

I opened the attachment and printed it, but I didn't let myself read it. I put it in a folder with Jodi's articles because it was late. If I got into the transcription of Jodi's notes and articles now, I'd be up until after midnight. I set it down, but kept my hand on it. I was torn. I wanted to open it, delve right in, and sort out the details, but was reluctant to do it.

I was getting deeper and deeper into the search for Jodi. I'd promised myself I wouldn't get mixed up in it, but here I was coordinating flyer distribution, volunteering for searches, and digging into Jodi's articles for clues. I put the folder down. I'd go through it, match up the articles and notes, then give it back to Nita and that would be it.

I went back to flipping channels. I knew I should go to bed, but I'd never mastered the art of going to bed early when Mitch was gone. Livvy wasn't the only one who had trouble falling asleep and I figured it was better to fall into bed totally beat and get a couple of really good hours of sleep than go to bed early and toss and turn most of the night. I settled in to watch a rerun of a home improvement show, but after thirty minutes of watching designers bicker and make outrageous choices, I went back to channel-surfing.

I paused on a classic movie station when I saw the title of the black-and-white movie was *His Girl Friday*. This was the movie that Jodi had liked, the one that inspired her to be a reporter.

I edged the sound up slightly and tried to follow the rapid-fire dialogue. I'd never seen the movie and it took me a little while to work out that Cary Grant in his role as Walter, a conniving newspaper editor, was using a story about a pending execution to lure his star reporter, Hildy—who also happened to be his ex-wife—back to reporting and, not incidentally, also back to him before she married a nice but dull insurance salesman and went off to the suburbs to have babies.

I watched Hildy stride into the press room, confident in her abilities and comfortable even though she was the only woman. She joked with the boys, who couldn't believe she was going to leave journalism, interviewed the condemned man, and then banged out an eloquent story on her manual typewriter with the ease and speed of a professional.

At the commercial break, I snuck into the kitchen to make popcorn and pour a tall Diet Coke. I was into the movie. No way was I going to bed any time soon, so I didn't worry about the caffeine. I grabbed a few Hershey's Kisses, too, for good measure.

I snuggled back into the chair and settled in to watch the movie. I was halfway through my popcorn when the sirens went off in the movie and I turned down the sound. The reporters scrambled from the pressroom to track down the story of a jailbreak. Instinctively, Hildy called in the news, then took off after the story, hiking up her skirt so she could chase the prison warden. She brought him down with a flying tackle so she could interview him.

No wonder Jodi had wanted to be a reporter after watching the movie. I was so immersed in it that by the time the credits rolled, I realized I hadn't eaten my chocolate Kisses. I untwisted the foil. The end of the movie had hit the perfect note. Justice was served and Hildy realized she was a reporter to the core and gave up her romanticized version of domesticity. She also realized she was still in love with Walter, which was no surprise since I didn't think there was a woman out there who could resist Cary Grant.

I rolled the foil into a ball and tossed it in the bowl with the popcorn kernels. Why couldn't they make movies like that today? I couldn't think of many recent movie roles that showed a woman that strong and confident. And as the acknowledged expert, too. Hildy was the best at what she did. She'd been a little mixed up about what she wanted in her personal life, but hey, that wasn't uncommon. At least she wasn't portrayed as a bumbling fool in every aspect of life, a movie formula that made me cringe.

I saw it was past midnight and groaned. I gathered up the dishes and went to coax Rex to bed in his kennel, still thinking about Jodi wanting to be like Hildy.

* * *

The next morning, I pulled into the garage and breathed a sigh of relief after dropping Livvy off at Mother's Day Out. We'd both been a little slow this morning, me because of my late night and Livvy because she spilled milk on her favorite shirt and didn't want to change clothes. I'd relaxed my parenting standards quite a bit since Nathan's arrival, but I had to draw the line at letting my daughter wear a wet, smelly shirt.

I climbed out of the car, unstrapped Nathan from his seat, then went around to the passenger side of the car to get the diaper bag.

"Not again." Another thin scratch wavered down the other side of the car.

An Everything In Its Place Tip for an Organized Party

Before the Party Checklist
- Make guest list.
- Send invitations via e-mail or snail mail two weeks prior to event date.
- Plan menu—finger foods work best if you're serving food from a buffet. If you're planning a sit-down dinner, use favorite recipes that you know taste wonderful. One or two new dishes are enough to stress out most hostesses. Also, when planning your menu, think about what can be prepared ahead and refrigerated or frozen to cut down on the amount of work you'll have on the day of the party.
- Party flow—decide on placement of food, drinks, and conversation area.
- Purchase nonperishable items.
- Purchase perishable items.
- Follow up with guests who haven't responded to invitation.

After the party
- Write thank-you notes for gifts received and to thank people who let you borrow items.
- Return rented and borrowed items.

Chapter
Twelve

I put Nathan down for his brief morning nap and went back to the garage, where I walked from side to side, looking at the twin scratches. Why would someone key my car? Twice? Had I made someone mad? Cut someone off in traffic and this was how they were getting back at me?

I ran my finger down one of the scratches and got an uneasy feeling. If it was intentional and not random, did that mean someone was following me around, watching me, and waiting for a moment when no one would notice them vandalizing my car?

But why would someone do that? The people around here practiced friendliness like it was an extreme sport, and as far as I knew no one hated me. I paused. Unless someone didn't like what I was doing to help the Find Jodi campaign? No, it couldn't be that. That idea was too far-fetched. It was a sign that it was indeed time to upgrade my wheels. I shook off the anxious feeling. It was bad luck, nothing more. I went to the kitchen desk. I had to focus and get some work done before Nathan woke up.

As I printed out the forms I'd need to take with me today to the meeting with Scott, I checked my e-mail. Nothing in the business account, but a new e-mail in my personal account from Abby.

Abby had taken a break from teaching after the birth of her first baby, Charlie. They'd moved to Taylor last October, right after Charlie was born. Abby and I spent from January to September doing mom things—library story time, picnics at the playground, outings to the mall, and even a trip to the strawberry patch. But her "sabbatical," as she called it, ended in September when she found a sitter for Charlie and returned to teaching.

She wrote:

Feels like it's been forever since we've seen each other. What's going on with you? For me, it's the same old thing—multiplication and cursive.

What's going on? Where did I start?
I replied:

For a change I have more happening in my life than laundry. Well, I have that, too, but there's other things— more interesting things—happening. Too much to tell you in an e-mail. Want to get together?

I didn't expect to hear back right away, but the computer dinged and I opened her new message.

Yes! How about after school today?

Can't. I have an actual, real, live possible organizing client. Tomorrow?

I hit REPLY and waited, but nothing came back. She was probably e-mailing during her planning period and had to go.

I paused to listen. I could hear Nathan shifting around. It wouldn't be long before he'd be completely awake and ready to play. It was strange that I could block just about anything out—the phone, the television, the dryer clunking away down the hall, the occasional jet from the base thundering overhead—but my senses were finely tuned to listen for those first rustling sounds coming from Nathan's room.

I jumped up and headed for the dishwasher. If I could get it unloaded before Nathan became fully awake, that was one less chore I had to do with him balancing on my legs.

I paused in the hallway to get my bearings and catch my breath. I shifted my portfolio from one hand to another and checked to make sure I'd brought my marketing packet. All present and accounted for. STAND certainly wasn't wasting money on classy digs. Glass doors lined a hallway of low-pile industrial-gray carpet. I headed for a door with a flag stencil.

I entered a small waiting area that was as bare as the hall-way, except for a receptionist's desk and two hard plastic chairs. Not a picture or plant in sight. Okay, this might not be the big-bucks client I'd been hoping for, but right now I'd just take a client with *some* bucks. Maybe STAND had saved their decorating budget for better use elsewhere. Like for a professional organizer.

A heavyset woman who looked like she was in her late forties sat at the desk stapling papers and chewing gum. Each time she banged the stapler her bracelets jangled and her huge hoop earrings rocked. She smacked her gum. "Can I help you?"

"I'm here to see Scott Ezell. I have an appointment."

"Sure." She tossed her head toward a door behind her and managed to chomp on the gum several times while also saying, "He's in there. Go on back."

The door was open and when I stepped inside I saw that the inner office was almost as bare as the front office, except for a table with four small televisions, all tuned to news channels and muted. Scott sat at a pressboard desk behind a laptop and a stack of papers. He was wearing a long-sleeved oxford shirt and dress pants, and his tie was patterned with a design of jet fighters. He stood up, extended one hand, and pushed his glasses up with the other. "Ellie. Good to see you again. Come in. Would you like some coffee or a Coke?"

It was never a "drink" or "a soda," only Coke existed, especially in Georgia. I declined and he said, "Well, let me get the worst part over with first." He walked to another door in the office and opened it.

So that's where they'd put everything. And I do mean everything. It was the "shove it all out of sight" ploy, a long-time favorite technique perfected by many kids as they "cleaned" their room. Shoving everything under the bed made the room look so much better, but it only delayed cleaning up the mess. Same principle here, just a door to hide the mess instead of a dust ruffle.

There were at least three filing cabinets that I could see. There might have been more, but I couldn't tell for sure because boxes were stacked to the ceiling and piles of paper tilted precariously on top of them. A coffeemaker sat on a TV tray crammed into a corner. Rolled banners leaned against a pile of Christmas decorations and five-gallon bottles of water. "You can see why we need someone like you. I don't have time to dig through here and Candy, you met her on the way in, she's not what you'd call the organizational type."

I pulled out my packet and said, "Why don't you glance through this and I'll take a look at what you have? Then I'll need to ask you a few more questions before I can give you an estimate."

"Sure. Have at it." Scott waved me into the storage area and went back to the desk.

I stepped across the threshold into the tiny square of open space and began scribbling notes as I looked through the file cabinets and peeked in the boxes.

Candy stuck her head around the door frame, and one hoop swung wildly against her cheek as she informed Scott,

"I'm takin' my break." She jiggled some change in her hand. "Anyone else want a Coke?"

"No, thanks," I said. Scott declined as well.

After a few minutes I sat back down across from Scott in another of the molded plastic chairs and worked through a few questions that helped me sort out exactly what clients expected the final result to be. "So, basically, you want an accessible filing system for the paperwork you deal with on a daily and monthly basis. You also need long-term storage for older items," I summarized. "As well as a place to store the Christmas decorations."

Scott smiled. "Got it in one." His phone clipped at his waist buzzed and he checked the display. "Excuse me. I have to take this one." He flipped his phone open and swiveled his chair slightly away from me.

I finished up my notes, then gazed around the room, waiting for him. He said, "Right. Press releases go out Monday and I'll follow up . . ."

Candy returned and walked into Scott's office. She slapped a bottle of Peach Snapple down on his desk and whispered to me, "If he doesn't have his afternoon tea he gets a headache and then he's a real bear to work with." She winked at me and headed back to her desk.

Scott swiveled back toward me, saw the drink, and shook his head. He twisted off the lid as he continued his conversation.

I switched my gaze away from him and focused on the television screens. Even though they were muted, it was hard not to watch them and try to keep up with the text that popped up.

The word *Nash* marched across the screen of the television that was tuned to a local station's early evening edition of the news. I recognized the stately black woman they were interviewing. I'd seen her at the Find Jodi meeting where she'd embraced Nita and comforted her. Now she was the one fighting not to cry. The closed captioning at the bottom of the screen read *Sherry Wayne, cousin of William James Nash, was visibly upset today after she learned the remains found earlier this week were those of her long-missing relative.* Sherry dabbed at her eyes with a tissue, shaking her head, but continued to talk. I went back to reading the crawl. *Wayne says the family is relieved to finally be able to bury Nash, but questions remain about his final hours.*

Now I understood Colleen's comment about Sherry being the only one who truly understood what Nita was going through.

Scott finished his call and turned up the volume on the TV. Sherry's robust voice quavered only slightly as she said, "We just want to know what happened to William. We'll keep pressure on county officials until we know the truth."

The shot switched to a view of the sheriff at a press conference. The reporter's voiceover intoned, "However, answers about this cold case with racial overtones appear to be a long way off." The report ended with the sheriff again asking for patience and reiterating that investigators were pursuing all possible leads.

Scott hit the mute button.

"Racial overtones?" I asked, puzzled.

Scott sighed and tossed the remote and his cell phone on the desk. "Sadly, the lynching of William Nash is one of the few claims to fame we have here in North Dawkins besides the large military base and our railroad depot."

"Lynching?" I'd never seen anything about that when I read up on North Dawkins before our move. I always like to know as much as I can about the town we're moving to. It helps make the move smoother and—usually—helps Mitch and me make a good decision about where to live.

"Yes, as awful as it is, it's about the only thing that happened here between the arrival of the railroad and the arrival of the Air Force base," Scott said.

"What happened with Nash?"

"Word around North Dawkins is that William wanted to

organize some sort of march or event in support of the Montgomery Bus Boycott. People say he was hanged on an oak tree out by the Taylor place, the one that's a B and B now, and then his body was tossed in the swamp over at the far side of the county."

"That's terrible," I said. It was hard for me to imagine what North Dawkins would have been like before the Civil Rights movement. All signs of segregation were gone now, at least on the surface. Black people and white people worked in the same offices, went to the same schools, and lived in the same neighborhoods. The only place I noticed a split along racial lines was on Sunday mornings when people tended to worship at either mostly white or mostly black congregations, which I thought was sad. Shouldn't churches be the first place for reconciliation? I supposed the difference in worship styles explained some of the division. I did see people with Confederate flag bumper stickers from time to time. The most popular one said IT'S OUR HERITAGE. BE PROUD OF IT. How can you be proud of something that included slavery? Obviously, race relations weren't perfect. "I wonder why I hadn't heard about Nash?"

Scott said, "People don't like to talk about it." His gaze was fixed on the monitors as he spoke quietly, almost to himself. Suddenly, he swung back to me and raised his eyebrows. "So, as for your fees . . ."

"Oh, of course." I handed him a sheet of paper. "This is a time and materials breakdown. The cost depends on whether you'd like to do some of this yourself or have me do all of it."

"I won't get it done and Candy—"

A shout from the outer office cut him off. "I ain't cleaning up that pile of crap. I didn't make that mess and I've got enough to do out here." This statement was followed with a resounding slap on the stapler.

Scott said, "Candy isn't one for tidying things up. And we have a big donor dinner coming up. She's got plenty to do with that, so we'd need you to do the work."

"Fine," I said as I wrote some figures down. I liked Scott's straightforward approach. So few people were honest with themselves when it came to cleaning out clutter or organizing things. Good intentions lasted only so long before they had to be backed up with solid hard work and realistic appraisals to see results.

I handed over my estimate and sat back in the chair. I'd gotten better at this part, stating my fees. I still felt a little nervous, but at least now I didn't apologize for charging for my services. It had taken a while to get over my feelings of awkwardness. I didn't charge an outrageous amount of money, but I'd had a few people in the past balk at my prices. They were polite to me, simply turning me down or telling me they were too busy at the moment, but I knew they were thinking, "Why would I pay this gal for something I can do myself?" The problem is that most people either don't actually get around to doing it themselves—we're all incredibly busy with our fast-paced lives today—or people get started, but don't finish. And there's nothing more depressing than a half-organized room.

Scott put the paper down and said, "This looks fine." Apparently, they had enough money in the budget to cover organizing, even if they didn't have enough to decorate, which was fine by me. We discussed payment and he wrote me a check, a deposit which I'd use to purchase supplies. I slipped the check into my portfolio and we worked out a schedule for me to return and work on the storage area during the next week.

I put my purse strap on my shoulder and prepared to stand up, but Scott was lounging back in his chair sipping his Snapple, which already had condensation on it. "Thank you for coming in today. I know Colleen probably tried to warn you off me."

"Well . . ." I wasn't sure how to answer that one.

He waved the bottle in the air. "Don't worry about it. I know she thinks I had something to do with Jodi's disappearance. I don't understand why she's so fixated on me, but maybe she'll let up since the remains weren't Jodi."

Somehow I didn't think that was going to happen. Colleen seemed pretty adamant in her dislike of Scott and her suspicions.

"No, I shouldn't kid myself." He put the bottle on the desktop and we both stood. "Thanks for coming in," he said as he walked me to the door. "We're looking forward to getting organized."

Candy snorted and said, "You're looking forward to it? You hardly ever set foot in there. I'm the one who's always looking for something or trying to find a place for more files. Whole place looks like Crooner's junk market."

"It won't look like that for long," I said before I headed out the door. I checked my watch. That hadn't taken as long as I thought it would. I felt rejuvenated, like I did each time I had a project spread out in front of me. Organizing wore some people down, but it had the opposite impact on me. I loved it. It energized me. I had time to pick up some file boxes and at least two sets of shelves. Better to get the errands done while I was without the kids. It was so much faster. I could be in and out of the store in under fifteen minutes.

Chapter
Thirteen

It took a bit longer than fifteen minutes to grab the supplies because of a snafu at the checkout. Of course, I picked the set of shelves without a bar code, but it was sorted out and I was sitting in the Jeep, supplies loaded in the back, peeling the foil off a Hershey's Kiss because I was starving. The peanut butter sandwich I'd had with Livvy and Nathan hadn't been enough to last me all day.

I steered the car to my favorite sandwich shop. I still had an hour before I was supposed to be back at home. Anna was warming up a frozen cheese pizza for the kids, a special treat that Livvy loved. I wasn't sure if she was more excited about having a babysitter to play with or the cheese pizza. I was just glad that she was over the stage of clinging to me and screaming for me not to leave. Unlike Livvy, cheese pizza wasn't my favorite. I'd much rather have a panini sandwich.

I was cruising through the parking lot, looking for a slot at the restaurant, when a car zipped out of a slot and across my path. I slammed on the brakes and my purse tumbled off the passenger seat onto the floorboard. The car whipped away down the aisle and after I loosened my grip on the steering wheel, I parked in the empty slot.

I grabbed my purse, which was an orange leather Furla tote, my nod to the fall season. I'd sworn I wouldn't be the mom wearing the cutesy sweatshirts and sweaters with ghosts and pumpkins. Actually, Abby made me swear not to buy any of those. I was pretty proud of my look today. I'd pulled it together without her help. Give me a room, a closet, or a filing cabinet and I'll have it sorted out in no time flat, but give me a closet full of clothes and I'm lost. I'm especially lost in a department store, where I have a tendency to only buy what's on sale and to fall victim to the latest craze that will be "out" in a few months. I thought my cream lightweight turtleneck and chocolate slacks looked pretty good. The bag was just the right accent—a little color, but big enough so that I could carry all my promotional material and not lug around a briefcase.

I put everything back inside my purse. I picked up the last thing, the file folder of Jodi's notes and article printouts. It slid in neatly. I paused with my hand resting on the edge of the thick folder. I'd been carrying it around all afternoon. I'd learned to grab anything I wanted to work on and take it with me. I never knew when I might have a few spare minutes while I was waiting at Mother's Day Out or the playground.

Why had I been so reluctant to even open this file? I was curious about Jodi and wanted to help find her, but something was holding me back. I'd been busy—that was true— any mom is busy, but there was something else. Some of the high I'd felt as I left STAND's office was leaking away and it was because of the notes. I'd been dabbling. I was good at stuff like this—putting little things in order to make a cohesive whole. Bringing order out of chaos, that was what I did. And I knew I could do it with these notes and possibly other things to help find Jodi, but I'd been holding back because of the promise I'd made myself—that I wouldn't get involved.

My phone chirped. It was Mitch.

"Hey, just letting you know we landed." Mitch liked to check in with me after a flight, which was really sweet, but I was usually going in so many directions that I didn't have time to wonder if he'd reached his destination or not. I knew he'd get there—wherever "there" happened to be that day. He was a resourceful guy.

"Oh, that's good," I said, trying to remember which leg of the trip he was on today. It was Tuesday, so he was in Japan. After a while all the TDYs started to merge together and it was hard to keep the destinations straight, except for those multimonth deployments to the Middle East. Those deployments were easy to remember. Thank goodness Mitch had put in his time there and wasn't scheduled to go back for a while. The shorter TDYs were a piece of cake compared to the deployments.

"How's everything going?" I asked.

"Uneventful."

"Always a good thing when you're flying."

Mitch agreed, then asked, "So, how did your meeting go?"

"Really good. I think Scott will be pretty easy to work with and the job isn't too overwhelming. So that's two paying clients."

"I'm glad for you. Anything else happening?"

I thought back over the days since he had left. Sometimes we didn't get to talk every day, especially if he was changing time zones. I told him Nathan's checkup on Monday went fine and that Livvy had scraped her knees—big drama and many Band-Aids involved. "And I'm staying up way too late. Have you ever seen *His Girl Friday*?" I asked.

"No, I don't think so," Mitch said.

Mitch was more of a sports kind of guy. Had he ever watched a black-and-white movie?

He said, "Hey, our bus is here, I've got to go." We said our good-byes and I put the phone away.

Inside the restaurant, I placed my order and snagged a high table by the windows. I put the folder on the table, still thinking about my unplanned movie night. I'd been acting like Hildy—trying to deny what I was really good at—arranging things in an orderly, efficient way—and pretending I wasn't interested in something that I was dying to know more about.

Who was I kidding? The Jodi Lockworth case fascinated me. I wasn't going to deny it anymore.

I ran my hand over the folder, then slid my finger under the edge and flicked it open.

An Everything In Its Place Tip for an Organized Party

Children's Party Checklist
- Make guest list.
- Reserve venue, if needed.
- Collect names and contact info for children.
- Mail or e-mail invitations.
- Order cake.
- Plan games or entertainment.

On the day of the party, don't forget
- Decorations.
- Cake.
- Ice cream.
- Candles.
- Matches or lighter.
- Knife to cut cake.
- Ice cream scooper.
- Plates.
- Napkins.
- Forks.
- Spoons.
- Door prizes for game winners.
- Pen and paper to keep track of gifts for thank-you notes.
- Camera with fresh batteries.

Chapter
Fourteen

I put Nita's e-mails on one side and the stack of Jodi's articles on the other side. I started with Nita's e-mails because I'd already looked through the articles. I worked steadily, matching notes with articles. The notes usually began with a date, location, and name of the person she was interviewing. They began in July and contained notes about back-to-school stories. She'd interviewed teachers for tips on helping kids with the back-to-school transition and a nutritionist for fresh ideas for packing lunch boxes. I found those articles and saw that she'd also included tips from local moms in both articles. I found her notes from the mom interviews in the next section of the notes that Nita had transcribed.

I heard my order number called and went to pick up my French dip and half salad, wondering if Nita really needed me to do this matching thing. It was going quickly. Was she being nice to me and letting me see what I'd found? I returned to the table and continued with the matching game between bites.

Jodi had written about the on-base youth soccer tournament, interviewed the new principal at North Dawkins High School, then interviewed Scott for the article I'd read earlier about his appointment as the director of STAND.

Since Colleen had such an aversion to him, I read Jodi's

notes of the interview carefully, but it was pretty basic stuff. His name, the date, exact title, his background, and some quotes about how vital STAND was to the community along with ideas he had to increase STAND's impact.

The first week of September, Jodi covered the dedication of the new courthouse complex and did a profile of Topaz, part of an occasional series about interesting local residents. I finished off my sandwich and salad, pushed my plate aside, and decided I had time for a few more lines.

I flipped to the next page of Nita's notes and saw a list:

Story ideas—
Identity theft prevention tips
Nash
Hurricane Katrina evacuees—any locals??

Nash? As in William James Nash? I skimmed the rest of the notes, but didn't see that name again. There were only a few more paragraphs of notes and I quickly matched up her interviews of local pumpkin patch owners to her Halloween roundup article.

I dumped my trash and hurried out the door, anxious to get home and check for more of Nita's e-mails after I freed the babysitter and heard all about their afternoon from Livvy. I paused in the parking lot as a satellite news truck from an Atlanta station lumbered by. What were they doing here in little North Dawkins? Not that North Dawkins was small in size, but it didn't have much that would interest viewers in Atlanta. It had to be something to do with the base, I decided, as I hopped in the Jeep and started for home.

I clicked the send/receive button on my e-mail again. Still nothing.

"Mom, are you ready for our story?" Livvy stood in the

living room wearing her pink pajamas with the feet, clutching *Sheep in a Jeep*, one of her favorite books.

"You bet," I said. I had been stopping by the computer pretty often, checking for another e-mail from Nita, but so far nothing, except a reminder from the Find Jodi campaign about the search coming up this weekend.

After completing the bedtime routine, I crept down the hall and into the living room. I didn't think Livvy would complain about not being able to sleep tonight because she and Anna had played the whole time. I wasn't nearly as wiped out as I usually was at the end of the day. Having a few hours on my own had refreshed me. Since my e-mail was being so uncooperative, I decided to focus on a few things that I'd let slide during the last few days.

Nathan's birthday party was coming up on Saturday and I still had so much to do. I definitely needed to update my lists. I jotted down the things I needed to pick up during the next few days, then called the parents to see who was actually planning to show up.

Even though Abby had let me know she was going to be at the party, I dialed her number. She answered on the first ring and I said, "Hey, it's Ellie. Hope I didn't wake Charlie."

"Oh no. He's sawing logs like a lumberjack."

"It's just not fair that you got the angel baby," I said.

"I know. I was so worried he'd be colicky, but he's been so easy. Of course, it makes me wonder what's coming, you know? It can't always be this easy."

"No, your next one will probably be a fright."

"Please, don't say anything about a next one. Jeff is already hinting that it's time to start trying again and I'm so pooped that I can barely stand up at the end of the day."

"I know that feeling. Do you have time to talk, or do you need to go?"

"No, I've got time. It feels like it's been a month since we've talked."

"I wanted to remind you about Nathan's birthday party on Saturday. Are you guys still coming?"

"*This* Saturday? I thought it was next Friday."

"No, next Friday is Mitch's promotion party."

"My, my. I'll start calling you Martha."

"Please. You know I'm no Martha Stewart."

"True."

"Hey! Should I be offended?"

"No way. That was a compliment. So. Your house is party central for the next two weeks. I'm writing a note right now so we don't miss anything."

I could hear drawers scraping in the background.

"Just as soon as I find a sticky note."

I had to smile because Abby and her reminder notes were usually soon parted. "How about I call you again next week and remind you about the promotion party?"

"That would be better. Hold on."

I heard the roar of the garbage disposal and shook my head. Charlie really could sleep through anything. The growling sound cut off. Abby said, "Mind if I put you on speaker for a second?"

"No."

The phone clicked and I heard the magnified sounds of a chair scraping across the floor and papers rustling. "I have fifty papers to grade tonight," Abby said, almost shouting.

How did speakerphones manage to amplify sounds, yet make everything sound tinny and farther away at the same time?

"Why don't you call me back later, if you've got a lot to do?"

"No. No, I'm fine. I can grade most of these papers on remote control. So, what's going on in your life that's too much to put in an e-mail?"

She was speaking in that hesitant stop-and-go way that people do when their attention is divided. I was tempted to tell her I knew she was busy and let her go, but I did want to talk to her. "Did you hear about those remains that were found in our neighborhood?"

"Ah—yeah," Abby said absentmindedly, but then she paused. The phone clicked as she took it off speaker. When she spoke again I knew I had her full attention. "Ellie, don't tell me—you're mixed up with dead bodies again?"

"Well, yes. I saw them when I was walking."

"Was it . . . gross?"

"No. I mean I knew it was human, so that was disturbing, but they were only bones."

Abby made an "ewww" sound and said, "The teachers at school were talking about it. Everyone thought it was that Jodi girl."

"I know. Did you hear the news?"

"Are you kidding? I'm doing good if I get to check the weather before I leave the house in the morning."

I gave her the details about the two men and she said, "Oh. Nash. I did hear that name today in the teachers' lounge. That must be why Kendra was acting so weird."

"Um, who's Kendra?" Conversations with Abby could make hairpin turns, but I could usually keep up. This time I was lost.

"Kendra Jenning. She teaches first grade. I'll have to ask Nadia for all the details—she's the expert on all things about North Dawkins, you know, since she's lived here *so* long."

Was that a bit of sarcasm in Abby's tone? Nadia could be a bit intense and focused. She was the perkiest person I'd ever met and she was also one of the most persistent people I knew. When you're constantly around someone who is perky and persistent, it can be, well, annoying. We'd discovered that when we met Nadia on the trip to Washington, D.C. Her obsession with photographing everything had irritated everyone in the tour group. Of course, she was blithely oblivious that the rest of us were ready to toss her camera into the Reflecting Pool if we heard the word *snappy* again. That was our attitude until we saw some of her pictures. They were amazing—interesting angles and unusual focal points. Really beautiful stuff, so we'd cut her some slack after that.

"Kendra is one of the sweetest teachers at school. She's what every mom wants to see when they drop off their little darling for the first day of school—she looks like an updated June Cleaver without the pearls. She's blond and always wears sweater sets. She'll help out with any committee and she's always so nice. I said something about Alexis Donogan's reputation as a little stinker being right on the money and she snapped my head off, then marched out of the teachers' lounge. I was so surprised, I asked if the body snatchers had been down in the first grade hall. It's just not like her to be so angry.

"Then another teacher said, 'We better not talk about the Nash thing anymore. I'd forgotten her family knows Coleman May really well.' Apparently, she grew up next door to the Mays and was like a granddaughter to them."

"Coleman May's the president of the homeowners' association here. What does he have to do with Nash?"

"I don't know. One of the teachers said that nothing had ever been proved, so we should drop it."

"What else did they say?"

"I don't know. I wasn't really interested. I like Kendra and all, but if she's going to be rude to me, well, whatever."

I knew Abby was shrugging dismissively. Other people's angst and blowups didn't bother her at all. She exemplified that saying "like water off a duck's back." Kendra's snappishness didn't really bother her. She didn't like it, but she didn't take it to heart and mull over it and worry about it. She went on with her day. Me, I'd have dissected the interaction and probably still be fretting over it.

"That's really interesting because I came across the name Nash in Jodi's notes."

"Jodi's notes? Where did you get her notes?"

I brought Abby up to date on how I'd found the notebook and she said, "My, my, my. You're right, all of that wouldn't have been easy to put into an e-mail. Well, you can meet Kendra yourself tomorrow. You are going to Jessica and Jasmine's birthday party, aren't you?"

"Oh. I'd forgotten." I looked at the calendar. "Yep. There it is on the calendar. We'll be there," I said, trying to remember what possible presents I had hidden away on the top shelf of the linen closet. "I think they invited all the neighborhood kids. Why will Kendra be there?"

"She's Jessica's piano teacher. She has a few students she teaches on weekends. Frankly, I don't know how she finds the time."

"Okay, enough about that stuff. What's going on with you?"

"Same old thing—school and Charlie. Nothing as exciting as you've been involved in, unless you count the fight I broke up on the playground yesterday."

"Well, you know my life is usually diapers and laundry." I glanced at the clock and saw it was almost nine. "I'd better let you go get those papers graded. See you tomorrow."

I hung up and raided the gift stash. I had a set of the first four books in the A to Z mystery series that I thought would be perfect for Jessica. Her younger sister, Jasmine, who was born four years and four days later—thus the joint party—would probably like the art set with crayons, paints, and stamps. I "wrapped" the gifts using bags and tissue paper and put them in the car.

I plopped down on the overstuffed chair and clicked the TV on. Just until ten, I promised myself. I was going to stay away from the movie channels tonight.

The news was on. The familiar picture of Jodi flashed on the screen. The reporter's voice-over stated, "The folks I talked to in the community said they expected the extra set of remains would be those of youth sports coordinator Jodi Lockworth, who has been missing since January eighth of this year." The photo of Nash that had been in the paper filled the screen. "Instead, it was another missing youth in the grave, one who's been missing over fifty years." The view switched to a live shot of the reporter pacing in front of a live oak. "But instead of bringing closure, the discovery has opened old wounds and drawn nationwide interest."

I flicked back and forth between the news channels. Nash's picture and a report of his identification were on all of them, along with hints about past racial tension in North Dawkins, but no details.

Guess I was wrong. There was news in North Dawkins.

Chapter
Fifteen

I went back to the computer and typed the name William James Nash in the search engine. The list of hits included all the recent news about the identification of his remains. I went to the *North Dawkins Standard* Web site and searched for articles about him, but that didn't bring up anything. I supposed the original articles about his disappearance were too old to be available online.

I started over with the search terms "William James Nash" and "lynching." The first line that popped up was a link to the Peach Blossom Inn. Not what I had expected.

I clicked over and scanned, looking for the name Nash. I found it on the page about the historic connections of the bed-and-breakfast.

Nestled between pecan groves, the Peach Blossom Inn is in the heart of historic Georgia in Dawkins County. Shopping and dining are minutes away, but history permeates every aspect of the Peach Blossom from the homemade peach ice cream that's served each night on the wide veranda to the massive live oak on the horizon, known as the Hanging Oak, rumored site of the infamous Nash lynching.

I sat back. Wouldn't a lynching be something you'd rather *not* put in your brochure? I read on and found several references to the spirit that was often seen wandering through the pecan groves at night. *Now I get it.* Nothing like a supernatural element to add cachet to your B and B.

"Do you have a local history section?" I asked the reference librarian, a young woman with a round face and thick dark hair caught back in a low ponytail.

"Our most popular section today." She came out from behind the large counter and led the way through the stacks. "Anything in particular you're looking for?"

"Information about the Nash lynching."

"You, too?" She stopped and ran her hand across several shelves. "This is our local history section, but I'm afraid we don't have anything on the Nash lynching."

"Nothing?" I asked as I did a quick check to make sure Livvy still trailed along behind me. After story time, she'd picked out two new books. She'd already sat down with her back propped against the shelves and was "reading" the pages. Nathan, strapped in the stroller, had three board books and was content to run his hand over the soft fur that represented a lion's mane. I switched my attention back to the librarian. Her name tag clipped to her jet-black sweater read DAWN.

"I'm afraid not. There's nothing more than rumor and innuendo," she said.

"I've done a search online and couldn't find anything except a reference in a B and B Web site. Internet searches are great, but sometimes they have big holes in them."

Dawn frowned. "That's true. I'm sure the Peach Blossom considers it marketing, but there's no evidence that the lynching ever happened."

Did that mean there never had been evidence or there had been evidence at one time and it had been destroyed?

"What about racist groups in the area? KKK? Anything like that?" I asked, skimming over the titles.

"No. I've done quite a bit of research into the history of Dawkins County," Dawn said. "I've traced my ancestors and helped other people with their family histories and I can assure you I've never come across anything like that. Here." She moved to the end of the aisle to a computer terminal. "I'll show you our search features and you can look up books as well as our online databases of periodicals and newspapers."

She showed me how to access the search. There was nothing about white supremacist groups in North Dawkins. There were two articles about Nash's disappearance. One described his last workday at the paper factory, but it was so short it barely had any information. The paper gave more coverage to the North Dawkins Women's Society Bridge Fund-raiser that took place that same night. It was pretty obvious that Nash's story wasn't a high priority in North Dawkins since the picture of several smiling women holding cocktails filled most of the lower half of the page. One of the women looked familiar. I read the cutline and smiled. ELEANOR RAWLINS, LEFT, JOINS AVA MAY AND DORTHEA CONNER IN CELEBRATING ANOTHER SUCCESSFUL FUND-RAISER. That *was* Dorthea with the dark lipstick and pearls.

The second article reiterated the same scanty info on Nash and stated that investigators were looking into the possibility that Nash was accosted. Hmmm . . . "accosted" didn't have the same connotations as "lynched," but it did indicate that investigators had suspected foul play.

I added two books about the Civil Rights movement to our stack. On the way to the checkout, I stopped at the reference desk and asked Dawn, "Why did you say that area was your most popular section?"

"You're the fifth person who's asked for information about Nash today."

* * *

The car was quiet as I drove home. Both the kids were still absorbed in their books, so I turned the kid music off. The silence was blissful.

Who else would be interested in Nash?

Lots of people. His name had been all over the news. But would that motivate someone to go to the library and do a search? After a second I had to smile at my speculations. It had driven *me* to do a search, after all.

I spent the next hour making grilled cheese sandwiches, changing diapers, doing dishes, and checking my e-mail. Still nothing from Nita. I didn't want to be a bother and call her. I knew she was very busy, but I really wanted her transcription of the rest of the notes.

Once I had Nathan down for his nap and Livvy humming away in her room with her stack of new books, I settled down on the couch to glance through the books I'd picked up about the Civil Rights movement.

I was surprised to learn that lynchings declined from about 1920 on, except for several well-publicized incidents from the '40s through the '60s. One name, Emmett Till, caught my eye. I'd seen it in the newspaper a while back. Till was lynched in Mississippi in 1955. Outrage over his death helped spark the Civil Rights movement and his case was one of several from that era that had recently been reopened.

"Mom." The exaggerated whisper came from down the hall. I stood up and looked down the hall. Livvy was leaning around her door frame. "How much longer until the party?"

"About an hour."

Her face scrunched in uncertainty. "That's about as long as *Sesame Street*," I said.

Her face cleared. "Okay."

"In fact," I said, checking the time, "*Sesame Street* is coming on in a few minutes. You and Nathan can watch it, and then we'll go to the party." I didn't have to check the TV schedule to know when the shows for the kids were on. I had the schedule memorized. I got Nathan up, changed his diaper, and then settled him in the living room.

"Can we watch *Tiger Gals*?"

"Nope." Already the negotiation had begun. Livvy felt she was too old for *Sesame Street* and wanted to watch the latest half-hour commercial disguised as a kids' show. "Today we're going to watch something educational. Nathan needs to learn his letters and numbers. You can watch your show next time." I didn't want Nathan to miss out on the little kid shows that Livvy had enjoyed so much.

The news was on and a familiar face surprised me. Nita Lockworth was talking about Jodi, giving the interviewer details about when Jodi disappeared. Jodi's picture flashed on the screen along with the eight-hundred number.

"Mom, *Sesame Street*, remember?"

I hid a smile because Livvy still enjoyed the show, even though she'd never admit she liked a "baby" show like that.

"Okay. Here you go." I switched the channel and went to our other TV and turned it on the cable news channel where Nita was still being interviewed.

She sat in a chair beside Sherry Wayne. They were outdoors with a row of trees behind them. The interviewer turned to Sherry.

"What's the status of the investigation concerning your cousin at this point? The incident with William Nash happened over fifty years ago. Have the investigators given you any indication that they'll be able to find out what happened? Who did this to William?"

Sherry tossed her head and said, "It may have been fifty years, but everyone in North Dawkins knows what happened the night William didn't come home. He was lynched. The sheriff needs to talk to Coleman May. He knows what happened."

The interviewer leaned forward. "Who is Coleman May?"

"He was the mayor back then and he didn't like the way things were shifting in 1955. I was just a girl then, but everyone in town knew the mayor didn't like what was going on in Montgomery—"

Here the interviewer jumped in and said, "You mean the bus boycott?"

She nodded. "Yes. Coleman May wanted to squelch anything like that here in middle Georgia. William was a warning."

"These are pretty serious charges." The interviewer was clearly delighted that Sherry was accusing someone of murder on his show.

"Plenty of Civil Rights cases are being reopened. No reason this one can't be reopened, too. Especially since it wasn't investigated properly at the time."

"Was there a federal investigation?"

"No. They were able to hush it up. But things have changed. There won't be no hushing it up now."

The interviewer turned toward the camera. "Two missing persons cases in this small southern town. A tragic outcome for one family and another still hoping for the best. We'll keep you updated on both stories. Coming up, which dancer didn't make the cut last night? Find out after the break."

I clicked through a few more channels and saw a taped interview with Nita and Sherry. They'd made the news show rounds this morning. That explained why I hadn't received anything else from Nita. She'd been busy getting as much publicity for Jodi as she could. And Sherry had accused Coleman May of being a murderer. I turned off the TV and went to get my shoes on. Coleman? He seemed sort of . . . fussy to be a murderer.

An Everything In Its Place Tip for an Organized Party

Cost-cutting Tips for Goodie Bags
- Use paper lunch bags instead of store-bought theme bags. You can personalize the bags with stamps or leave them plain.

- Avoid prepackaged "party favors." Often these favors are expensive, considering the number of items in each package and the quality.
- Here's a few inexpensive goodie bag alternatives: large packs of gum, stickers, pencils, and sculpting clay can be purchased for a few dollars each and used to fill goodie bags. Add prepackaged raisins, popcorn, or fruit leathers for healthy alternatives to candy. Try to include things related to the party theme: for a movie party, include microwave popcorn; for a swimming party, include goggles or sunscreen. Another option is to skip the bag entirely and give each child one inexpensive gift, such as a puzzle or book.

Chapter
Sixteen

"What does that sign say?" Livvy gripped the edge of the door and strained to see out the window.

"It says 'North Pole.'"

Livvy was out of the car almost before I'd brought it to a full stop. By the time I'd transferred Nathan from his car seat to the stroller, grabbed the diaper bag, stowed the presents in the stroller, and locked the car, she'd followed the arrow on the sign and disappeared around the side of the house.

A cool breeze rattled through the bronze leaves and swept across my face. I was glad I'd dressed the kids in jeans and long sleeves since the humidity was down today and fall was in the air.

Livvy came motoring back into sight. "Snow! There's snow! See!" She hopped, pointing through the gate. "It snowed."

"But only in Jessica and Jasmine's backyard. Interesting." White blanketed the entire backyard. On one side, the white stuff was piled up and kids were attempting to make a snowman. A dusting of snow covered the huge igloo positioned in the middle of the backyard and a few flakes still clung to the giant bouncer that filled the other side of the yard.

Livvy didn't hear me; she was letting a woman in a red shirt with furry white trim on the neckline and cuffs wrap a scarf around her neck as she said, "Welcome to our winter wonderland!"

I recognized Jessica and Jasmine's mom from the car pool line at Mother's Day Out, but we'd never met. I handed her the gift bags and introduced myself.

She put the bags on a picnic table crowded with other gifts and said, "Hi, I'm Juliet. We're so glad Livvy could come."

"I'm sure you can tell, she's excited to be here."

"Oh, the snow. I know. Isn't it great? Just add water and instant snow. Totally biodegradable, too. I love the 'wow' look on the kids' faces—and the parents', too." She adjusted her Santa hat. Incongruously, she was wearing Bermuda shorts and Clark sandals. "The girls want it to snow so badly and you know we hardly ever get any here. If we do, it's a fluke and only enough to cover the ground, so I figured we'd give them snow for their birthday."

"Where did you find the igloo? Did you make it somehow?"

"Heavens, no. Styrofoam blocks. It's amazing what a party planning company can do. I used Party Hearty out of Atlanta. Wait until you see inside the igloo. Go on, take a look," she urged. "Help yourself to the food. We'll have cake later. And don't forget to get the kids' portraits drawn," Juliet said as she pointed to a table set up on her back porch where Topaz sat, making rapid strokes on a sketch pad. A little girl posed stiffly on a bench. "I have a local artist doing portraits of the kids. So much more special than photos, don't you think?"

I was actually speechless. All of this for a kids' birthday party? Juliet shooed me in the direction of the igloo. "Go ahead, check out the inside."

Cold air gushed down the short entry, which was tall enough that I didn't have to stoop down. It was as cold as my freezer. We emerged from the corridor into a small round room with a fire blazing at the center. I did a double take.

Surely, Juliet didn't have a real fire in here with twenty kids running around? I looked closer and realized it was made of strips of orange and yellow cloth that fluttered as air pumped over them from below. Fog curled up the edges of the room, engulfing tables where food flanked two snowmen ice sculptures. Wow, indeed. What was this, a birthday party for two kids, or a fund-raising bash?

I found a plate and loaded it with snack foods, making sure to get some crackers and cheese for Nathan. Balancing my food and a drink I'd poured from a large punch bowl, I steered the stroller with one hand back into the sunlight.

Juliet was hurrying across the snow, but she stopped and asked, "Did you like it?"

Um, like it? I actually thought it was a bit much for a birthday party, but I tried to be diplomatic. "It wowed me all right."

"Good! I always feel a little sorry for the girls since their birthdays are only a couple of days apart. I want to do something spectacular for them, so they'll each feel special." She bent over the stroller and spoke to Nathan in that singsong voice people use with kids. "I heard you have a birthday coming up soon," she said, poking him in his tummy.

Nathan grinned and reflexively gripped his stomach.

She poked again. "You're going to be one!"

Nathan giggled.

She stood up and said to me, "That's a big birthday, their first. I remember Jessica's first birthday. We had a petting zoo. The kids loved it. What are you going to do?"

"Umm . . ." Suddenly my idea of a party seemed rather banal. "Birthday cake and ice cream in the backyard."

Her eyebrows crunched together. "Oh," she said uncertainly. "Well, I'm sure that will be . . . nice. You might think about that petting zoo idea, though. It would be a birthday he'll never forget. Now, I have to check the temperature in the igloo." She patted my arm, then hurried off.

"A birthday he'll never forget," I muttered under my

breath. "Like he's going to even *remember* it in the first place. He's going to be *one*."

"What are you talking to yourself about?"

I turned to find Abby standing beside me, balancing Charlie on her hip and holding a plate of food in the other hand.

"Oh, nothing. Just grousing." The boys spotted each other and we made our way over to a corner of the yard with a sign that read LITTLE ELVES PLAY AREA. We deposited Nathan and Charlie in the fenced-off area stocked with toddler toys and sat down on some chairs. The "snow" was pretty thin on the ground there and the boys examined it for a moment, then went for the toys.

"I'm having a mental block. What did you do for Charlie's first birthday?" I'd never ask that question of Juliet. She clearly intended her parties to be events and would be hurt if people didn't remember them, even years later. But with Abby I could honestly say I didn't remember and she wouldn't care. "Why can't I remember? It was only a month ago."

"Family party."

"That's right. Lucky you. You didn't have to plan a birthday party that rivaled the Academy Awards After Party."

"Not quite so lucky. I did have both my parents and Jeff's parents staying at our house. Remember?"

Abby's duplex in base housing gave new meaning to the word *minuscule*.

"So. Are you planning a big shindig like this for Nathan?"

"Honestly, no, but I'm starting to feel like the underachieving mom after the tea party birthday party and now this. Cake and ice cream in the backyard seem a little passé."

"Stick to your guns. This is overkill."

"I'm going to. What will these kids expect for their sixteenth birthday?"

"A Hummer?" Abby said, then saw Charlie, Nathan, and another boy all with a death grip on the same toy. "I'd better break that up before we get to the screaming stage," Abby said, and entered the corral.

She sorted out the boys, then returned to the chairs. "So, what have you done today?"

"Story time at the library."

"I miss story time. I'm already looking forward to next summer when we can go with you," Abby said. "I love teaching, but sometimes feel like I'm missing so much time with Charlie."

"Are you thinking about quitting?" I asked, surprised. Abby had never waffled about going back to work.

"No, not really. I just feel guilty sometimes that I'm not with him all the time."

"Abby, I'm with my kids almost all of the time and I still feel guilty."

Abby transferred her gaze from the boys to me. Charlie abandoned the truck and Nathan pounced on it. "When I'm doing laundry and dishes and all that routine stuff that I have to do, Livvy's constantly asking me to play with her and Nathan wants my attention, too. So while I'm cleaning the bathroom, I'm feeling bad that I'm not playing hide-and-seek."

"So you're saying no matter what I do I'm going to feel guilty." Abby laughed. "Great! Thanks, that makes me feel so much better."

"Sorry, but it's true."

"Yeah. I think deep down, I already knew that," Abby said. "So, what's going on with the Find Jodi stuff?"

"I don't have any new transcripts from Nita and I can't find out anything about William Nash's death. It's weird, there's not even any news coverage about the lynching. I checked the newspaper archives at the library today and there wasn't anything. I did see Sherry Wayne on the national news. She practically accused Coleman May of Nash's murder."

"You're kidding."

"Nope. She said he knew what happened that night."

A voice sounded behind us, "Hey, ladies! Happy snow day!"

Nadia perched on the chair beside Abby. I was glad to see she didn't have her camera with her. No "snappies" today, thank goodness. She leaned across and tapped my knee. "I hear you're working on the missing persons case." She leaned back and her dark hair swayed against her earlobes. Petite, perky, and curvy, Nadia was the epitome of cute. Today she had on a red cardigan trimmed in plaid over a long-sleeved white shirt, dark jeans, and red boots. Very festive. Usually smiling and upbeat, she always made me think of a cheerleader.

Her daughters rushed up, miniature versions of her with their long dark hair held back with matching red plaid bows that went with the trim on their sweaters, which also matched the trim on Nadia's outfit. Just thinking about the time it would take to coordinate all those clothes made my head hurt. And Nadia did it every day. "Mommy, mommy, can we go in the jumper?" they shrieked, bows quivering.

"Yes. Off you go," she said, and waved them away. "So, do you have any leads on what happened to Jodi?"

"I'm not really investigating anything. I'm just helping Nita Lockworth."

"Right." Abby exchanged a look with Nadia.

I shrugged. "Sure, I'm curious. After all, it's more interesting than cleaning and figuring out what we're having for dinner."

"There's Kendra," Nadia said, and waved to a young woman entering the backyard, who hugged the birthday girls and then moved in our direction. She was tall and skinny and had wavy blond hair and pale skin sprinkled with freckles.

Nadia introduced her to me and said, "Ellie has a knack for figuring out puzzles. She's interested in Jodi Lockworth and that poor William Nash."

At the name Nash, Kendra stiffened. "I'm sick of people spreading rumors about Mr. Coleman. He didn't do anything that people are saying he did. He's too sweet."

Nadia wrapped her arm around Kendra's shoulders. "I know it's upsetting, but you should tell Ellie about the Coleman May you know. So far, all she's heard are those rumors. Shouldn't she hear what you have to say, especially since Sherry is being so vocal?"

Kendra shook her head. "Since Sherry's been on TV, everyone's forgotten about how nice Mr. Coleman is. I haven't. He's always been nice to me."

"So you've known him a long time?" I asked.

"Yes, since I was five. He was always outside working in his yard and there weren't that many kids on our street, so I'd ride over. I had a bell on my bike and I'd ride up his sidewalk, ringing the bell. It drove my mom crazy, but he didn't mind. He'd let me ring it all I wanted. And he'd talk to me while he worked. Mrs. Ava had a crystal candy dish on their hall table. When I left to go home, she'd give me a piece. She was sick a lot, but on the days she was feeling good she'd always bring out the candy. They were either peppermints or butterscotch. Or sometimes, if it was really hot she'd bring me a glass of lemonade when she brought one out for him. They were so sweet. He was always taking care of her, watching out for her. When she died it was incredibly sad. My mom and I used to go over there after that, to cheer him up. He kept that candy dish full and always gave me some when we left."

I tried to ask my next question as delicately as possible. "You know what the rumors are. Was he racist?"

Kendra had been leaning toward me, but now she straightened up. "He's over eighty years old. He grew up in a different era."

I took that as a yes.

Kendra's lips thinned as she pressed them together; then

she said rapidly, "I know what you're thinking, but using derogatory names and physically harming someone are two different things. He'd never hurt anyone. You should talk to his family. His son Durwood lives here and his granddaughter, too. They know him even better than I do."

Nadia said, "Durwood May? Isn't he the mayor?"

"Yes," Kendra said, "and his granddaughter is Colleen Otway."

Chapter
Seventeen

"Colleen Otway is his granddaughter?" I asked. She hadn't mentioned anything about being related to him at the homeowners' meeting. In fact, I didn't even see them speak to each other that night.

Kendra continued. "She lives right around the corner from me. I never really got to know her until she moved into my apartment complex—she didn't visit her grandpa that much—but she's as nice as can be. She can tell you what a sweetheart he is."

"Miss Kendra," a voice called. "Come see our snow angels." I turned to see Livvy flailing on her back in the snow along with some of the girls.

Kendra said good-bye and I leaned back in my chair.

"That was interesting," Nadia said, her eyebrows arched. "You're going to talk to the granddaughter next, right?"

"I suppose so." And get a hold of Nita.

Topaz approached the fenced-off area. She looked as eccentric as always in her low-slung jeans, starburst peasant blouse, and a belt of metal medallions that matched her dangly metal earrings. A red Santa hat topped the highlights that striped her dark hair. She said, "Okay, it's the little guys' turn. Ready to be sketched?" Topaz asked the boys. They stared at her, wide-eyed.

"This is Topaz, a friend of mine from high school. Instead of doing photos, Juliet is having all the kids sketched," I explained.

"Oh, hi," Abby said. "Don't worry about sketching the boys. They're fine. Just let them play."

"Nope, I have to sketch every kid here. Juliet's orders. Who does this one belong to?" she asked, pointing to Charlie.

Abby bristled. "This *boy* is my son, Charlie."

Topaz leaned over to pull him out of the play area. "Let's start with Charles."

As soon as she slid her hands under his armpits, Charlie wailed.

Abby was at the fence in an instant. "It's Charlie," she said, taking him from Topaz and walking a few steps away.

Topaz looked perplexed. "None of the other kids cried."

"Why don't you just sketch Nathan inside the play area?" I said, shooting for the least problematic solution.

"Sure, I can do that," Topaz said, and placed her sketchbook on the fence.

"I think Charlie needs a diaper change." Abby marched inside.

I exchanged glances with Nadia, then looked back at Topaz. Her back was turned to me, but I could see the unhesitating black strokes on her sketch pad. In just a few seconds, she caught the essence of Nathan as he hunched over his toy, his face intent with concentration as he tried to stack rings on a pole.

"That is beautiful, Topaz," I said when she handed me the drawing. "I can't believe how fast you did that and how much it looks like him."

Nadia said, "You have quite a talent."

Topaz shrugged. "Thanks. I don't think about it. It's like an instinct, something I've always been able to do. I used to sketch in the margins at school all the time."

I smiled. "That's funny. I don't remember that at all."

"Oh, I kept it pretty well hidden. Couldn't have Mrs. Daniel yelling at me for doodling instead of taking notes."

"Have you sketched my girls?" Nadia asked.

"Everything's on the porch. Want to take a look?"

Nadia and Topaz headed for the porch and I saw Abby take a circuitous route back to me to avoid them.

She set Charlie beside Nathan and said, "Kind of bossy, isn't she?"

When I got home a few hours later, I had an e-mail from Nita with more of Jodi's notes, but I didn't even get to open it because Livvy dropped her snow globe from the birthday party goodie bag on the kitchen floor. I spent a good portion of an hour drying tears and keeping the kids and Rex out of the kitchen until I could sweep up the glass fragments mixed with glitter.

After that fiasco, it was time to fix dinner. Once I had both of the kids tucked in bed, I went back to the computer. Rex rested his chin on my leg and fixed his brown eyes on me. Even the dog wanted my attention.

I rubbed his ears as I opened my e-mail, then tossed his tennis ball while it printed. Rex settled down to gnaw on the tennis ball as I skimmed the first lines of the e-mail. I didn't see the name Nash. I went back to the top and slowly worked my way through the notes, matching them with Jodi's articles, which included a feature on an elementary school hosting a local author and the articles on the Jackson Hollow debate. I read those notes and articles slower, but it seemed to me that Colleen was right.

Jodi had been pretty even-handed in her coverage. She'd quoted Scott's arguments and the council's concerns and then interviewed the residents of the neighborhood. Of course, they'd been impassioned and emotional. Their homes were at stake. Thinking about it from Scott's point of view, I could understand why he wouldn't be too excited about the articles. It did make him and STAND look as if they wanted to kick people out of their homes. But on the other hand, was keeping a small neighborhood intact worth risking the possible closure of Taylor Air Force Base, which employed most of the town? Her last entries were story ideas for January about resolutions.

I leaned back in the chair, frustrated. Everything seemed pretty straightforward. No extra notes about Nash. Had she even pursued her idea for a story about him?

I picked up Rex's tennis ball and bounced it once. He'd been twitching as he dozed, but once that ball hit the floor, he was up and ready to play. After a few more throws, I called him outside. I went through the screened back porch and onto our small concrete patio; then I threw the ball as far as I could. It was dark now and Rex shot though the pool of light from our floodlights into the darkness around the pines at the back of the yard. A few seconds later, he reappeared.

As I tossed the ball and he trotted back and forth, I thought about what I was going to say to Nita when I called tomorrow. I still didn't see why Jodi hid the notebook. All the notes seemed innocuous, even the one jotted mention of Nash. There was nothing there that I could see that needed to be hidden.

Rex was walking back now, so I called him inside and put him in his kennel for the night. I grabbed the file again and curled up in the overstuffed chair. I wanted to go over everything one more time. I'd used a red pen to check off each item in Jodi's notes as I found the information in one of her published articles. I scanned down the list of checkmarks until my vision went bleary. I took a break, downed some Hershey's Kisses with a tall glass of milk, then went back to the list.

On the last page, I found three names without a red checkmark: Sherry, Rosalee, and Mary. They were at the end of a long interview with the Jackson Hollow residents, so I told myself not to get too excited. I'm sure that a reporter wasn't always able to use every bit of information and research in the finished article, but I double-checked and their names weren't in any of her articles. Sherry could be Sherry Wayne, but who were Rosalee and Mary?

Thursday morning I pulled into Nita's driveway and parked under a magnolia tree. I'd called her and told her I wanted to drop off the notes and articles. I grabbed the folder and used it to shield my head from the rain as I sprinted up the sidewalk to the shallow concrete steps of the modest rancher she and Gerald lived in on Scranton Road. It seemed a bit ironic to me that Gerald had built so many of the new homes in our subdivision, yet he and Nita lived in a rambling '60s rancher. Of course, he had taken care of his daughter, I thought as I rang the bell. He'd made sure she had a brand-new house to live in with all the latest amenities.

The porch was barely wide enough to protect me from the rain. A storm had rolled in during the night, banishing the crisp fall weather. Now the blazing leaves hung limp and wet under the slate-colored clouds.

Nita opened the door, looking as neat and trim as she always did in a crisply ironed orange shirt with jack-o'-lanterns embroidered on the collar points. "Come in. What a dreary day. No little ones with you today?"

"No, it's Mother's Day Out for my daughter, and Dorthea agreed to watch Nathan for me since I have an appointment after this."

"Well, don't let me keep you," she said as she led the way into a sunken living room where a huge brick fireplace filled one wall. "Were you able to find any discrepancies in the notes? I have to say nothing leapt out at me as I worked on transcribing them."

"I only found two things that didn't match any of her articles." I flipped to the passages. "Two lists, one of story ideas and another of names."

Nita picked up the paper and I couldn't tell if she was disappointed or not. "I did notice the name Nash when I transcribed the notes, but there was nothing else about him?"

"Not that I could find." I sighed. "Here's the other list." I turned to the pages at the end.

"Sherry. That could be Sherry Wayne. And Rosalee . . . I know that name." She tapped her lips with her fingers. "Where have I heard that? It's an unusual name."

The phone rang and she said, "I better get that. Excuse me."

She picked up the phone in the kitchen. I couldn't hear her words, but she hung up quickly, then hurried back into the living room. "Ellie, dear, I appreciate all your work on this and I hate to rush you out the door, but I have to leave right now. Can I write you a check later?"

"Of course," I said, already walking to the front door. I didn't doubt Nita for a moment. This clearly wasn't a ploy to get out of paying my fee. Heck, I'd have done it for free, but I could tell by the quiver in her voice and the constricted look on her face she was worried. "Do you need anything? Can I help?"

"No, thank you. I need to go," she said as I stepped out the door.

"All right, well, I'll get in touch later—" I stopped. I was talking to a closed door. It must be something urgent for her to completely abandon me on her doorstep. In the South, leaving usually took at least as long as the visit, I'd found. I recognized her at the wheel of a gold Taurus that zipped past me on the road as I drove to STAND's office.

In the parking lot, I hauled my bin of supplies out of the Jeep. The cars on the interstate whipped by, a continuous drone of wet swishing in the distance. The dreary weather had settled into a steady drizzle.

Today Candy's earrings were scarecrows and jumped as she folded letters and stuffed envelopes. "Hey," she greeted me. Between chomps on her gum she said, "Scott's out today, but he said for you to go on back. Have at it."

"Great." I hefted my plastic bin into the other office. I turned on the light with my shoulder blade, set down the bin, and pushed up the sleeves of my sweatshirt. I'd worn work clothes since I was going to be mucking out the storage area and I knew it would be a dusty job.

After setting up my supplies—trash bags, marking pens, and labels—I opened the door, flicked on the light, and got to work sorting. It was actually nice to be on my own in the beginning stages of an organizing project. I moved quickly, shifting through boxes and stacks of paper. Some of the items I'd have to check with Scott about whether or not to keep, but most of the stuff in the storage area was pretty obvious. It went in either the trash bag or the "keep" pile, which I divided into long-term storage and current files.

After about an hour of working, I heard Candy shout, but I couldn't understand what she said.

I went to the doorway. "Excuse me?"

"What?" Candy spun from her monitor. "Oh, sorry. I won the auction. On eBay." She swiveled her computer monitor toward me. "I collect vintage sewing patterns. This one is very World War II. Look at those shoulder pads. They don't design clothes like that anymore."

"That's interesting. I haven't heard of that type of collecting before. Do you make the clothes?"

"Nah. I just like having the patterns. I collect Depression glass, too." She clicked her mouse, studied the screen and said, "No good Depression glass today. Sometimes the best place to find that is at Crooner's. You never know what he's got in that junk pile of his."

Candy stood up and caught sight of the storage area behind me. "I didn't think it could look any worse, but it does," she said, surveying the drifts of paper and bulging trash bags.

"It may look bad, but this is the first step to clean it out.

You have to get everything out and sorted." I showed her the different piles and asked if the office had a shredder.

"Sure," she said, and pointed to a tiny one.

"Umm . . . I think you're going to need a bigger one." I reached for my notepad. "Either that or a shredding service. How much shredding do you do a week?"

Candy shrugged. "No idea. I don't shred."

Obviously, no one did. I made another note to talk to Scott.

Candy said, "You want a Coke or anything? It's break time."

"No, I'm fine," I said as I dragged the trash bags with papers that needed to be shredded over to one side of Scott's office. I looked up to see Candy, hovering uncertainly in the doorway. "I probably shouldn't go off and leave you in the office alone."

"Oh. Right. Sure, I understand." I grabbed two bags of trash. "I'll run these out to the Dumpster."

Candy looked relieved. "Anything else to take?"

"One more," I said, and handed her the last bag of trash.

We made the trek outside through the thin drizzle and dumped the trash. On the way back inside, Candy stopped. "Well, what's going on over there?" she asked as she looked at the vacant lot between the office park where STAND was located and a Quick Mart, a convenience store on the corner.

An Everything In Its Place Tip for an Organized Party

Party Countdown Checklist (Three to Four Weeks Prior)
- Compile guest list.
- Decide on theme.
- Set date and time.
- Set budget.
- Order, print, or hand-write invitations.
- Contact and reserve venue, if needed.

Chapter Eighteen

Equal amounts of official government police-type vehicles and news vans filled the street beside the vacant lot by the Quick Mart. Beyond the vehicles I could see a dozen people, maybe more, milling around the lot.

A reporter setting up her camera waved to someone in the crowd. A woman with short blond curls, wearing an orange shirt, detached herself from the cluster of people and shook her hand dismissively at the reporter. "I think I know her," I said. "I'll be right back."

I stepped carefully across the strip of brown grass and mud, wishing I'd grabbed my jacket before heading outside. Even though it wasn't a downpour, the drizzle was cold. I suppressed a shiver and held my arms tighter to my body.

"Nita," I called. "Are you all right?"

She looked up, startled. When she recognized me, she relaxed a bit. "Ellie, what are you doing here? I'm fine. Just on my way to rest in my car for a little while and warm up."

She didn't look fine. She looked pale and chilled. I saw her gold car parked at an odd angle, hemmed in by the hulking official SUVs.

"I don't know if you'll be able to get to it without soaking your shoes," I said, pointing to the only path, which was basically a mud puddle. "Why don't you come over here to this building? I'm working over there, at STAND's offices."

She glanced back at the flurry of uniforms and I said, "Scott's not there. I think you'll be able to see what's going on from inside and I can get you a cup of coffee."

"That would be wonderful."

I put out my arm to support her, but she picked her own way across the patchy grass and mud to the sidewalk where Candy still stood with moisture dotting her bangs.

I was about to perform introductions when Candy said, "Mrs. Nita, what are you doing out here in this awful weather? Come inside with us and warm up." She linked her arm through Nita's and drew her inside the building. I should have known they knew each other.

My shoes were muddy, so I paused to wipe them off and by the time I got inside STAND's office, Candy had Nita seated in Scott's chair and was brewing coffee for her.

I pulled out the tube of foam cups I'd found earlier and handed one to Candy. She poured a cup for Nita, then raised the coffeepot and looked at me.

"No, thanks. I'm not big on coffee," I said.

Candy replaced the coffeepot, then turned back to Nita. "You stay here as long as you want, Mrs. Nita. There's no need for you to stand out there in the cold. I'm sure you can see just as much from these windows as you can outside."

Nita hadn't stayed in Scott's chair long. She'd gravitated to the windows and stood staring out, holding the coffee, but not sipping it.

She looked over her shoulder and said, "Thank you so much, Candy. I do appreciate it."

Candy waved her thanks away. "It's the least I can do. You and Mr. Gerald were so sweet when we were building our house." She looked at me and explained. "Mr. Gerald let me change my mind three times on the tile and I don't know how many times I switched the drawer pulls. You stay here as long as you want, Mrs. Nita. I'm going to the vending machine. Want a Coke? Snapple?" she asked me again.

"Sure," I relented. "I'll take a Diet Coke."

Candy must not have felt the same qualms about leaving me and Nita alone in the office, because she left without a backward glance.

Nita continued to stand with her back to me, staring out the window at the dreary scene outside. I was dying to know what was going on out there, but she'd seemed so shaken when I first saw her face. And now she was clearly in her own world, unaware of me.

I decided to leave her alone and went back to work cleaning up as best I could. I'd finished the first stage of organization, sorting through everything. During my next work sessions I'd organize the paperwork and arrange everything on the new shelves. One of the secrets to successful organization was breaking the project up into smaller pieces. Besides being frustrating, trying to finish a huge project in a couple of hours wasn't realistic. I tugged boxes and stacks into a semblance of order, then sat down in one of the uncomfortable office chairs to write a note for Scott and bring him up to date with what I'd done.

"We've been searching in the wrong place."

I raised my head.

She sipped her coffee, then said, "All this time we've been so focused on Magnolia Estates. We should have been looking here."

Nita turned from the window, took a seat at Scott's desk, and pulled her small computer out of her purse. "We have to move the search here," she said.

"What's going on out there?" I asked.

"The night Jodi disappeared there was one charge on her credit card. It was from that convenience store. She bought two bottles of water, an energy bar, and a map of Florida."

I looked out the window at the store. "Yes, Colleen told me about that. Was she on the store's surveillance video?"

"No. By the time we realized she was gone, they'd already taped over that day's video. They have an old security system and still use tapes, instead of digital recordings." Nita tapped her stylus on the desk. "Davey thought she'd caught a ride with someone and was on her way to Florida. That's where he focused, but I know that's not like her. Since her car was in her garage, I assumed she'd run to the Quick Mart, then returned home." She stopped tapping. "I was wrong."

"Have you changed your mind? Now do you think she was getting ready for a road trip?" I asked.

"No. I don't. I really don't. No one's found any trace of her on the road or anywhere in Florida. I'm still positive she wouldn't leave town without telling someone. We were so focused on Magnolia Estates that we overlooked this place." Nita sighed wearily, then rubbed her forehead. "The police received a tip this morning about evidence in that lot. They found a plastic bag with two water bottles and an energy bar."

"But how can they know it belonged to Jodi? Anyone could have left it out there."

"A receipt." She removed her hand from her forehead and looked forlorn as she said, "It had Jodi's credit card account number on it."

"And it survived this long?"

"Yes, it was faded, but readable. Davey tells me a tightly sealed plastic bag preserves what is inside it very well. The handles were tied at the top, locking out the moisture."

"Where's the map?" I wondered.

Nita sighed again. "I don't know. And I don't know why the bag would be in the middle of that field." She looked scared again and I hated to think what scenarios were running through her head. She visibly pulled herself together and tapped the screen while murmuring, "E-mails, phone calls, notify the media." As she said the last phrase she looked up at me again.

"I think I need your help again, Ellie. I'm concerned about what might have been overlooked."

"The lot was searched before? When she disappeared?"

"Yes, and I don't understand why they didn't find it. But that's not what I was talking about. I've got to stay focused on the media and keep Jodi's picture out there. Gerald isn't good with television. Truth is, I'm not either, but of the two of us, I'm better at it and I'm her mother, so that's a link the newspeople want to talk about, a hook."

She wasn't bitter, just stating facts, and I knew she was right. The media thrived on stories of beautiful young women in danger, and a compelling news hook was an interview with family members.

Nita said, "It's all very draining. I'm not normally a person who'd seek out this type of attention and it fatigues me. Besides constantly being 'on'—do you know what I mean?— there're so many news shows now. I can't turn down anyone who wants an interview. It could be the one that helps us find Jodi."

For a few seconds I had a glimpse of what she was going through. I knew I worried and fretted over my kids constantly, but how could you deal with the worry and anxiety that Nita and Gerald felt every day?

"It's wearing me out. And, frankly, I can't do the media part of this right now and focus on anything else. I have to do that because they're fickle. A few days, maybe only a few hours, and they'll have moved on to something else. What I've been trying to do for the last few days is go back through everything the police didn't take after she disappeared. I know they looked through everything, but I can't help feeling that they might have missed something. If they missed her notebook and a plastic bag in that field, who knows what else they might have missed?"

"Now, Mrs. Nita, you know that field was one of hundreds of sites we searched in the days after she disappeared."

We both turned. Detective Dave Waraday stood in the

doorway with Candy hovering behind him. She said, "He was looking for you, Mrs. Nita." She squeezed past him and came into the room to hand me my Diet Coke; then she retreated to the front office as she said, "Y'all are welcome to stay back there as long as you need."

I stood up. "I've finished here. I'll leave you two," I said as I placed my note on Scott's desk.

"No. Don't go, Ellie," Nita said. "I want Ellie to go through Jodi's papers again. She's already found several things in Jodi's notebook that weren't mentioned in her articles." Nita switched her gaze from Waraday back to me. "Will you be able to help me out?"

"Of course, anything you need. Why don't you call me later and we'll talk about it?"

"I think it would be better if you stayed. I'd like to discuss what you found in Jodi's notes with Davey," Nita said, nodding Waraday into the other visitor's chair.

"Fine. I want to keep tabs on anyone who's dabbling in my investigation." He sat down, but didn't look happy. He looked like a kid who'd been summoned to the principal's office.

"Oh, she's not dabbling," Nita said with a tight smile. "She's helping. I know how overextended you are, investigating William Nash and Jodi. Tell him about what you found," she said to me.

"There were two lists, one of story ideas, which mentioned Nash, and another with three names. Sherry, Rosalee, and Mary."

Waraday stared at me for a moment and I shifted uncomfortably in my chair. The bright fluorescent office lights highlighted his smooth, unwrinkled face. Not even a single crease under his eyes. I wished my skin looked that smooth. But when I looked at his eyes, I noticed his gaze was hard and appraising. "And you think this means . . . ?"

"Well, I think it means she was interested in Nash and made a note to talk to his cousin Sherry."

Waraday sat for a moment with his elbow on the armrest of the chair, his chin propped on his hand. He shifted his gaze back to Nita. "I'll check into it," he said slowly.

Nita smiled. "Thank you. I'll make sure you have copies of all Ellie's notes. Now, I should go back out there. Are they still searching?"

"No, ma'am. They're done. The plastic bag was the only thing we found and we're sending it to be analyzed now. We should have results in a few days."

She nodded and stood up. "Ellie, would you be able to come by my house tomorrow and look at Jodi's things? I'd like you to see what there is and tell me how big a job it will be."

Waraday and I stood, too. I went to get my bin of supplies. Tomorrow I had to prep for Nathan's birthday party. "How about now?"

"Let me check and see if any of the reporters would like an interview first. How about we meet at my house in about an hour?"

I nodded and Nita stopped to pat Candy on the shoulder. "Thank you, dear, for the coffee and the rest. I feel much better."

"No problem. You be sweet, Mrs. Nita," Candy called as Nita left.

I told Candy I'd be back next week to finish the storage area and then I left through the door Waraday still held.

"Here, let me," he said, gesturing to the plastic bin I was carrying.

"Oh, that's okay. I've got it," I said, pacing down the hall quickly to walk with Nita.

He caught up with us and opened the outer door for me. "At least let me give you a hand while you get your keys out," he said, and I realized I was going to have to set the bin down anyway because he was right, I didn't have my keys out like I usually did.

I handed the bin over and dug my keys out. Waraday followed me to the Jeep and stowed the bin in the back. As he shoved the hatchback door closed, he said, "Mrs. Nita's interest in this case is understandable. What I don't understand is why you're involved, Mrs. Avery."

At the mention of her name, Nita walked back to us and said, "I'm paying her to help out. She's an organizer and I need a little organization in my life right now. She's a kindhearted person, Davey." Nita turned and stepped carefully through the mud to the throng of people by the Quick Mart.

Waraday watched her for a second, then refocused on me. "Sure, you're an organizer, but you seem to be almost as interested in Jodi's case as her mother. I find that odd."

To tell or not tell? Did I let him in on the fact that I'd had a few run-ins with criminal investigations in the past? He was going to find out anyway, if he hadn't already. Wouldn't any investigator worth his salt have already checked me out, since I was the person who'd found the human remains?

"Well, I'm assuming you've already talked to Oliver Thistlewait, so I don't need to tell you I've been able to . . . contribute to several investigations." Thistlewait was with the Office of Special Investigations at Greenly Air Force Base. Our paths had crossed when we lived there.

He raised his eyebrows slightly. "Yes, I spoke to him a few days ago. He was very complimentary about you."

"I bet." That popped out before I could stop myself. "I'm sure he's glad I don't live anywhere near Greenly Air Force Base now. Let's just say I don't think he was ever thrilled to see me."

"Nevertheless, he said you're a good observer and have a knack for finding things out."

That assessment surprised me. It wasn't at all what I would have thought he'd say about me. "Well . . . maybe it's because I like things organized. I can spot things that don't fit or, sometimes, what's missing." And when things didn't fit, it irritated me to no end, but Waraday didn't need to know that. I moved around to the driver's side of the car and opened the door. He didn't seem to have anything else to say and his long silence was making me uncomfortable.

I climbed into the driver's seat and reached out to pull the door closed. "I'm sure Nita will let you know if anything turns up."

He caught the door before I could close it and said, "Jodi's belongings were searched. We pulled anything that impacted the investigation."

"But isn't it possible that something could have been overlooked, missed—" I glanced at the field. "Something that might not have seemed significant ten months ago, but might be important now?"

"It's possible," he conceded. His gaze was on the field as he said, "You do your search, but realize that the best hope we have of finding out what happened comes from hard evidence like fingerprints and Jodi's movements on that last day. Not from speculation."

"What are you saying? That you don't want me to look through Jodi's things?"

"No. If you find something, bring it in, but don't get Mrs. Nita's hopes up."

"This was her idea, not mine."

"Have a good day, Mrs. Avery." He closed the door, then tapped the side of the car as he went around behind it on his way back to the field.

Chapter Nineteen

"It's all in here in the garage," Nita said. She opened the door and I followed her down a short set of stairs. A blue Jetta took up one side; the other was stacked with boxes. Nita's gold Taurus was parked in the driveway and Gerald wasn't home, so the blue car must be Jodi's.

"We have her furniture in a storage unit," Nita said as she walked down a narrow path between the boxes, scanning the writing on the sides of them. "Of course, this is just what was left after the investigators took what they thought was important. The FBI still has her computer."

"The FBI is involved in Jodi's case?" I asked, surprised.

"Yes, there are several agencies involved in her case. The FBI, the GBI—that's Georgia Bureau of Investigation— the sheriff's office. Some are more involved than others." She sounded weary and her shoulders drooped as she ran down the list. She stopped about halfway down the aisle and rested her hand on a stack of boxes. "Everything is labeled. These were from her office at the house. This is where I think you should start."

"It doesn't look like you need any help with organizing anything," I said doubtfully.

"No, I know where her things are." She ran her hand over

the tape that sealed the box before continuing. "Honestly, I can't bear to look through Jodi's life right now. Every small thing will bring back a memory. I'd get lost in memories." She blinked a few times, then said briskly, "I can't allow myself to do that. There's too much to do."

I nodded and swallowed. If Nita wasn't going to cry, I wouldn't let myself either, but I could see how torn up she was.

"I'll leave you to look around."

Nita left and I sighed. She'd described all this stuff as Jodi's life, but it was a life on hold, frozen until there was some resolution. Maybe it was because it was gloomy in the garage— there was only one window and one overhead light—but a feeling of sadness seemed to permeate the place. Once, when Mitch and I were looking at houses, we stepped inside the front door and I knew immediately that neither one of us liked the dark, almost sad, room. Our agent had scurried around opening curtains as he said, "Sometimes houses get in a funk. They have a bad vibe to them."

This garage definitely had a bad vibe that made me want to get out. I gripped the corner of the tape and pulled. The rip seemed to echo around the open space. I pulled back the flaps and dug into the box. We'd moved so often I was pretty good at assessing what was in a box by looking at a few things on the top layer or two. This one held personal bills. The next box was clippings of her newspaper articles. I heaved those aside and opened the third one. It contained more articles, office supplies, and some framed photographs wrapped in newspaper. The next box held thick spiral-bound notebooks. The covers had looping handwritten titles, Mass Communication Research Methods, Public Relations, and History of Information.

Jodi was a keeper. She didn't throw things out. She hung on to stuff, even her old college notes. I flipped through a few and found the same indecipherable shorthand. I moved that box to a different stack. I bet Jodi had packed these when she finished college and hadn't opened them since.

I went through the rest of the boxes, then dusted my hands on my jeans and went back up the steps and into the kitchen. Nita was sitting at the kitchen table, which was covered with papers. She waved me over as she spoke into the phone. "Right. Saturday. You'll send out the e-mail? Thank you." She hung up. "I had to get in touch with Colleen since she maintains the Web site for us. We've got to get the word out about the change in the search location."

Did this woman never get tired? She seemed to always be juggling some aspect of the search for Jodi. If it wasn't TV appearances, then it was searches.

"What do you think?" Nita asked.

"Well, there's only three boxes from her office. Why don't I start with those? Would you mind if I took them home? If you're uncomfortable with that, I completely understand. I might not be able to get back here until later next week." I didn't know if she'd let the boxes out of her house since each item connected with Jodi seemed special to her, but if she let me take them, then I didn't have to spend time in the depressing garage.

"Of course you can take them. I know you'll take good care of everything."

She wanted to help me carry the boxes, but I wouldn't let her. She stood beside the Jetta and watched. "Thank you, Ellie." She handed me a check. "This is for your help with Jodi's notebook."

I thanked her and she went back inside, the garage door slowly rolling down on the artifacts of Jodi's life. I had just enough time to run by the store and pick up Nathan's birthday present. A plastic sandbox, even the small one, was just too noticeable to stick in the shopping cart without Nathan seeing it. The days when I could buy presents for the kids while they snoozed or cooed while strapped into the front of the cart were over.

* * *

I stepped out of the shower the next morning and heard a tap on my door. I slapped on some lotion and struggled into my clothes. I checked the clock as I hurried through the bedroom. Six-ten. Livvy was even earlier today than usual. She had the uncanny ability to wake up only seconds after I did each morning. I had no idea how she did it. Did she hear the hot water running? More likely it was some sixth sense that let her know people, adult-types, were up and moving around and she should get up, too.

The quiet tap sounded again before I opened the door. Livvy smiled up at me from under the brim of her flowered baseball cap. She'd dressed herself in a pink top with flowers that matched the cap. She'd paired it with an orange skirt and mismatched socks. Her hands clasped behind her, she twisted from side to side. "Good morning, Mom! Nathan is still asleep. I was very quiet."

"Good morning," I said as I opened the door wide and dropped a kiss on her head. She skipped past me and dove for the bed, delighted. She'd scored some one-on-one mommy time.

"You look nice. Good job dressing yourself." I went back into the bathroom and combed my hair. I didn't realize until I became a mom that my attention was the prize that both Livvy and Nathan competed for. It could really wear me out, especially when it started at six in the morning.

While Livvy played with my makeup brushes I clicked on the blow-dryer and worked my hair over until it was only damp, then pulled it back in a ponytail. No time for anything else because by now Nathan was demanding to be let out of his crib.

I scooped him up, snuggled him close. For a couple of precious minutes he burrowed into my shoulder; then he wiggled impatiently. He had things to do—furniture to try and climb, crumbs to search for on the floor, and a sister to annoy. I changed his diaper, dressed him, and released him to explore.

I went into the kitchen and put on some water to boil for oatmeal. "A man is coming to our door," Livvy reported from her post at the narrow window beside the front door.

I frowned and went to look. The man looked respectable enough—suit and tie—even a little familiar. He rang the bell and I opened the heavy front door. The glass screen door still separated us. A volley of deep barks came from the back-yard. Rex had heard the doorbell.

The man hesitated a moment as the barks sounded, then realizing the dog wasn't in the house, asked, "Mrs. Avery?"

Livvy had been standing under my arm, but she scampered off.

"Yes," I said slowly. I couldn't place him, but I knew I'd seen him before. He reminded me of a highly polished stone. Everything about him seemed to gleam—his dark hair, his teeth, even his eyes. And his skin looked odd; it was too smooth and had a funny cast to it. He shifted and I realized he was wearing thick makeup. As he moved I saw the street behind him was lined with satellite trucks. A woman strode up my sidewalk.

Even though the brunette's hair was smooth instead of that intentionally messy style like it had been the last time I'd seen her, I still recognized Chelsea O'Mara, a reporter with *24/7*, a news magazine that specialized in sensational-ized news.

The man pulled open the glass screen door and said, "Good morning! I'm Skip Collins."

That's where I'd seen him. He was a correspondent for one of the cable networks. I wanted to blurt out, "You look so much better on TV," but instead, I pulled the screen's han-dle to close the door, but he held tight. "Please, don't go. I'd like to ask you a few questions about Jodi Lockworth. You want to help find her, don't you?"

I yanked on the handle, but his grip didn't loosen. Behind him, Chelsea pounded up the steps and tried to wedge herself in front of him, saying, "Is it true that Jodi Lockworth said she'd return to this house before the end of the week?"

I felt a surge of panic. They wouldn't force their way inside, would they? I pulled on the handle as hard as I could, but with two people bracing it open I couldn't close it. I let go and reached back to close the front door. A clicking sound came from behind me as Rex rounded the corner from the kitchen, his paws slipping and sliding on the hardwood floor. He spotted the two strangers at the door and let out another volley of deep barks.

They let go of the door and nearly fell backward down the steps. The glass door closed on its valve, causing Rex to do a face-plant into the plate glass, leaving a huge slobbery mark. He kept his nose pressed to the glass, alternately growling and whining, not sure if the people were bad guys who needed a bite taken out of them or if they were good guys willing to play a little fetch.

I nudged him out of the way with my foot, closed the front door, and slid the dead bolt into place.

"I opened the door for Rex. He wanted to come inside," Livvy said from the kitchen. Behind her, steam rose from the boiling water.

"Thank you, Livvy, you did great. I wanted him inside, too."

I dumped oatmeal into the boiling water. It's funny that no matter what crisis is going on, the basics, like keeping the kids fed on a reasonable schedule, take top priority. I lifted a slat of the plantation blinds that I hadn't opened yet. Four satellite trucks and seven or eight people milled around on the street. Not on my lawn, so I didn't think they were technically on my property.

The phone rang and I jumped. I took a deep breath to calm down. Okay, I was a little on edge. I recognized Abby's number on the caller ID.

As soon as I said hello, she said, "Ellie, your house is on TV."

"Now?" I asked. "Right this minute?" I slanted the blind up again. I'd missed the guy with a camera stationed across the street, getting a wide shot of our house.

"Channel forty-two," Abby said over Charlie's jabbering in the background.

I heard a splat behind me and spun around. "Hold on. I forgot about the oatmeal." I sprinted into the kitchen, stirred the oatmeal, then grabbed the remote and turned on the TV. Both kids were by my side instantly. Livvy said, "Channel twenty-seven, Mom. Twenty-seven."

She was already savvy enough to know which channel to tune to for her shows. I tilted the phone away from my chin and said, "We're not watching kid shows this morning."

"That's our house," Livvy said.

An Everything In Its Place Tip for an Organized Party

Party Countdown Checklist (Two Weeks Prior)
- Address and mail invitations or send e-vites.
- Reserve rentals with rental company and/or contact friends and ask to borrow items you'll need for the party.
- Plan menu.
- Order cake, if needed.
- Plan flow of party. Where will you put the food, the drinks, the kids, and the pets?
- Make shopping lists.
- Make to-do list. Include things you want to accomplish around your home, but don't get too carried away. You don't have to redecorate your house. Entertaining can be a great motivator to get little items accomplished. Now is not the time to put in

a pool, but cleaning the carpets would be manageable.
- Plan decorations.
- Purchase nonperishable items.
- Follow up with guests who haven't responded to the invitation.

Chapter
Twenty

"**O**ur house is on *TV*," Livvy said, delighted. "Let's call Grammy and Nana so they can see it, too."

"Let's not," I said. I didn't want to attempt to explain what was going on to both sets of grandparents. Livvy's face fell. She loved making long-distance calls to her grandmothers.

"For one thing, it's too early. Maybe later."

Livvy thought everyone was as delighted with dawn as she was. She huffed and stomped off down the hall.

Nathan had levered himself up and had his face planted directly in front of the TV. He put out his pudgy finger and pushed the button to turn the TV off. He grinned and punched the button again.

I said to Abby, "Can you hold on for a second?"

"Sure."

Nathan aimed for the button again. I caught his hand and held it. "No." I pointed to the button and repeated, "No." I let his hand go and, just like I knew he would, Nathan reached for the button again. I repeated the word *no* and picked him up. He knew exactly where he was going—his room for a time-out. The howling started immediately.

After I put him in his bed, I shut the door on his wailing. I absolutely hated this part of parenting. I knew he'd only cry for a few seconds. And when I went back to get him after one minute he'd be fine. It didn't matter, though, I still hated being the heavy, the one who had to hold the line.

I picked the phone back up. "Okay. I've got one kid mad at me, the other screaming at full volume, and my house is on national TV."

"Sounds like a typical morning. Except for the TV part," Abby said.

I turned the TV off. There was no way I could hear it now anyway. "So, what are they saying?" I went into the kitchen, pushed the oatmeal pan to the back of the stove, and pulled out the juice and milk.

"That Jodi will be back before Halloween."

"What?"

"I know. It sounds crazy, but they're reporting a rumor going around that Jodi has never missed her mother's birthday and she'll be home to help her celebrate. Nita's birthday is October thirtieth."

"Then why are they at *my* house? Shouldn't they be at Nita's? Not that I'd wish that group of people on anyone, but she *wants* to talk to them. I don't."

"Apparently, they got a tip that Jodi left evidence in her house, telling where she'd be."

I pursed my lips. Well, they were half right. There had been evidence in the house. But as for telling where Jodi was . . . so far it hadn't been very enlightening about that subject. "You know, I didn't try to keep the discovery of Jodi's notebook quiet and Waraday hadn't warned Nita and me not to talk about it, so I suppose if someone was asking questions it wouldn't be too hard to find out about it. That could be the source of the rumor about evidence in our house, but the part about Jodi returning, I don't know where that came from. Are we still on TV?"

"Yep. Your pumpkins look great. Nice arrangement on the steps. You should add some cornstalks, too—"

"Abby! This is not the time to focus on decorating."

"Sorry. Do you want me to come over there? I could, I don't know, create a distraction."

"No distraction creation." Abby had a tendency to create distractions without meaning to. Who knows what she'd do if she was *trying* to create a disturbance? "At least not yet." I scooped the oatmeal into bowls and transferred them to the table with the phone tucked between my shoulder and ear. "I was planning on staying home this morning anyway. I have lots of party stuff to do, like bake Nathan's cake and make the goodie bags. The reporters will get bored and be gone in a couple of minutes."

They were still there at noon. We'd baked a cake, had lunch, and played two games of Jack and the Beanstalk in which Livvy was the director of our little play and I had to be the giant and the cow. All those activities occurred between fielding several phone calls from curious friends and neighbors.

I stuffed the goodie bags and iced the cake. They were still there. It was almost one o'clock and I had a serious case of cabin fever. It's one thing to stay home all day by choice; it's quite another thing to know you can't leave. Well, I supposed we could leave, but I didn't want to brave the wall of reporters. Two satellite trucks were blocking the end of the driveway and I didn't know if they'd move.

I had things I needed to do, including buying the candle. Even though it was just one candle, we definitely *had* to have it. Can't have a first birthday party without a candle. And I needed to pick up ice cream, balloons, and a few essentials, like diapers. Nathan was napping now and I'd been planning on making a run to the store after he woke up. I'd been so sure they'd lose interest and leave after a few hours.

I wished there was some way to get word to Mitch about what was going on. He was flying home today, so I couldn't get in touch with him until he landed at the base later to-night. For a few seconds, I considered calling the command post and asking them to patch me through to the plane, but I discarded the idea almost as quickly as it popped into my head. That seemed a little extreme just to warn someone that the press was camped out in front of their house. I settled for calling his cell phone. I didn't know how to summarize everything that had happened in a few quick sentences, so when his voice mail switched on I said, "Mitch, call me before you come home. Don't worry, everyone's fine, just call when you get this."

I raised one of the slats of the blinds and saw Coleman at the center of the cluster of reporters. Well, if anyone could get them to leave, he could. The homeowners' association probably had a "no assembly without a permit" clause.

I dropped the slat and paced around the dining room. Soft singing came from Livvy's room, where she had a huge game going that involved spreading toys over every surface.

I made a list of things I needed at the store, then checked the street again. Coleman was arguing. I could hear his raised voice through the window, but the reporters weren't moving. I paced around the dining room again, running through my mental checklist of things I needed to do to get ready for the party. I was going to clean tomorrow before everyone arrived because otherwise it was a wasted effort. If I cleaned today, the house would look good for about fifteen minutes.

I paced some more, trying to think of something to do to get my mind off the circus in the front yard. I couldn't work in the box room right now because I'd wake up Nathan. Surely there was something else I could sort or organize?

Jodi's boxes. I dragged them from the garage into the study and planted myself on the floor with the boxes encircling me. I settled down to some serious paper sorting. Twenty minutes later, I was about two inches deep into the box and had several stacks of paper.

I unfolded another crumpled receipt and put it on one of

the stacks. Apparently, any time Jodi charged anything or paid a bill she tossed the receipts and statements in this box.

I stopped when I reached the halfway point and stood up to stretch my legs. Nothing remotely exciting or interesting had showed up as I shifted through the papers. Jodi paid her bills on time and her bank statements looked pretty normal for a single working girl. All in all, the papers seemed to indicate she had an ordinary life. Maybe the FBI would find something on her computer.

I stepped over the paper piles and angled up a slat of the blinds. The scene out front hadn't changed, except Coleman was gone. Everyone else was still there. I dropped the blind back into place and sagged against the window frame, rubbing my forehead.

Somehow I had to clear the street before tomorrow. We wouldn't have any guests for Nathan's party if they had to fight their way through reporters and satellite trucks. If Coleman couldn't make the reporters leave, I doubted my pleas would make any difference. And if I went out there to talk to them, I'd end up on the news for sure. Short of calling in a bogus anonymous news tip myself and directing them to some other part of town, I couldn't figure out how to get rid of them. They had more patience than I'd given them credit for. I was almost sorry I hadn't taken Abby up on her offer to create a distraction, but she was at the school at the moment, so I couldn't get her help until later anyway.

The phone rang and I grabbed it before it could ring again. I didn't want any extra noise disrupting the last few minutes of nap time.

Mitch said, "Ellie, are you okay?"

"Yes," I said cautiously. "Why? Did you get my message?"

"I did. Are you at home?"

"Yes. In fact, I'm kind of stuck here."

"I can see that."

"You can? You're watching the news?"

"Yep. We have a couple of hours on the ground before we

take off again, so I'm waiting in base ops. They have the news on. What's going on?" His tone was concerned.

I summarized the rumors and told Mitch about the plastic bag found yesterday. "Apparently, the identification of William Nash was what drew the national media here in the first place, but now they've latched on to Jodi's story, too. What are we going to do?"

"Wait them out." He took the news in stride, which amazed me.

"But we have Nathan's party tomorrow."

"If they're still there, we'll move the party somewhere else. Or we can postpone it."

I rubbed my forehead. "You say that so flippantly. Move it. Postpone it. I've done a lot of work to get ready for his party. We can't just move it. Where would we move it?"

"I don't know. Maybe Jeff and Abby's house?"

"Okay," I said grudgingly. "That's a possibility." She *had* offered to help me out.

"Besides, the press has a very short attention span. They'll probably be gone before I get home tonight."

"I hope so, but I thought they'd be gone in a few hours and they're still there. I think Jodi was researching William Nash."

There was a pause and he said, "I thought you weren't going to get involved in this."

"I think we're past that point. It's sort of overtaken us. Besides, I am interested in what happened to Jodi. I can understand the media attention. I want to know what happened, too. I'm looking through some of Jodi's boxes for Nita. If I can find out what she found out—"

Mitch interrupted me, his relaxed tone gone. "You could be in a lot of danger if it's what led to her disappearance or possibly got her killed."

"Mitch, I'm strictly on paper patrol. You know I'm good at stuff like that—sorting, shifting, catching little details."

He paused again and finally said, "I know you're going to

do it anyway, no matter what I say, so just be very careful. Stick to the paper trail."

"That's my plan," I confirmed.

He asked, "Have you talked to them, the press?"

"No!"

"Good. Just leave them alone and they'll lose interest. I have to go. I'll call you when I land tonight."

We said our good-byes and hung up. I paused as I put the phone back, thinking about what Mitch had said. "Just leave it alone" was his way of handling things. He was good at waiting things out and he believed that things worked themselves out. *Que sera sera* and all that. My way of handling things was more carpe diem.

I heard Nathan shifting around. Time to get back on mom duty. I got Nathan up and had to smile back at him because he was so delighted to see me when I pushed open his door.

I picked up him, showered him with kisses that made him giggle, then put him down on the changing table. As I unfastened the snaps on his outfit, I glanced out his window into the backyard. I wished it would rain. Showers might drive the reporters away. At least I could be pretty sure there weren't any reporters in the backyard since we had a wooden privacy fence on all sides and the back gate was secured with a heavy-duty lock. There wasn't an alley, and the woods behind our fence stretched out to the gravel access road.

While I was changing him, Livvy appeared in his doorway. Her supersonic hearing had detected the slight noise from his room. "Is rest time over?"

"Yep. You can come out of your room," I said. I grabbed the last diaper and taped it on Nathan, looking at the back gate thoughtfully.

Livvy bounced. "Are we going to get the balloons? Is it time?"

"Almost. Go get your shoes. I have to make a phone call."

Chapter
Twenty-one

Twenty minutes later I'd revised my wishes for the weather and hoped the rain held off for at least another couple of minutes. I had Nathan strapped in the backpack. I was carrying his car seat and had the diaper bag slung over my shoulder. Livvy had on her pink rain slicker and rain boots. "I hope it rains," she said, unfurling her princess umbrella.

I whispered, "Remember to be very quiet." I unlocked the gate and checked the woods. I couldn't see very far into the dense foliage, but there was no one in my immediate line of vision. I nodded at Livvy and she solemnly nodded back. We stepped through the gate and I relocked it.

"Okay," I said, keeping my voice low as I reached down to pick up the car seat and diaper bag. "Close your umbrella. Are you ready for a hike?"

"Yes! Can we pick flowers?"

"No," I said rather sharply. I softened my tone and explained, "Some plants can make you itch if you touch them. And I don't think there will be any flowers this time of year anyway." I put out my hand, she put hers in mine, and we walked down the tiny path that wormed its way through the trees. It was just wide enough that we would walk side by side. Livvy smacked at dead leaves with her furled umbrella as we went along. It was only a few minutes before we reached the gravel path where the heavy silver car was idling.

Dorthea emerged from the driver's seat and took the diaper bag from me. "Did anyone see you?" I asked.

She shrugged. "They saw me, but they didn't care."

"That's good," I said as I secured the seat belt to Nathan's car seat and transferred him into it from the backpack. Livvy had a special strap holder to keep the seat belt at just the right place for her, so I buckled her in and then dropped into the passenger seat, tired from carting all the kid paraphernalia.

Livvy's voice piped up from the backseat. "Do you have a quarter for me today, Mrs. Dorthea?"

I cringed. "Livvy, it's impolite to ask for a present."

"Oh, I don't mind," Dorthea said, digging in her pockets. She pulled out a coin and held it up. "Well, look here." She eased the car down the gravel path and I said, "Thanks for helping me out."

"Glad to do it."

"I don't know how we'll get back inside without someone seeing us." A balloon bouquet was pretty hard to hide.

Dorthea touched the brake as we emerged from the trees where the gravel path met the paved neighborhood road. She turned away from the conglomeration down the block at my house and said, "I'm sure something will work out."

I studied the cars, trucks, and people milling around until Dorthea turned the corner and she said, "I've never seen anything like that. In fact, I don't think North Dawkins has ever had this much attention or excitement, except when Jodi first went missing."

"You've lived here a long time?"

"All my life. Hard to believe we have all these fancy stores and restaurants. When I was a girl, North Dawkins had one road and it didn't even have a name." She looked over at me and said, "They named it in the '70s. Tarlton Street."

"That's pretty amazing," I said, considering Tarlton was constantly snarled with traffic now. "So, what was it like around here in the '50s?" I asked.

"Like most small towns." Dorothea shrugged. "We had the base by then and there were always handsome flyboys about town. We had a bank and the train was still important, but North Dawkins was nothing like it is now. If we wanted to do any shopping we went up to Macon or Atlanta."

"Was there a lot of racial tension?"

She tilted her head back and forth. "There was some. Some white people thought black people had to be kept in their place. My granddaddy was like that, but not everyone felt that way. Of course, there are some people who still feel like that today. We had a dustup at Magnolia Estates a few years back when the Websters sold their house to that nice black family. You know the Calvertons, across the street? They were upset and said their property values would go down. Ridiculous, but thank goodness the rest of the neighborhood didn't feel that way.

"I know my daddy thought segregation was evil. Not just wrong. Evil. So opinions varied, but we didn't have the marches and demonstrations. As strange as it sounds, I think the air base made North Dawkins more . . . cosmopolitan. That's an odd word to use to describe North Dawkins, isn't it? But we had all kinds of different people coming and going. Broadened our horizons, I suppose."

"Did you know William Nash?"

"You knew everyone, but things were still segregated then. I knew who he was, but I didn't *know* him. I was older than him and he went to a different school. He lived in one of those tiny houses at the corner of the state highway and Scranton Road."

"The houses past the antique place? What's it called? Crooner's?" I asked.

"That's it. No antiques there. It's a junk market." Dorthea

snorted. "I can't believe the county lets Crooner get away with that eyesore."

"Who else lived out there?"

"No one, really, except for a couple of houses way down at the end of the road." Dorthea had navigated through our neighborhood and stopped by the second pond to wait for an opening in the traffic on Scranton Road. As we whipped past the houses she waved her hand at a rancher set back from the road. "That was where Coleman and Ava lived. They only had a couple of neighbors," Dorthea said, indicating three smaller houses a bit down the road. She nodded at the last one. "There's my old house."

"I think I met a girl that grew up in one of these. Kendra Jenning."

Dorthea nodded. "The Jennings lived there for years, too. I think they've moved up to Atlanta. It's so hard to keep up with everyone now."

I glanced back to check on the kids. Livvy was putting the coin in her pocket, then pulling it out, then putting it away again, and Nathan was snoozing.

"Now that I think about it, everyone who lived on Scranton Road has moved on to some place new, except for Nita and Gerald. Even Coleman's moved to Magnolia Estates. That stunned everyone."

"Why?"

"Well, he'd lived on Scranton Road forever. Ava died—oh, I believe it was about 1992."

It always amazed me when people could pinpoint a date in their memory so exactly. Everything was moving so fast now in my life I usually had a hard time remembering what day of the week it was.

Dorthea continued. "He was devoted to her. Her death crushed him. She was delicate. Some folks said he spoiled her, but she wasn't in the best of health and he took good care of her. I remember when he bought her a brand new car.

That caused quite a stir. They drove up to Atlanta one weekend in their old car and came back with a shiny Bel Air." Dorthea laughed. "He said it was a late Christmas present, but everyone said that car was really for Coleman because after that he drove her everywhere, even the grocery store.

"He was devastated when she died. He retreated to that house and didn't do much for a couple of years. In fact, I think the whole town felt it. She was the quintessential southern lady. She had a Christmas tea at their house every year and the whole town was invited. She ran the volunteer program at the library and was a member of all the clubs—garden, bridge, the rose society. I don't know how to describe it, but she had a spark, an excitement that could move people and she was always on some crusade or another. First it was the library. She did most of the fund-raising for that and then she was on to, let's see, was it the campaign to plant trees and flowers at the entrance to North Dawkins or was that later? I can't remember now, but she was always doing something.

"After she died, he didn't run for mayor. He got a civil service job at Taylor and worked there. Never showed any interest in remarrying. And let me tell you, several of the ladies around here had their eye on him. If he'd so much as smiled at one of them, they would have had him marching down the aisle before he knew it. So everyone was as shocked as all get out when he moved to Magnolia Estates."

She spent the rest of the drive describing the history of the various areas we drove through. It was interesting, but my thoughts were stuck on this nice-guy view of Coleman. Could a man who took care of his sickly wife murder someone?

We arrived at the store and I had to focus on checking off my list, but I was still contemplating those questions on the drive home. The Mylar balloons bumped around the ceiling of the car, which delighted Livvy and Nathan. I debated about asking Dorthea another question. Finally, I shifted so that I could see her better.

"Do you think Coleman had anything to do with William Nash's death?"

"No, I don't."

"Why?"

"Why are you asking about him?" she asked, cutting a quick glance at me.

"Well." I took a deep breath. "I think Jodi was researching Nash and if she uncovered something about Coleman being involved, then perhaps . . ." I trailed off.

Dorthea was shaking her head. "Coleman's not like that. He has a don't-rock-the-boat kind of personality. A stickler for rules. You know what he's like with the HOA. I can't imagine he'd ever be able to go that far outside of normal actions."

"But if he's racist, if those are his norms, then he might have seen killing Nash as acceptable."

Dorthea shook her head, one decisive shake. "That's about as likely as Coleman approving Bridget Sanders's request to build a backyard playhouse and paint it hot pink. I'm telling you, there are some things that just wouldn't happen."

I propped my elbow on the armrest and leaned my head on my hand. "Well, was there anyone else around that time that you can think of who might have wanted to hurt Nash? Or any black man to make a point?"

"What point was there to make?"

"Wasn't Nash organizing a march to support the Montgomery Bus Boycott? Scott Ezell told me that was why Nash was lynched. To make a point about desegregation."

Dorthea turned the wheel and we glided past the pond and fountain at the neighborhood entrance. "Now that you mention it, I do remember something like that making the rounds. Just whispers, but it doesn't sound like William. He was a very quiet man and didn't put himself forward. I can't see him leading anything."

"But the lynching was common knowledge, right?"

"There were whispers, but that's all I remember. North Dawkins certainly wasn't a hotbed of desegregation feelings."

"There weren't any other incidents?"

"No," she said derisively. "Unlike the image some people have of the South, the KKK didn't exist in every town."

A balloon floated forward and I batted it back to the backseat, which set Livvy and Nathan to giggling. They were so engrossed in the balloons that they weren't paying any attention to the conversation in the front seat.

"People here might not have liked desegregation, but no one was foolish enough to dress up in sheets and burn crosses."

Maybe the lack of information in the news archives at the library was not because news had been suppressed, but because there really wasn't any news? Then why was Nash killed?

"Don't turn here." I realized we were about to turn onto our street. "Go around the back way and drop us off on the gravel path."

"Let's take a peek." Dorthea eased the car into the turn. "Well, look at that." The street was empty except for the normal scattering of a few parked cars.

"What happened?"

Dorthea smiled. "I think Nita decided that she should have a press conference this afternoon about the search tomorrow."

I heard the garage door go up and I met Mitch in the kitchen. He parked his rolling suitcase, put down his flight bag, and kissed me. "Kids asleep?"

"Yes, even Livvy," I said.

"And the media siege is over?" he asked.

I relaxed into his arms, glad to have him back. "Yes, Nita

called a press conference this afternoon and they haven't been back. I don't know what's keeping them busy, but I'm glad they're not here."

"We could turn on the news and find out."

"No, I've had enough of that for today. I have a better idea. How about a date?"

Mitch looked over my shoulder. "Do you have the sitter hidden around here?"

"No." I took his hand and pulled him into the living room. "Since we can't seem to get out of the house for a date, I thought we'd have one here." I'd spread a tablecloth over the coffee table and tossed big pillows on the floor. "You know that new Chinese place we've been wanting to go to? I've got takeout," I said as I lit the taper candles in the new candlesticks. "We can eat in here while we watch a movie. Unless you're too tired?" Sometimes the time zone changes wiped him out after a trip.

"Too tired for a candlelight date with my wife? I don't think so."

"Good." I wrapped my arms around his neck. We kissed again, slowly; then I leaned back. "There's one good thing about you having to go out of town so much."

"What's that?" he asked, interspersing his words between kisses on my neck.

"The coming home bit is nice."

He smiled slowly. "I have to agree."

"You know, we don't have to eat right now. We can warm it up later."

"Excellent idea."

An Everything In Its Place Tip for an Organized Party

Party Countdown Checklist (One Week Prior)
  • Prep food—cut, chop, and arrange whatever you
    can ahead of time.

- Prepare and freeze some food, if possible.
- Pick up any items that you're borrowing from friends.
- Iron tablecloths and napkins. Polish silver, if needed.
- Clean house.
- Clean out the refrigerator and freezer.
- Follow up with guests who haven't responded to invitations.

Chapter
Twenty-two

The next morning, I leaned over to kiss Mitch good-bye. "I'm leaving," I whispered. "Kids are still asleep." He murmured an agreement and I picked up the laundry basket. I had no doubt that the kids would make sure he was awake shortly. I sneaked down the hall to the laundry room at the opposite end of the house. I might as well throw in the first load since I had several piles of dirty clothes to wash today. It was so far away from the kids' rooms, it wouldn't wake them.

The laundry was like the Hydra that grew two heads for each one Hercules cut off. Every time I washed a load of laundry, twice as many dirty clothes seemed to sprout in the hampers. Too bad I couldn't cauterize the hampers like Hercules did. But we couldn't really have flaming hampers. Or dirty socks, for that matter. As I reached the end of the hall, I frowned.

What was that smell?

I pushed open the laundry room door and immediately recoiled at the rotten egg smell. I shut the door and hurried back to the bedroom. I was fairly handy at minor household repairs, but I knew nothing about gas leaks. I shook Mitch awake. "There's a natural gas leak in the laundry room."

"What?" he said blearily. He came fully awake when I repeated my news.

He paced down the hall and checked the laundry room. "Yep. That's natural gas, all right." He shifted the dryer a bit, then worked his hand into the space and closed a valve. He opened the tiny window above the dryer. "That should do it. I'll fix it after it airs out." He pulled the door closed and rubbed his hands through his bed head. "Good thing that door closes on its own, or else the whole house would smell like that."

"So it's not dangerous?" I asked as he ambled back to our bedroom.

"Not now. If that had been open all night and you made oatmeal for the kids, there could have been an explosion, but it's good now." He rubbed his hand over his hair, which was sticking straight up anyway.

"Why don't we call the rental company? They'll send someone out to fix it."

"Nah, it's not that hard and it's a Saturday. It'll probably take them until Monday to get someone out here. I'll have it fixed before you get back," he said as he climbed back into bed.

"I wonder how it happened?"

"We probably bumped it or it just wasn't on the valve really well to begin with."

"I was throwing the tennis ball with Rex yesterday. He chased the ball in here and slammed into the dryer when he lost his footing on the tile floor."

"That probably did it. See you later," he said with his eyes already closed.

The sun wasn't even above the trees when I parked at the edge of the Quick Mart's parking lot beside the shuttered stand that sold boiled peanuts. My breath came out in little white puffs as I hiked down to the cluster of people gathered at the edge of the vacant lot where the plastic bag had been found. I'd learned last winter that southerners do get a taste of winter. In middle Georgia the temperature could dip into the thirties overnight. There was rarely any snow, but it did get cold enough that gloves were required. After the sun cleared the trees it would warm up, but it would still feel like fall.

I saw several news crews inside the convenience store and pulled the brim of my baseball cap lower over my eyes. I'd dressed more for warmth than for anonymity in a long-sleeved shirt, down vest, jeans, boots, and gloves, but now I was glad that my hat hid my face, at least a little bit. Only Chelsea O'Mara and the male reporter knew what I looked like, and I hoped to steer clear of all the press today. They hadn't reappeared last night. So far they hadn't shown up on our street and I hoped it would stay that way, but I knew it was a strong possibility that they would be back and it irritated me. I didn't like being held hostage in my house.

I spotted Colleen's mustardy hair frizzing out from under a black ski cap, and hurried over to her. "Colleen! Hi!" I said.

She was sipping on a cup of Starbucks coffee and murmured hello. It didn't look like she was a morning person and normally I would have felt bad about forcing her to chat with me when she clearly wanted to be left alone, but knowing that reporters could descend on my house at any moment . . . well, let's just say that situation removed some inhibitions.

"This looks like a good turnout," I said as I scanned the growing crowd.

"Pretty good." She sipped her coffee and gazed listlessly at the office park where STAND's offices were located.

I needed something to wake her up since the caffeine obviously wasn't doing it. "Is Scott here?"

She shrugged. "No idea. Probably. He wouldn't want to break his perfect attendance record. Unfortunately, we can't bar him since it's open to the public."

At least she was focused on me now. "Colleen, did Jodi ever talk about what she was working on for the newspaper? Especially during those last few months?"

"Nothing specific. Sometimes she'd mention an interview

or something, but only in general terms. I've gone over every conversation we had during those last few months and I can't remember anything specific. Believe me, I've tried. The only thing that sticks out in my memory is one time. She was working on a story and said she might not be at the *North Dawkins Standard* much longer." She finished off her coffee and tossed it in a trash can.

"And she never indicated what she was working on?"

"No." Colleen sighed. "I've gone over that conversation again and again in my mind and she didn't mention anyone or anything. In fact, it was more of a throwaway line. We were talking about whether she should paint the dining room in her house and she said she might as well wait and see if her story panned out. If it did, she might be able to get on at a bigger paper, like the *AJC* in Atlanta. I know the story had to be something big. I have no idea what it was."

Something big. I'd say the Nash investigation would qualify as something big. It had certainly drawn national media attention. And Colleen was Coleman May's granddaughter. Maybe that's why Jodi hadn't mentioned she was investigating Nash's disappearance.

"Did she ever ask you any questions about your grandfather?"

Colleen's head whipped toward me and she said, "No. Why?"

I wasn't sure I wanted to take the conversation in this direction, but I didn't have a glib answer to throw her off either. Dang. I should have thought this one through, because coming up with stuff off-the-cuff was not my strength. In fact, I tended to get tangled up in my own words and trip myself up. By then it didn't matter because my hesitation gave me away.

"She was looking into the whole Nash thing, wasn't she?" Colleen turned away from me, her head thrown back and her hands braced on her hips; then she spun toward me again. "How? How do you know?"

"It was in her notebook. Just his name, nothing else, so I

don't know how far she got in her research, or even if it was only a story idea. She did know Coleman was your grandfather, right?"

"Yes," she snapped.

"I only asked because I'd never have known. That night at the HOA meeting, I had no idea. Someone else told me you were related."

Her hands, balled into fists, were still braced on her hips. "Look, I don't broadcast it, okay? We're not . . ." She shrugged and said, "Close. I hardly ever saw him when I was a kid. I lived in Seattle until I was ten, and I only remember one time that we came out to visit them. Grandfather made me a tire swing in the backyard and Grandma Ava let me play with her jewelry." She sighed and shook her head. "It was cheap costume stuff. You know, the chunky brooches with lots of stones made into flowers or animals?"

I nodded. "My grandmother had the exact same stuff."

Colleen smiled, more relaxed. "Yeah. Well, to a four-year-old those sparkly things were amazing. I loved the panda bear pin. Anyway, Grandma Ava let me play with them one afternoon. I had them spread out across her bed, every brooch, necklace, and earring."

Colleen's mood shifted and her face shuttered. She pressed her lips together, then said, "I don't know how long I'd been in there playing, maybe an hour, but she came back later and freaked. She screamed at me. I don't mean she yelled at me to put everything away. She lost control, shrieking. I was so scared. I thought she was going to hurt me. I used to have nightmares about it." Colleen took a deep breath, seemed to shake off the memory. "Anyway, my mom packed our stuff that afternoon and we left. I didn't see them again until I was ten and my dad got a job here. That's kind of late to bond, you know, especially when your parents don't get along with your grandparents. Makes it difficult. Looking back now, I can see that my parents kept us away from them, even after we lived here. We hardly ever saw them."

"Was your grandfather volatile, like your grandmother?"

Colleen made a snorting noise. "No. Meek as a lamb, my mother used to say about him. That's why the whole Nash thing is absurd. I wish Jodi had asked me about it. I could have told her he'd never do anything like that."

She must have seen the doubt on my face, because she said, "I can understand why you'd think I might have a slanted view of my grandfather, but honestly, I hardly know him at all. I was only at his house that night of the HOA because of the connection to Jodi. You should talk to my mom. She'll be in town this weekend. She can tell you about Coleman."

Wouldn't any family member have the inclination to cover for a relative?

"She's never liked my grandparents, so you can count on her to give it to you straight," Colleen added. "She even went back to her maiden name after the divorce. That's why my last name isn't May."

She focused on a movement behind me and I turned to see what she was staring at. "I knew he'd show up," Colleen said, her gaze focused on Scott as he walked into the Quick Mart.

"I didn't recognize him with the baseball cap," I said. He was back to his rumpled look in a University of Georgia hooded sweatshirt and worn jeans.

"Are you kidding? He's got to be here to see if we find anything else that might implicate him. At least he had the courtesy to wear red. We'll be able to keep track of where he is."

"Colleen, do you really think he'd do something like tamper with evidence, if he found anything?"

She sent me a withering look and said, "I can see he's charmed you, too."

"I wouldn't say he's charmed me, but so far, he doesn't seem like the type of person who'd hurt someone he didn't agree with. Maybe argue them to death, but as far as physical harm goes, I don't know. Do you know Candy? His receptionist?"

Colleen nodded and said, "Yeah, her daughter is in my science class."

"Well, Candy doesn't seem to be at all intimidated by him. In fact, she's kind of, well, motherly isn't the word, maybe bossy is a better choice, but she does seem to like him in a grudging way. And she doesn't seem like the kind of person who'd take crap from anyone."

Colleen smiled. "You're right on that."

"Morning, ladies."

Colleen and I both startled at the sound of a voice behind us. Scott stood a few feet away, holding two cups of coffee. He held one out to Colleen. "Thought you might need some more caffeine. It's not Starbucks, but it is coffee. Cream, no sugar, right?"

Colleen stared at him for a moment before she said, "Ah, right. Thanks."

She took the coffee and he raised his cup before moseying off to join another cluster of people.

"Well, that was unexpected," I said.

Colleen rolled her eyes. "He was just being nice."

"He sure didn't bring *me* any coffee."

Nita broke away from a tight circle at the edge of the vacant lot, a clipboard in one hand and a megaphone in the other. She raised the megaphone. "Good morning. First, I want to say thank you to each one of you for coming out today. I can't tell you how much it means to us that you're taking time out of your schedule to help us find Jodi. That's why we're here today, to make sure every inch of this vacant lot is scoured. We want to do this search as thoroughly as possible, so I've asked Detective Waraday to instruct us on the appropriate way to conduct this search."

She handed the megaphone off to Waraday.

"We need everyone to line up across this side of the lot."

Waraday waved his arm, indicating the shorter end of the lot near the Quick Mart. We moved down and formed a rough line along the boundary of the lot. I ended up sandwiched between Topaz and a burly man in an insulated flannel jacket and work boots.

"How are you doing?" I asked Topaz.

"Great! Just got back from Jekyll Island yesterday," she said as she tucked the longer side of her striped hair behind her ear. "I had two stores that sold out of my stuff, so I had to get out there. I wished I could have stayed because it's so nice there—no crowds at all—but I felt like I should be back for this. I had no idea it would be so chilly." She pulled her fuzzy multicolored scarf tighter around her neck, and her dangly metal earrings shivered.

Waraday's voice came over the megaphone again. "Everyone spread out a little. You need space to move, but not too much. Good. Looks good. Now, we're going to stay in this line and cross all the way over to the woods on the far side. For those of you who have the office park directly in your path, just wait for the rest of us to go around it and then get back in position on the far side. Move slowly. The most important thing is to stay low to the ground. If you see something, raise your hand and we'll halt the line. I'll send someone to assess what you found and then we'll all move again on my signal. The woods on the far side will slow us down a bit, but it's important to stay in line."

Someone down the line shouted, "How far into the woods are we going?"

Waraday said, "All the way to Elliott Road. That means we'll have to go around the lake. Use the same technique as with the office park. If the lake is directly in your path, drop back, let the line move around it, then take your place on the other side. This lot has been searched once by crime scene technicians, but there are a lot more of you than there were on that team. We may find something new, we may not, but the important thing is that if you see anything—paper, cloth, any disturbances in the dirt, digging, raised mounds, anything like that—raise your hand and let us check it out. Everyone ready? Okay, check the area directly in front of your toes. Anyone see anything?"

I didn't have anything to report since I only saw wisps of grass, which were still green because of all the recent rain.

"Okay, let's take one slow step and check again. Remember, the lower you can get, the better."

We moved forward at a "Mother May I?" pace, one baby step at a time. We'd gone about three steps when Topaz squatted down and delicately moved a few blades of grass. Then she popped up and waved her hand. "I see something." A ripple of excitement moved through the line. "I think it's a gum wrapper."

Waraday approached, squatted to examine it, then placed it in a bag. "You're right. Gum wrapper." The tension eased as he noted the location, then said, "The smallest things can be important. Don't overlook anything." He gave the signal for us to move on.

I didn't see anything more interesting than dirt, sticks, grass, and a few vines, but the line stopped moving several times. Each time word traveled down the line that it was a relatively minor thing. A scrap of paper, an empty can of motor oil, and a handmade garage sale sign all turned up and were carefully bagged and logged.

I had to admit that Waraday certainly was making every effort to do a thorough and professional search. Our line crawled past the office park and across the rest of the open area. We'd just entered the woods when a shout went up from a guy down the line. By then my shoulders, back, and thighs were screaming. Who knew searching the ground was such a good workout? I stretched and realized the people had gone extremely quiet. "What is it?" I asked Topaz.

"A mound of dirt."

Chapter
Twenty-three

"Oh no," I said as the line began to collapse around Waraday. He stood up and pressed the air with his palms. "Stay in your line. We'll let you know what we find."

I realized I'd instinctively stepped forward and into the area in front of Topaz, so I stepped back. Waraday called in a woman from the sidelines and they carefully probed the stack of leaves, then removed a few of them. After a few minutes of both of them examining the ground, they stood up, walked carefully a few feet farther into the woods, and checked the ground again. I felt sick to my stomach and looked around to locate Nita. She was at the far end of the line, tensely waiting, her hand gripping Gerald's.

Waraday walked back, speaking through the megaphone as he went. "It's an old dirt road that winds around the lake and comes out on the other side at Elliott Road. The slight mound is the middle of the track between the two ruts made by the tires."

I swear that everyone in that line breathed a sigh of relief at that moment. Someone slapped a man on the back and said, "Congratulations, Henry, you found a road." Nervous laughter followed and we resumed our trek through the woods, which was much slower going.

I halted at the edge of the lake and studied the water as it lapped gently against the grass. "I'm surprised it's so big. I had no idea this was back here."

"Me either," Topaz said.

The man beside me said, "Used to be the best place to swim. Old Cotner, he didn't care if you came out here in the summer."

"Really? Is it deep?" I asked, surprised.

"Probably about fifteen to twenty feet." The man pointed to a high outcrop on the far side and said, "Deep enough to dive anyway."

The rest of the searchers had made their way around the lake, so we took up our position on the far side and continued to the road without anyone else calling the line to a halt.

"Thanks for your help, everyone. You did an excellent job. We'll check everything that was found today. Don't be discouraged because there wasn't a dramatic find. Sometimes it's the smallest things that break a case." Waraday handed the megaphone back to Nita, who still looked a bit pale.

"Let me say again how much we appreciate your help today. Thank you." She turned immediately to Waraday and began talking to him, occasionally glancing at the lake.

Topaz and I made our way back to the Quick Mart. The boiled peanuts stand was open now and had several customers in line. "Well, that was a bit anticlimactic," Topaz said.

"After that scare with the mound of dirt, I'm glad we didn't find anything else. Nita looked awful," I said.

"We still haven't had a chance to catch up. Do you want to go have a bagel? I haven't had breakfast and I'm starving," Topaz said.

"Oh, I'd love to, but I have a birthday party for my son in a couple of hours." I still had some cleaning to do and a couple of last-minute details. "Why don't you come by and have a piece of cake? We're in Magnolia Estates and we'll be partying all afternoon, unless we have to close it down because of the media." I glanced back and saw that Nita was surrounded by a huddle of reporters and photographers.

"Oh, I heard about that. Can you believe you live in the house where Jodi lived? How strange is that?"

"It was really strange yesterday. Hopefully today will be normal. Please come by if you have a chance."

"Well, I have to deliver a special order out that way this afternoon. I'll try to drop in."

I was stopped at a light on the way home when my cell phone chimed. I opened it, expecting it to be a call from Mitch, but it was a text message. I clicked over and stared at it.

Did you think the keying and gas leak were random incidents? They weren't.

"What?" I frowned and looked at the phone number the message was sent from, but I didn't recognize it. A car horn sounded and I jumped. The light was green. I hit the gas and tried to concentrate on driving.

The keying on my car and the gas leak were intentional? Someone was following me around and keying my car? And they'd been in my house? A frisson of cold fear crept through me and I pressed harder on the gas pedal. I wanted to get home, see that everyone was okay. Thank goodness I was close. I careened down Scranton Road and took the turn into the neighborhood too quickly. My heart was fluttery in my chest. I turned onto our street and my eyes widened. There was a car from the sheriff's office parked in our driveway.

From that moment until I got inside was a bit of a blur. I only remember tearing into the house and running directly into Mitch.

"Whoa. Are you okay?" he asked as he held my upper arms.

"What's wrong? The sheriff's car . . . why is it here? Is everyone okay?"

"Yes, we're all fine, but you don't look so good."

I still held my phone clamped in my hand. I held it out and hobbled over to a bar stool. I felt like I had casters on my shoes. I collapsed onto the stool and said, "I got a text message saying that the keying and the gas leak were intentional. Then I saw the sheriff's car and I—" I put my hand over my mouth because I didn't want to go back to the horrible thoughts that had raced through my mind.

"Hi, Mom," Livvy said from the table. She had a Pop-Tart clutched in one hand and a sippy cup of milk in the other. Nathan grinned happily at me through jelly smears on both cheeks. At least, they weren't fazed by this.

Mitch hugged me. "I was about to call you. The gas line had been cut."

A deputy walked through the dining room and smiled at the kids on his way over to us. Mitch said, "Deputy Walsh, this is my wife, Ellie."

"Ma'am." He nodded at me, then said, "There's no sign of forced entry on any of your doors. Most likely, someone slipped in through one of the open windows. Probably the one in the kitchen, since it faces the backyard."

Someone had been in our house while we were sleeping. I rubbed my hands over my face and leaned against Mitch. He put his arm around my shoulders and said, "I'm changing the locks today, just in case. I think we should bring Rex's kennel in from the garage and we're setting the security system from now on. No sleeping with the windows cracked either."

"Of course."

"You need to see a text message I received this morning," I said to the deputy. Mitch handed him my phone and I described how my car had been keyed.

"Do you know anyone who'd want to harm your family?" Deputy Walsh asked.

"No," I said, frustrated and scared that this was happening to us.

"Any ideas why someone would send you a threatening message, possibly vandalize your car, and break into your house?"

"No! I don't think I've made anyone mad. Lately, the only thing I've done differently is take a few organizing jobs and get involved in the Find Jodi campaign."

Mitch said, "You found Jodi's notebook."

"I know, but that hasn't really helped the investigation and I haven't found anything in her notes either."

The deputy looked from one of us to another, then glanced at the kids behind us. "Maybe someone thinks you've found something."

"Well, then I have to stop doing anything to help find Jodi. It's too dangerous."

"I think it's about time for the goodie bags," I said to Mitch. I'd seen several moms checking their watches and murmuring about having to leave soon to make it to the next soccer game or karate class.

"I'll get them." Mitch took my empty paper plate and stacked it on his.

"Don't forget the balloons," I called as he headed for the house. Amazingly enough, our day had settled back into a fairly normal routine after the deputy took down the information from the text message and left. There's nothing like kids to keep your life normal. The birthday party had gone off as planned.

Dorthea stood beside me scraping the last of the icing off her paper plate with a plastic fork. "Delicious. And you made it yourself?"

"Yes," I said. Unlike the are-you-crazy looks I'd gotten from some moms today when I brought the simple cake out, Dorthea said, "It's nice to have a homemade cake instead of one of those garish ones from the bakery."

I breathed a sigh of relief as I surveyed the backyard.

"Turned out fine, didn't it?" Dorthea asked.

"Yes, it did," I said, still half amazed that everything had gone so smoothly. Not only was the street clear of reporters, but the kids seemed to be having a great time. After spending some time in Dorthea's arms—she was his new favorite person—Nathan parked himself in his sandbox and hadn't moved from it. He was busy scooping sand into buckets, then tipping them over on his bare toes. I adjusted the umbrella so that it shaded all the kids in the sandbox. The sky was still clear and it had warmed up to a perfect seventy degrees. Nathan had smeared cake all over his face and opened his presents. He didn't understand everything, but it didn't take him long to realize that ripping the paper off packages was a lot of fun. Now the kids were running around the backyard, playing on the swings and in the sandbox. The only glitch was a seating shortage. The adult guests outnumbered my lawn chairs.

A rumbling sound came from the trees behind the backyard. "What's that?" I asked.

"A dump truck," Dorthea said. "They've begun clearing the lots behind you. Phase Two is open. I expect the developer will pave that gravel path in the next couple of weeks and then we'll have dump trucks bouncing through the neighborhood constantly. And dust. The dust they kick up coats everything."

"The lots around the little cemetery?"

"Well, I don't know if it's those specifically, but it's that section."

We both turned to gaze at the wall of tall trees behind the house. Dorthea said, "Those trees will be gone in a few months."

"I hope they leave a few. For privacy. They make a nice buffer."

"I wouldn't count on it. It seems most of the developers like to raze the trees. We were lucky on this street because Gerald Lockworth built most of these houses and he likes to keep some trees. Gives the landscaping some depth. We do have other streets that looked like Sherman just marched through."

Her face turned more serious. "Have you heard they're going to search the lake?"

"No. The one near the Quick Mart?"

"Yes. Nita's found a dive team in Florida and convinced Waraday to let them search the lake. I forgot the fancy term she used . . . wasn't forest, but something like that."

"Forensic? A forensic dive team?"

"Yes, that was it. I sure hope all they find is Cotner's old pickup."

"What? There's a pickup at the bottom of the lake?"

She nodded, but the hint of a smile on her face made me say, "I think there's a story behind that statement."

She broke into a grin and said, "That lake used to be the place to go when I was a teenager. Not much to do around North Dawkins back then."

"A man at the search mentioned that it was the local swimming hole."

"During the day it was the swimming hole. At night it was the most romantic spot on earth. Frank and I would go there and park on that dirt road and watch the moon sparkle on the water. Old man Cotner didn't care. In fact, I don't think he knew that it was such a popular spot. He didn't come out that way very much since his house was over on the other side of his property. Today, it's on the other side of the interstate.

"Anyway, one night, Frank and I were out there late, the only ones, when we heard a terrible racket. It was Cotner driving his old pickup and towing their car. He drove it right up to the edge of that high ledge. I thought he was going to keep right on going, but he stopped with a few inches to spare. Then he got out and we could hear the clink of chains. He went around to the back of the pickup. The next thing you know, he gave it a couple of shoves and over it went.

"It was like something out of a movie. It nose-dived down into the water and there was a tremendous splash. It was so quiet I swear you could hear those bubbles popping. He stood there for a minute. Then cool as you please, he cranked up the car and left. His wife was tooling around town in a new car a couple of weeks later. The story was that the pickup had been stolen."

I raised my eyebrows. "You and Frank didn't say anything?"

"When you're sixteen insurance fraud is not what you're worried about. We weren't supposed to be there in the first place."

"But you said he didn't care if people were around the lake."

"Right, but *my parents* would have cared and I wasn't about to say a word and lose my chance to see Frank. Besides, it all comes out in the end. Tomorrow everyone will know he pitched his old pickup into the lake."

"Why didn't the swimmers notice it?"

"It was in the fall and no one was swimming then, but it wouldn't matter because that lake is so deep. By the time summer rolled around, it would be good and settled into the lake bed. Well, I should be getting back home. Thanks for inviting me over."

"Thanks for coming," I said, marveling at the stories people have. You just never know what people have seen.

Bridget, my neighbor down the street, finished reapplying sunscreen to her youngest daughter's face, then stood up and joined Abby, who was walking in my direction. Bridget called, "Great party. Very . . . quaint."

"The kids seem to be enjoying it," Abby said.

"I've thought about getting a sandbox for Geneva and Gabriella. Were you able to find noncarcinogenic sand?"

"Ah—no. I bought the play sand at the store."

Her eyes widened. "Oh, that stuff's terrible. The dust can cause cancer." She checked on her kids. They were both playing by the swings.

Abby and I exchanged a glance. "I'm pretty sure it's the

same type of sand that we played in when we were kids. We turned out fine," I said.

"Well, you can't be too careful."

Mitch came out of the house holding the balloons and goodie bags. Bridget said good-bye and was one of the first parents to round up her kids and leave.

"She couldn't get out of here fast enough, could she?" Abby said.

"Earlier, she asked if I'd used any artificial sweeteners in the cake."

"Is she for or against them?"

"I have no idea. I told her it was all organic ingredients."

Abby gave me a look. "You've never been into organic stuff before."

"Sugar and chocolate *are* organic."

Nadia joined us and her girls chorused, "Thank you for inviting us."

"Glad you could come."

"I really loved this. A retro party! What a great idea, an old-fashioned birthday. Can you believe the kids had never played Pin the Tail on the Donkey? Amazing!" She swung toward Abby. "We're still on for tonight?"

Abby said yes.

"Great. I *so* need a break. We're going to have so much fun." Nadia glanced at me and said, "Ellie, you should come, too. It's a girls' night out. We're going to the Peach Blossom for dinner and then getting a manicure."

Abby added, "We're going to gorge ourselves and not have to get up from the table once during the whole meal."

"Sounds fun. I'll talk with Mitch and let you know."

Mitch was making his way around the lawn, handing out balloons. Nadia called out to him, "Mitch, you don't mind if Ellie comes with us for our girls' night out, do you?"

"Nah. Jeff will have Charlie?" Abby nodded and Mitch said, "He can come over here and watch the game with me."

"Terrific!" Nadia said. "Our reservations are for six-thirty. You know where it is, right? Out on Sanders?"

"Yes, I know. I'll meet you there. Oh, there's Topaz."

I walked over to her and she said, "Looks like I'm late."

"No, come on in. Have a piece of cake." I guided her over to the table with the cake and cut her a generous chunk. "We've got juice bags and water bottles," I said, opening the ice chest.

"Water, thanks," Topaz said.

"We're a little short on chairs, but I see one over there by the patio."

"Oh, this is fine." Topaz sat down cross-legged in the grass and propped her water bottle against her knee.

I grabbed a water bottle for me and sat down beside her. The party was in its last stages and I didn't see anything I had to do, except clean up later.

"I'm going to have to find some more chairs before next weekend," I murmured more to myself than to Topaz. I figured we were going to have around fifty adults at the promotion party.

"This is killer," she said, pointing to the cake with her fork. "I saw some chairs at Crooner's place on the way over here. They were wooden folding ones."

"That would be good. How many?"

"Well, it's hard to tell with all that crap he has out there, but I think about eight, maybe more."

"I'll have to take a look. I'll figure out something. I might have to rent some."

"The closest rental place is up in Macon. What's coming up next weekend?" Topaz asked.

"Another party. Mitch got promoted."

"Congratulations."

"Thanks."

"You don't sound very excited."

"I'm happy for Mitch about the promotion, but"—I wrinkled my nose—"I hate hosting parties. I'm terrified I'm going to forget something essential or that I'll give everyone food poisoning. Then there's the flow of the party, making sure everyone is having a good time."

"Oh, I love parties. I think if I didn't have Found Objects I would have been a party planner. I love the energy and all the interaction. Let me know if you want some help."

"Why don't you come?" I asked impulsively. "You can help me make sure the party's fun." Topaz had the perfect personality, outgoing and energetic, to be the life of the party.

"Sure. I'm always up for a party."

"Wonderful. We'll see you next weekend. The party starts at six. It's a come-and-go, so feel free to drop in when you can. Enough about parties. We've got some serious catching up to do. Do you ever go back to Texas?"

Topaz smiled briefly and said, "It's better if I don't go back there."

"Oh." I didn't know a lot about Topaz's family, but I did remember that her parents were divorced and she didn't get along with either one.

"Well, have you kept up with anyone from high school? Like who was it you used to eat lunch with every day? Samantha? Or was it Savannah? I can't believe I can't remember."

Topaz gazed across the yard and shook her head. "Samantha. It was Sam, for short. Nope. I haven't seen anyone."

"Well, what about Michael Kommer? You've seen him, right? Can you believe that?"

"No," Topaz said, puzzled.

"He's an anchor on ESPN."

"No! Seriously? I don't watch sports."

"Yes, Llano Estacado High's one claim to fame."

"I'll have to check it out. What about you? Have you stayed in touch with anyone?"

"Not really. A few Christmas cards here and there, but that's all. Moving every few years makes it hard. That's no excuse, I know."

Topaz frowned as she cracked open the water bottle. "You

don't have to have any excuses. That was high school. It's over. We were forced to spend time with those people. You don't have to keep it up your whole life."

"I suppose you're right. It *is* good to see you again, though. I wonder what happened to Jeremy Hoskins?" He was *the* guy, the one everyone had a crush on.

Topaz shrugged and sipped her water. "Who knows with him."

"Probably a lawyer like his dad."

"Probably."

We both fell silent, watching the kids race around the yard with their balloons trailing along behind them. I searched for something else to talk about, but couldn't think of anything else high school related.

It appeared we didn't have a lot to say to each other after the initial "how have you been?" stage. A little girl from down the street fell and scraped her elbow on the brick steps, and by the time I'd found the Band-Aids, the party was breaking up and Topaz left with the other guests.

An Everything In Its Place Tip for an Organized Party

Party Countdown Checklist (One to Two Days Before)
- Purchase perishable foods.
- If you're preparing food trays yourself, cut and arrange food, then refrigerate.
- Set the table or arrange buffet.
- Wash serving pieces.
- Set up decorations.
- Pick up fresh flowers.
- Choose the music.
- Touch up the house—concentrate on the entry and the areas where the guests will be and give the bathrooms another cleaning.

Chapter
Twenty-four

A couple of hours later, I put on my turn signal and pulled into a small gravel parking area beside the homemade sign that read ANTIQUES. I had a few minutes before I was supposed to meet Abby and Nadia at the Peach Blossom. I might as well knock something off my to-do list, if I could.

Crooner had some prime property because of his location on a fairly busy state highway. Five flags, a mixture of the Georgia state flag, the Confederate flag, and the Stars and Stripes, were spaced along the lot. They hung limply in the still air, but on windy days the snapping flags drew attention to the business.

I passed the first flag, a Confederate flag, and spotted the chairs Topaz had mentioned. They were spaced in two rows beside a decrepit wicker chaise longue and a metal office desk. Everything Crooner had was out in the open, and as far as I knew, he never moved anything inside. There wasn't any cover or roof anywhere to store anything if it rained. In fact, I'd driven past here many times when it was raining and everything stayed right where it was, in the open. Rain or shine, Crooner's antiques were always exposed to the elements. The wicker chaise longue certainly had taken a beating—I thought I saw some mold—and the desk was rusty.

Hopefully, Crooner's prices would be better than anything

I could find at a big box home improvement store here in town. Dorthea had offered to let me use her lawn chairs and I knew Abby would bring some over, too, if I asked. I thought we could get by if I could find a dozen more chairs. I counted the wooden folding chairs. There were ten and they were in good shape. I thought they'd do.

Out of the corner of my eye, I could see a black man making his way through the accumulated junk toward me, humming a tune I couldn't identify. "Can I help you?" He walked with one leg held straight and I wondered if he'd hurt his leg recently or if he always walked with a limp.

"How much are these chairs?"

He pulled off his baseball cap and scratched his short gray hair. "Oh, I picked those up at an estate sale last week. Haven't had 'em long. And they're in real nice shape."

I had to agree with him. Made of a light wood covered with a shiny varnish, they looked like the best thing on his lot.

He shoved the cap down and put his hands into the pockets of his thick barn coat. "Twenty dollars."

"For all ten?" I asked, amazed. Okay, maybe that's why there were always cars in the little gravel parking lot.

He chuckled. "No. Each."

"Too steep for me," I said, and moved away.

"Now, don't be hasty. Maybe we can work something out."

I paused and looked back at the chairs. Even at twenty dollars each they were close to the same price I'd pay for metal folding chairs at an office supply store. I knew because I'd checked online before I left the house.

"Well, they are nice, but I just need them for one party. I hate to pay more than ten bucks apiece for them."

"How about we meet halfway at fifteen?" he offered. "I'd even load them up for you."

"Sounds good," I said.

"Come on back here to pay," he said as he made his way

to the closest of two tiny houses perched at the far end of the narrow lot. His uneven gait made him lurch from one side to the other as he climbed three stairs to a screened porch. He held open the screen door for me, then went to a desk that was a match, rust and all, with the one I'd seen outside beside the chairs.

Just like the lot, there was stuff everywhere—old lamps and fans, rusty advertising signs, and piles of yellowed magazines. He went back to humming the same tune as he wrote my receipt.

I handed over my check   I didn't think he was set up to take debit cards—and asked, "Was this the house that William Nash lived in?" I tried to see past the accumulation of stuff to the lines of the house. About all I could make out was a door from the screened-in porch to a microscopic kitchen area.

"Yes, ma'am, it was. He used to keep an eye on me when I was outside," he said with a nod of his head toward the small patch of land between the house and the railroad tracks that ran a few feet behind the houses.

"So you knew him?"

"Oh yeah. I lived in the house next door." He tapped the receipt. "My name and number's on there. You call me, if you're looking for something in particular. Dressers, bureaus, hutches, anything you want, I can be on the lookout for it."

I glanced at the receipt as I folded it. "You're Crooner?" I asked, confused. I glanced at the open box of Confederate flags on the floor.

He saw my glance and winked. "I don't have to like something to sell it. If I only sold what I liked, I'd be a lot shorter on cash today, that's for sure."

I followed him outside. Talk about your pragmatic attitudes. I supposed it was his business and if he wanted to sell Confederate flags, then he could. Despite the limp, he was able to stack and load the chairs quickly. "So, is it true, what I've heard about Nash, that he was organizing a march to support the Montgomery Bus Boycott?" The question was out of my mouth before I had time to check it. Habits are hard to break, especially when you're naturally curious. *You're not interested in Jodi or Nash anymore*, I silently lectured myself. *No more questions.*

He shook his head. "That was a sad business—one of the saddest things I've ever seen in my life. Why are you interested in what happened so long ago?"

"All the news coverage has made me curious," I said.

He focused on gently positioning the last chair in the Jeep. "That's what folks said."

"Has anyone asked about him recently?"

He firmly closed the hatchback door and turned to me with eyes narrowed. "Are you one of those TV people?"

"No. No, I'm not," I said quickly, and he looked a bit disappointed. "You want the reporters here?"

"A little free publicity couldn't hurt, 'specially if it drew those Atlanta folks down to do some antiquing on the weekend." He laughed as he said that, then called over his shoulder as he shuffled over to help a new customer, "You take care, Mrs. Avery."

Abby and Nadia were already seated, chatting with a tall, curvy woman standing beside their linen-covered table, when I arrived at the Peach Blossom. I'm fascinated with how quickly Abby gets to know people. Couple her instinctive bonding with our location in the South—where people strike up conversations over grocery carts and gas pumps—and she's like a veritable information vacuum. Give her a few minutes and she knows all sorts of details about people—jobs, schools attended, family background, even recent surgeries.

I pulled out a chair and greeted everyone.

Abby said, "Ellie, this is Kate Navan, the owner. We were admiring her pictures on the wall."

"Nice to meet you," I said. "Your inn is lovely." I'd taken a good look at a huge live oak in front of the house when I arrived. It had to be the tree mentioned in the brochure, the Hanging Tree. With the mention of the hanging on the inn's Web site, I'd almost expected the place to emphasize the macabre, but it had a serene atmosphere. Sconces glowed along the pale cream walls. Low vases of fresh flowers rested on each table and there was an incredible view of a peach and pink sunset through a set of French doors, which opened onto a veranda.

The house was obviously quite old. It had wide wooden-planked floors that creaked and windows with slightly wavy glass. As I looked around, I noticed all the windows and doors had transoms over them, which I'd seen in other older southern homes. They were to help the air circulate throughout the house.

"Thank you," Kate said with one hand braced on her rounded hip and the other on the back of the only unoccupied chair at our table. She glanced around and said, "I know it looks great now, but you should have seen the place when I first got it. Those pictures do not show how decrepit it was. Rotting wood and dirt, everywhere. We had to totally redo everything. Practically rebuilt the place from the ground up. New wiring, new drywall, new plumbing, new roof . . ." She shook her head and laughed, her white smile flashing against her mahogany skin. "My poor daddy. He worked so hard. He said this was my college fund and inheritance all rolled into one. Now, what are you ladies having tonight?"

"Well, I'm definitely having the cheesecake," Nadia said.

"Chocolate cake with ganache, for me," Abby said.

"Count me in for the chocolate," I said.

The Peach Blossom had some trendy items on the menu, but most of the food was authentic southern cuisine. I settled on chicken-fried steak, green beans, and mashed potatoes. I figured if I was going southern, I might as well go all the way. Kate didn't write anything down, only nodded as we gave our orders. Then she brought us a basket of soft, warm bread and real butter.

Abby and Nadia chatted about school and I buttered my roll, thinking about how Crooner had neatly slipped out of answering my question about whether anyone had been asking about Nash. He'd distracted me with his own question.

"Yoo-hoo," Abby said, waving the bread basket at me. "You seem a bit preoccupied."

"Sorry," I said, and took another roll from the basket. "There's just a lot going on." And a lot I didn't understand.

"Jodi?" Abby asked, and I nodded.

"I didn't want to say anything at the party today, but someone's threatening us." I described everything from the keying of the car to the text message.

Nadia said, "I can't believe you're as calm as you are right now."

"Well, I've made a resolution. No more questions. No more curiosity."

"But did you find out anything that would threaten someone?" Abby asked.

"No," I said. "I can't find anyone Jodi talked to about Nash. Isn't that what a reporter would do? Interview people?"

"Sure, but maybe she was doing background research first?"

I shook my head again. "Nope. I've checked most of her papers and I can't find anything on Nash. No notes, nothing."

"Maybe it wasn't on paper. Maybe it was on her computer," Nadia said.

"The FBI has her computer. I bet they'd have already found it if it was on her computer."

"Oh," Nadia said, "I've been meaning to tell you that Jodi and Topaz didn't get along."

"Really? Jodi wrote a profile about her for the newspaper and there didn't seem to be any animosity there. In fact, the tone of the piece was pretty flattering."

Nadia shrugged and said, "All I know is what I heard."

"Who said this?"

Nadia looked at Abby for help. "Remember last year, when

the FBI questioned some teachers? It caused quite a ruckus, let me tell you. But I never knew who actually said they didn't like each other."

"I wasn't there last year," Abby said.

"That's right," Nadia said. "You fit in so well now that it seems like you've always been there."

"So it was a rumor?" I asked.

"I don't know. I know the FBI asked about it."

"Wait. What am I doing? I just vowed not to be involved in Jodi's case anymore and I'm asking you questions about this. You guys have to help me stop it."

"Sorry, honey. You're right. We'll keep you in check," Nadia said as she patted my hand.

Kate came by and topped off our glasses of peach iced tea, one of the signature menu items that drew people to the inn.

Abby asked her, "How long have you owned the Peach Blossom?"

"For fifteen years." Kate surveyed the room. She seemed satisfied that the rest of her customers were being well taken care of because she continued. "My daddy complains about all the work it took to bring this place up to snuff, but he's the one who found it for me. Land prices were starting to take off around here. That was the beginning of the growth boom and there was no way I could afford anything. I never did understand why the owner sold it to me at such a good price, but Daddy said to lowball him. I did and it worked."

She transferred the iced tea pitcher to her other hand and pointed to a photo on the wall. "There we are on the day I signed the papers. I wasn't sure I'd get it. I wanted it so bad and I was afraid a developer was going to come in and raze the house and build a subdivision. But I got it. Course, after we found out how bad it was, structurally, I almost wished he hadn't taken my offer. Daddy still says I should have gone out and bought a new house. It would have saved him so much work, but it wouldn't have had the feel of this place."

"No." I glanced at the six framed black-and-white photos on the wall beside us. "This place feels aged. You can't create that. Is this your dad?" I asked, pointing to one of the pictures. She nodded.

"I think I just met him. He sells antiques?"

She rolled her eyes. "Well, he calls them that, but I doubt there's much on his lot that would qualify as a genuine antique. I wish I could get him to close that place down, but he's not about to retire. 'What would I do all day?' he asks me. He fell and broke his hip last year and I thought that would do it, but no, he just totters on."

I looked at the picture of Kate and her dad. They were both smiling as Kate dangled a set of keys from her fingertips. Several overgrown bushes almost obscured the house in the background, but I could see a few rickety steps, peeling paint, and a tilting handrail around the porch.

"Crooner. Is that a nickname?" I asked as I studied the picture. His face was more gaunt today, but otherwise he looked the same.

"Yes. He's got a beautiful voice. My grandmother called him her 'little crooner.' It stuck. Pretty soon everyone called him Crooner. When he was a kid he sang all the time. My grandmother said he had music in his soul. She wanted him to sing in church, but the one time he got up there—he was about seven—he froze up. Couldn't make a sound. Still can't sing in front of people to this day. It's a shame, too, because he really does have a nice baritone voice. He won't even sing for me, but I've heard him when he didn't know I was there."

"He was humming today."

She nodded. "I think my grandmother was right. He does that all the time. He can't sing, but he hums, usually without realizing he's doing it. It's like he can't completely hold back the flow of music. Well, let me go check on your entrees. They should be up any minute."

By the time I'd devoured my southern dinner and chocolate cake, I'd learned that Kaitlyn Foster, one of Nadia's third-grade students, was a challenge—they called her precocious—and that there was a controversy because one of the teachers wanted to use a new spelling curriculum next year.

We paid our bill and Kate walked us out to the porch, where we paused in the cool night air to zip up jackets and find car keys. "Is that the tree?" I asked Kate. It was dark now, but a floodlight at the base of the tree highlighted the twisted branches towering above us.

"What tree?"

"The Hanging Tree. I read about it on your Web site."

"Is that up again?" she said, aggravated. "My daddy is my webmaster, but he's going to lose that title if he can't keep to the content I want. I've told him to take that off of there, but he keeps sneaking it back in. Says it's a draw."

"What's a draw?" Abby asked.

"A rumor that a man was lynched and hung from that tree," Kate said, shaking her head. "That is not what I want to be known for."

"If it makes you feel better, everything I've heard about the Peach Blossom was about how nice it was out here and how good the food is," I said.

Nadia nodded. "And now we know what we heard about the food was true. I may not fit into my pants tomorrow, but I don't regret it. That cheesecake was the best I've ever had."

"Well, that's sweet of you to say," Kate said, calming down a bit.

"So, do you think the rumors about the tree are true?"

"I have no idea. All that was way before my time and, frankly, I don't see what good it does, hashing up all that stuff now. You ladies have a good night. Thanks for coming out."

We meandered down to the gravel parking area and I couldn't help but look at the tree in the moonlight.

"Kind of creepy, isn't it?" Nadia said.

The air was completely still and the only sound was the loud crunch of gravel under our feet. "Yeah, it is," I said, thinking that a man may have died a horrible death here. The floodlight only lit part of the tree. Above, against the blackness of the sky, I could see more twisting branches.

Maybe it was the darkness, but the place disturbed me. I didn't want to linger. "Come on," I said, "we don't want to be late for our manicures."

Melissa's was a little place in a strip mall that only did manicures. I parked and blinked at the light pouring out of the windows. After the darkness of the inn, the light was almost dazzling.

We walked inside and a woman with a nose ring and a shaggy haircut waved to us and said, "Yeah! Our last appointments of the day." She sorted us out along a line of manicurists. Nadia and Abby were seated at side-by-side stations and fell into talking about their classes. I ended up at the far end of the row. The woman who'd welcomed us sat down across from me. "I'm Melissa," she said as she shifted bottles of nail polish, then picked up my hands and examined my nails.

"Are you always this busy?" I asked. There were about ten manicure stations and each one was filled with a customer on one side and a manicurist on the other.

Melissa kept her head bent over my hands as she clipped my nails. "Yes, especially in the evening."

"Ellie? Is that you?"

I leaned forward and looked down the row of stations. Colleen waved, flashing a French manicure. I smiled back since Melissa had placed my hands in a tray to soak. Colleen pointed to a woman on the other side of me and drew a frown from her manicurist, who was waiting to finish her nail polish. "That's my mom. I told her you had some questions you wanted to ask her."

I turned and smiled at the woman. I could see the resemblance in the shape of her face. And she had the same frizzy hair, but hers was cut even shorter and made a halo around her face. "Hi. I'm Ellie. I'd shake hands, but I don't think that would be a good idea," I said.

"No, probably not. I'm Rosalee."

Chapter
Twenty-five

I turned toward her, yanking my hands out of the solution. "Too hot?" Melissa asked.

"Ah, no. Sorry." I plunged my hands back in. "Rosalee?"

"Yes. Is something wrong?"

"No. Not at all. It's just that I've been looking for a person named Rosalee."

"Well, Colleen told me you were helping Nita and had some questions about Coleman, but she didn't say you were looking for me."

"Honestly, I don't know if you're the Rosalee I'm looking for or not. I didn't know that was your name. Colleen said I should talk to her mom. She never mentioned your name."

"Well, why did my name surprise you?"

Melissa pulled my hands out of the solution, patted them dry, and rubbed lotion on with deep massaging strokes. It felt great and normally I would have thoroughly enjoyed being pampered, but I was so focused on Rosalee that I barely noticed. "I'm helping Nita Lockworth in her Find Jodi campaign." I stopped myself. "Well, I was. Now I'm more of an interested bystander, but since you're here and I'm here, we might as well talk and maybe we can figure out if you're the Rosalee from Jodi's notebook." I described the notebook and how I'd helped Nita match the notes to stories. "She'd written Nash's name in a list of possible story ideas. There was also a list of names that didn't match anything else she'd written. Rosalee was one of the names. Did she ever contact you, ask you any questions?"

"No, I never heard from her."

"Oh." Maybe I was completely wrong and Jodi wasn't planning to write a story about Nash.

"I suppose she could have called when the power was out and I might have missed it," Rosalee said as she put her hands in front of a small fan to dry the polish. "My husband—my second husband, not Colleen's father—and I run a camp for kids in Maryland. We're less than an hour away from the nation's capital and we're never really sure we're going to have power. Amazing, isn't it? We do have several generators, but it takes a while to get them all working. Colleen said you wanted to know about Coleman. I suppose you've heard the rumors about him and Nash."

"Yes. Do you think they could be true? That he could be involved in any way?"

Rosalee snorted. "Absurd."

I'd glanced at Melissa, who was using some evil-looking instruments on my cuticles—painless, I should add. I looked back at Rosalee. "Really?"

"Yes," Rosalee said. "I don't know how much Colleen has told you about her grandparents, but it was not a good situation for a child and I tried to keep her out of it as much as possible."

"Not good? In what way?"

"Ava was an alcoholic," Rosalee said matter-of-factly.

"I've never heard that."

"Well, you can believe me or not, but it was true."

I said, "I thought she was sickly."

Rosalee gave a sharp laugh. "Right. That's what Coleman said to cover for her. The technical term for it is enabler. His son, my first husband, Durwood." She shook her head. "Exactly like his father. I didn't realize how bad it was. When Durwood and I first married we lived in Seattle and rarely saw his family. The few times we visited were short stays, just a couple of days, and Ava was able to hide her drinking then. I certainly wasn't aware of it. A few years later, after we had Colleen, we went for a longer visit and Ava had deteriorated by then. Of course, I had no idea she was that bad until I saw her screaming at Colleen."

"Everyone else I've talked to has mentioned she was sick, but no one's said anything about drinking," I said, amazed and still not totally convinced.

"Because Coleman hid it. He did everything he could to keep it a secret. Durwood did, too. Once I realized the extent of the problem, I wanted to get her help, but no. That was impossible. Then people would *know*." Rosalee rolled her eyes. "So idiotic, to live like that, in denial. Of course, by the time Durwood's job brought us here, I knew and kept Colleen away from them. Eventually, Durwood and I divorced—too toxic. I made sure Colleen was protected from the lies and cover-ups."

"What color?" Melissa asked.

"Oh. I'd like a French manicure."

Melissa sighed. "French manicure. Always a French manicure. Nobody wants color anymore."

Rosalee shouldered her purse and picked up her keys with two fingers, careful not to mar her new polish.

"Wait, before you leave, tell me more about Coleman," I said.

"There's nothing to tell. He's meek as a lamb. He ran around his whole life cleaning up Ava's messes."

"Would you say he was prejudiced?"

"Of course. He never made any bones about that, but would he kill someone? No. Maybe that's why Jodi didn't get in touch with me. Maybe she found out how ridiculous that idea was."

We walked outside twenty minutes later and I scanned the parking lot. "Didn't I park right beside you?" I asked Nadia.

"Yeah." She clicked her key chain. Her minivan beeped and her doors unlocked. "Right here—" Nadia broke off.

"My car's gone," I said, staring at the empty parking space.

"And you probably should contact Detective Waraday with the sheriff's office," I told the police officer who was taking my statement. "There was an incident at our house this morning . . . threats and a break-in."

Officer Kinsawa did a double take, then said doubtfully, "Yes, ma'am. If you'll wait here for a moment, I can have an officer take you home."

"Oh, you don't have to do that," Nadia said. "We can take her home."

Once we'd established that I wasn't just crazy and my car really had been stolen, I'd called Mitch, the police, and my insurance company. We were still in the parking lot of Melissa's, but it was now closed.

The officer came back and said, "We've had a call about an abandoned car on fire, a Jeep Cherokee. It's not too far from here."

I rode with Nadia and Abby, hoping that by some strange coincidence it was someone else's Jeep Cherokee on fire. We followed the police car to a deserted parking lot in the older section of town near the base. The fire was out by the time we arrived, but a fire truck was still parked near the burned-out carcass of a car. "Do you think that was my car?" I asked, leaning forward. I recognized the basic shape, but I couldn't quite match the metal shell to the car in my memory.

"I can't tell," Abby said. "It might as well be a big piece of charcoal."

We all got out of the car and followed Officer Kinsawa. "Don't get too close," he warned as we walked through the film of water covering the parking lot. The smell of burnt fabric and hot plastic filled the air.

I heard a firefighter speaking behind me saying, "Doused with gasoline and set on fire. It was the upholstery that did most of the burning."

I looked at the remnants of the military identification sticker that expired in a month at the top of the windshield, then circled to the back and saw the yellow ribbon bumper sticker. "It's mine," I said with a sinking sensation.

Abby patted my shoulder and said, "Oh, Ellie, I'm so sorry."

"You know, there was one problem with that vow I made not to be involved in figuring out what happened to Jodi."

"What's that?" Abby asked.

"The person who's doing this doesn't know about it."

"Come on, honey," Nadia said, steering me back to her minivan. "Let's get you home."

"Mitch, what are we going to do?" I rubbed my hand over my face and paced around the kitchen again. He caught me and stopped my pacing. "We're going to be very careful and hope Waraday wraps this up soon."

"Right. We have to hope for that," I said, but I knew what I had to do. I didn't bother to say it aloud, because I knew Mitch would disagree and I was too tired to argue. Jodi had been missing for months and who knew how much longer it would be before there was a resolution to the case? I had to go back over those notes and look through the boxes from Nita. It didn't matter if Mitch wanted me to stay out of it. It didn't matter if I tried to stay out of it. We were in the middle of it and we weren't getting out until Jodi was found. And, obviously, I wasn't very good at leaving things alone anyway.

*   *   *

"Watch me, Mom! Watch me!"

I looked up from my stack of papers. Once Livvy was sure she had my attention, she clambered up a rope grid and onto the platform of the play equipment designed to resemble a ship.

"Good job, sweetie," I called out, and went back to sorting papers after a quick check to make sure Nathan was still engaged in his favorite activity, piling sand on his toes. It was another spectacular autumn day, so nice that we had to spend at least part of it outside. The insurance company had arranged for a loaner car for us while our claim was processed, and even though I missed the Jeep, I had to admit the new minivan was nice.

"Just act like it's a normal day and try not to worry. That's the best thing for the kids," Mitch had said before he left for work that morning. He was right. There was nothing more normal than a picnic on a nice day and it got us out of the house for a while. I'd been flinching at each noise, so I'd loaded the stroller and a blanket in the new minivan along with the last box of Jodi's papers. I'd figured once we'd eaten our peanut butter and jelly sandwiches and fed the crusts to the ducks, I'd be able to finish sorting out the papers while the kids played on the playground.

"Watch me, Mom! Watch me!" Livvy shouted again, this time from the top of the slide.

I suppressed a sigh. My plan wasn't working out quite like I'd hoped. "Okay, go ahead." I had to work on these papers. I wouldn't have time tomorrow since it was my last day to work with Scott and I had to finish his storage room. "Oh, look. Here comes another girl. I bet she's your age. Why don't you see if she wants to go down the slide with you?"

I finished sorting the receipts by date, then pulled the last pile into my lap to look through them. Most of them seemed normal enough. Jodi bought groceries, filled her car up with gas, went out to eat, and bought several gift cards. I switched to her credit card statements and frowned. There was a charge for Beach Vacation Rentals in Destin, Florida, during the week after Christmas. I scanned through the rest of the statements and found a charge at a gas station in Pensacola. I reviewed the rest of the statements again, but didn't see any more charges in Florida.

I gazed across the playground, automatically checking on Livvy as she and her new friend scampered under the monkey bars. Nathan had moved on to the panel of knobs attached to disks. He stood, wavering slightly, as he carefully gripped each knob and twisted.

Surely, someone investigating Jodi's disappearance had checked out these charges. I couldn't imagine it would have gone unnoticed, especially since Peter Yannis lived in Florida.

I pulled out my phone. Nita answered on the second ring. "Ellie, it's lovely to hear from you. How are you?"

"Fine, fine. I'm looking through the last of Jodi's receipts and charges. There's two charges in Florida."

"One of her good friends from school moved down there. Jodi visits Tracy at least once a year. Jodi says it helps her recharge."

"So it's been checked out? Waraday knows she went to Florida between Christmas and New Year's?"

"Yes, of course. In fact, it was one of the first things they checked on. Because of Peter Yannis."

"And they didn't find anything?"

"No. Peter lived in Jacksonville and Jodi went to Destin. It's a shame, really, that Tracy wasn't there. At least, if she'd been there she might have talked to her and Tracy might know something that would help us out now."

"She didn't see her friend when she went to Florida?"

"No. Tracy had a business trip. She'd started a job with one of the big hotels there and had a training meeting she had to go to. Jodi went down anyway. She loves the beach, especially the Gulf. It's so beautiful down there with all that white sand. Anyway, Tracy offered to let her stay at her apartment while she was gone, but Jodi didn't want to do that. She found a vacation rental and stayed there for a few days."

"So she went down there quite a bit?"

"Oh yes. We used to go there on family vacations when she was little. I could hardly get her to come out of the water. I think she was more excited than Tracy when Tracy moved down there."

"So she went to take a break, to get away?"

"Yes. She sat on the deck and walked on the beach. Best therapy in the world, I think. The water is so relaxing."

"Hmm. Okay. I haven't seen anything else out of the ordinary."

"Oh." Her voice, which had been so lively when she talked about Jodi and their beach vacations, had flattened. "Thank you for looking, Ellie. There has to be something, somewhere. Something that will tell us what happened."

"I'm sorry." I think it was her unfailing politeness coupled with the sheer depression of her tone that nudged me to say, "I can look through everything again. I probably won't be able to do it until later in the week, but if you don't mind if I hang on to the boxes until—"

"Yes, why don't you do that? Take one more look. You keep the boxes as long as you need."

"Okay. I'll call you in a few days." I had another call coming in, so I switched to it.

It was Detective Waraday. He said, "We were able to trace the text message sent to your phone. It was from a disposable phone that was purchased in Macon."

The small flare of hope I'd felt at his first words died away. "So there's no way to know who bought it?"

"I'm afraid not."

"Well, thanks for letting me know."

"You take care, Mrs. Avery." He emphasized the words and I knew it wasn't just a casual good-bye.

"I will." A shadow flickered over the bench and I realized

another mom had arrived at the playground. I piled the paper-work back in the box, careful to keep it in order, then shifted it to the ground to make room on the bench.

I threw a quick smile in the direction of the person who'd taken a seat at the end of the bench. My smile froze and I quickly shifted to grab the box and stand up while doing a quick scan of the park.

"It's okay. No photographers, I promise," Chelsea O'Mara said. In her posh pantsuit and heels, she looked like she'd been teleported to the playground from a boardroom. "Please don't go. I know I'm the last person you want to talk to, but we might be able to help each other out."

I paused with the box balanced on my knees. "Why?" I glanced around the park's expanse of grass dotted with magnolias and pines. It really was empty except for Livvy and her friend chattering away, the other mom, and Nathan, who'd moved on to the steering wheel, which he was spinning enthusiastically.

"I think we should trade information."

An Everything In Its Place Tip for an Organized Party

Party Countdown Checklist (The Big Day)
- Finish preparing food.
- Make or pick up food trays.
- Purchase ice.
- Pick up balloons—helium balloons usually last one day, so don't pick them up the day before. Mylar balloons last several days.
- Pick up any last-minute items you've forgotten.
- Set up drink stations and appetizers.

Chapter
Twenty-six

"What?" Was she crazy? I was not going to develop any sort of relationship with someone in the press, especially Chelsea. Except for closing the door on her a few days ago, I'd only encountered her once before when she covered a big story I'd gotten involved in when we lived in Vernon, Washington. Despite that brief acquaintance, I knew that the tactics she used to cover a story were about as classy as the tabloid television show she worked for.

"About the Jodi Lockworth case," she continued.

I cut her off. "I don't have anything to trade. Shouldn't you have this conversation with the police? Detective Waraday, for instance?"

Chelsea made a face. "Come on! You're living in the house she lived in. After what happened in Vernon, I can't imagine that you'd let that interesting detail go without at least being curious."

I set the box down carefully, thinking what an odd contrast we were. We probably looked like "before" and "after" makeover pictures. With my hair caught up in a droopy ponytail and scuffed tennis shoes and denim jacket, I'd definitely be the "before" picture. "Sure, I was curious. Who wouldn't be? But that doesn't mean I'm asking questions or trying to figure out what happened."

"Of course you are," Chelsea said. "*Everyone* in North Dawkins is trying to figure out what happened. You're just a little more persistent than most people *and* you have access to her house and the people close to her. I saw you chatting with Nita Lockworth and I heard you've been helping her out." Chelsea's gaze switched to the box and she looked like she wanted to rip the top off.

I propped my feet on it. "All that's true, but I really don't know anything that would help you out." But even as I said it, I thought that if she knew something that would help with finding Jodi, it would be worth it to talk to her. I was at the point that I was willing to try anything so I could stop jumping at each sound and worrying that someone was trying to break into our house each time the wind rattled the window screens.

Chelsea ignored me. "Okay, I'll go first. William Nash's hyoid bone wasn't broken."

"Hyoid?" I frowned at her.

"God! Don't you watch *CSI*? Hyoid bone. It's in the throat and when someone is hanged it breaks."

"How do you know this?"

Chelsea's lips curled. "Even though Detective Waraday has been less than forthcoming, I have some contacts in the GBI."

"The Georgia Bureau of Investigation," I said thoughtfully. "So that means the lynching story isn't true."

The pleased look faded from her face. "I don't know. It's still possible he was the victim of racial violence, but just not hanged. There were also multiple rib fractures, a broken femur, and a wrist fracture."

"Wow." We were both quiet for a moment. "That's . . . pretty severe."

"I know." Her somber tone matched mine. "I assume you've heard what Sherry Wayne has said about Coleman May?"

"Yes."

"Well, I've been doing a little research on him. Except for practically giving away property, I can't find anything on him."

"Giving away property?"

"Yep." She reached down and pulled some papers out of the side pocket of a leather computer bag. "He owns seven pieces of property around North Dawkins, most of them rentals as well as two undeveloped lots in your neighborhood and his current house. He also owned two other houses, but sold those cheap, years ago." She handed me the papers and I flipped through them. "That's all the public records on him," she said with a sigh.

"You sound disappointed."

"Public records can be a gold mine of information. Unfortunately, they haven't been too helpful here."

I stared at the addresses of the properties Coleman had sold. 123 Clifton Avenue and 5296 Sanders Road. "Sanders Road. Where's that?"

"South of town. Not much out there, but why he'd sell that low, I don't know. I've talked to a few people about the market around here and he could have sold that for much more, if he'd held out."

"Maybe he needed the money," I said thoughtfully, making a mental note to look up the addresses when I got home. "Know anything else about Coleman?"

"Not much." I handed the papers back. I was surprised. She was doing her homework on the story. My opinion of her edged up a notch. She'd been fair with me and had actually told me a few things I hadn't known. I decided I'd tell her what I'd found out, so far. Little that it was, I didn't see how it could hurt. "All of this is strictly off the record."

She nodded and I raised my eyebrows.

"Off the record, I got it," she repeated.

"Well, everyone I talk to says Coleman wouldn't have hurt Nash. Says he's not the type to go for violence. Apparently, he'll talk about how much he doesn't like African-Americans, but he wouldn't actually do anything to harm someone."

Chelsea said, "Sure."

"I know. Everyone is adamant on that point, though. His ex-daughter-in-law called him meek."

"I've heard you found Jodi's diary."

I laughed. "I wish. We might have some answers if I'd found her diary. I found her reporter's notebook. It was in shorthand, her own version, so Nita had to translate it."

"Oh, that's good." Chelsea's eyes widened. "A notebook in code."

"This is still off the record. When Jodi's found you can use it."

Reluctantly, she said, "Okay. It's going to make such a good story. Do you still have it?"

"No! I gave it to Detective Waraday."

"So, what did it say?" she asked eagerly.

"It was notes on her stories, interviews, a couple of possible story ideas, that sort of stuff. It did mention Nash. Have you researched the lynching?" I asked, hoping to distract her from asking any more notebook questions.

"Yes, and I haven't found much, which I suppose isn't that odd. It would be something people would want to cover up. I haven't been able to track down anyone who'll admit they were there."

"Speaking of rumors, how did everyone hear about Jodi supposedly returning before her mother's birthday?"

Her eyes narrowed. "That one was weird. We were all camped out at the sheriff's office, waiting for any news on Nash, when Skip packed up and got out of there fast. He hardly ever moves fast, so I knew something was up. I followed him. Later, I found out he got a tip with the story and your address."

"He was specifically given my address?"

"Yes. I guess the person with the tip thought they'd better spread the word. By the time he got to your house, there were three other reporters arriving besides me."

Chelsea's phone rang as I noticed the other mom and little girl were leaving the park. It was nap time anyway and there's never a better time to leave than when a playmate leaves. I quickly called to Livvy that it was time to go. Chelsea clicked her phone off. "The divers have arrived to search the lake. I've got to get out there. We'll talk again soon."

I was surprised to find Mitch at home when I arrived.

"What are you doing here?" I asked as I came inside, carrying Nathan on one hip and lugging the remnants of our picnic in my other hand.

"Well, that's some welcome," he teased. "Can't I come home in the middle of the day for no reason?"

"You're never home in the middle of the day for no reason."

"I can think of a few good reasons to be home in the middle of the day," Mitch said with a slow smile.

"Right. What's really going on?"

"Crew rest. I have an early flight tomorrow."

Livvy barreled past me. "Dad's home! Dad's home!"

He squeezed her into a hug and looked at me over her head. "That's the kind of greeting I like. How's my girl?"

"Good!" Livvy shouted. She wiggled free and raced off down the hall, postponing the inevitable. She knew nap time was near and she often disappeared right before. Her strategy was to stay clear of me because then I couldn't tell her to go to her room for her quiet time.

I went to Mitch and kissed him. "How's that?"

"Better."

"I'm glad to see you."

"Really?"

"Yes. Really glad," I said, and kissed him again. "Crooner got in four more chairs. I saw them on my way home. If I hurry, they'll still be there. I'll get them while Nathan's napping."

Mitch followed me into Nathan's room. Nathan hung limp in my arms. He'd worn himself out at the playground. "You don't have to worry about the chairs. People can stand up and eat. Happens all the time at parties."

As I changed Nathan's diaper, I said, "Mitch, think about the last party we went to. Were people eating standing up?"

"No, but that was at my squadron commander's house. We're not the squadron commander. We don't have to have chairs."

I snuggled Nathan close for a few seconds before putting him in his bed. "Face it. We're not college kids anymore. We're moving up into the big leagues—parties with chairs instead of only pizza and beer." I kissed him on the cheek and said, "Back in a flash."

The chairs were still there when I wheeled into the gravel parking area a few minutes later. The flags were fluttering in a lazy way as a gentle breeze moved through the air. I made my way through a mishmash of rusted machinery that I couldn't identify and beat-up display cabinets that had their glass replaced by chicken wire.

The chairs looked good. They were almost the same color, maybe a little darker stain than the ones I'd already bought, but it was close enough. I heard humming and turned to see Crooner. "Afternoon. I see you spotted the rest of the chairs."

"Yes, I did. I'll take them, as long as they're the same price."

He hesitated for a second, then nodded and said, "Sure. Sure. Let me load 'em up for you."

After he'd stowed them in the minivan, I followed him across the lot, his lopsided gait making our progress slow.

"I met your daughter the other day. She told me how much you helped her with the Peach Blossom. It looks wonderful now."

He laughed. "Would'a been a lot less trouble to build a new building, but Kate wouldn't hear of it."

We went inside and he went back to humming quietly as he wrote up the receipt. I wrote another check. If anything, the place looked more cluttered than it had the last time. I briefly considered giving a pitch for my organizing services, but quickly discarded the idea. I had a feeling Crooner would dismiss me out of hand. Kate was probably the person to approach. She might be able to convince him he needed some organizational help.

When I handed the check over I said, "You know, you never answered my question last time I was here."

He grinned as he stamped the back of the check, then slid it into a cash box. "What question was that?"

"Whether anyone else had been asking about Nash."

"Nope, can't say that I've had anyone out here asking after him."

Can't say? Did that mean he hadn't had anyone asking about it or he wasn't going to tell me if someone had been around? He handed me the receipt and I folded it in half, then paused as I noticed the address and phone number printed on the bottom.

"This is 123 Clifton Avenue?"

"Yes, ma'am," he said as he flipped the cash box lid down.

"That means you bought this property from Coleman May."

Crooner slowly pushed the latch down on the box. "Yes." He turned away and raised his arms a little as he walked, to help him pick up his pace. He braced the screen door open and gestured for me to go first.

I went slowly down the steps, thoughts tumbling through my mind. Another property south of town sold cheap, too, on Sanders Road. The Peach Blossom was on Sanders Road, I suddenly remembered. I got to the bottom and turned back to look at him. "Coleman May sold this property to you and he sold another house to Kate. Both of them below market value. Far below, from what I understand." I cocked my head and waited to see what he'd say.

He shrugged. "He needed to sell." He angled his stiff leg down the steps as he braced his arm on the banister, then brushed past me and busied himself with straightening one of the tilting flagpoles.

I glanced at the two houses so close together and thought

about the last time I was here and what he'd said then. I hurried over to him. "You said that what happened to Nash was the saddest thing you'd ever *seen* in your life. What did you see?"

"I never said I saw anything."

"But you used that word, 'seen.' If you hadn't seen something wouldn't you have used the word 'heard?' It was the saddest thing you'd ever *heard* in your life?"

He gave the pole one final twist into the ground. "Those are just words. Seen, heard. There's no difference." He turned his back and made his way to the screened porch.

I hurried along behind. "You know about the missing woman, Jodi Lockworth, right? You've got to have seen her picture. It looks like she was researching Nash and Coleman. If her disappearance is connected with Nash, you could be the one to help find her."

"Her disappearance doesn't have anything to do with what happened to William Nash."

"How do you know?"

He gripped the handrail and looked back over his shoulder at me. "I just know."

Chapter
Twenty-seven

"Please, wait," I said, trying to keep him from going inside the house. "You don't have to tell me. Just call the sheriff's office and tell them. Ask for Detective Waraday. If Coleman killed Nash and Jodi was researching Nash, then Coleman would have a reason to make sure Jodi stopped researching. You could be the key to a break in the case. And that's not even considering what happened to Nash. If you know something about how he died, you could give his family the answers they're looking for."

His gaze wandered over the flags and the sporadic traffic flying by on the state highway. I prayed that a car didn't turn into the parking area, because if one did, he'd be off in seconds to see if he could make a sale and I could tell he was debating whether or not to tell me something.

"Fifty years. It's been over fifty years and Nash's family still doesn't know what happened," I said quietly.

He swiveled fully toward me and his harsh tone hit me like a physical shove. "You think I don't know how many years it's been? You think it was easy to see his mama suffer day after day? She lived right beside us. I saw her every day." His voice broke and he wiped his hands over his eyes. "Every day."

I'd taken an involuntary step back at his angry tone, but with his head bent and his shoulders slumped, he looked harmless enough. I stepped closer and put a hand on his shoulder. "You must have been a kid. How old were you?"

He stepped back and leaned back against the handrail. His eyes were dry. "Ten. Old enough to know what I saw, but I'm not going to talk to any police about it." He had a set look on his face. "I'll tell you and you can tell them."

"I don't think they'll take my word . . ."

"It was late and I was supposed to be asleep, but I was hangin' out my window. My mama would have tanned my hide if she saw me doing that, but she was always tired, what with working two jobs. I'd go to bed and not ten minutes later, she'd be dozing in her chair. I could pretty much do what I wanted. I'd climbed out of my window and shimmied down the roof over the front porch plenty of times to meet my friends, and I was about to do it again. I was waiting for William to go past. He was fifteen or twenty yards down the road when I spotted him, walking."

"Wasn't that road pretty busy? Why was he out there?"

"He walked to work every day at the paper factory. It's only two miles up the road and back then there wasn't that much traffic. Just had to watch out for the eighteen-wheelers."

A four-mile round-trip to get to work and back. I didn't think there were many teenagers who would do that today.

Crooner swallowed. He spoke slowly, his gaze fixed on the piles of run-down furniture. "It truly was the most awful thing I've ever seen in my life, when that car hit him." His gaze switched to me and he was intense, focused on me. "It was one of those things that you see and then you wonder, just for a second, if your eyes are playing tricks on you. But that sound of metal hitting flesh and bone, well"—he shook his head—"I'll never forget that as long as I live."

Just to be completely clear, I said, "You saw a car hit Nash?"

"Yes. It was over in a couple of seconds. The car was wavering all over the road, and then it swerved to the right, onto the shoulder, and hit him. Didn't slow down or nothing. He went up on the hood for a second, then went flying through the air, like someone tossed a rag doll. He landed in the drainage ditch."

He stopped and I said, "Then what happened?"

"The car went on and it was quiet. Real quiet."

"Did you recognize the car?"

"Yep. It was Coleman's car. Mrs. Ava was driving."

"Ava May hit William Nash and drove off?" I repeated, stunned.

"That's what happened. I got down there as fast as I could, but there was nothing to be done for him. He was gone. I wasn't sure what to do. I decided I'd better go home and wake up my mama, but about then, a car came along the highway, driving real slow, and I got out of there. I went backward into the trees and waited."

"Why?"

"Why?" His voice was incredulous. "Because I was ten years old and I'd just seen a woman run over my neighbor."

"Sorry. I'm sorry. It must have been very traumatic."

"It was Coleman May in the same car. Mrs. Ava was with him in the passenger seat and she was drunk. I could tell by the way she was slurring her words and sliding down in the seat. She kept saying, 'I didn't see him. I didn't see him,' but with her words all drawn out. It took Coleman a while, but he finally found Nash. He took something out of the trunk, a sheet or tarp. Something white. He rolled William up in it and lugged it to the car. He put it in the trunk and drove away."

"What did you do?" I asked again, trying not to imagine how dreadful it would be for a kid to see something like that.

"I ran home, jumped on my bike, and followed him. I had to see what happened. It was dark and there weren't many people on the roads. I kept to the shadows and followed him back to Scranton Road. He took that cut-through road, so it was only about a mile. I thought he was taking William back to his house, but then he turned at the old Chauncey place and went to the family plot. I watched him bury William." By now his face was expressionless and his voice had taken on a mechanical quality. "I waited until he left. Then I went home."

"What happened then?"

"Then I kept my mouth shut." He turned to me and said, "Who was people going to believe? A black boy or the white mayor?"

"But you knew where he was buried. You could prove it."

"It was 1955. It didn't matter what I knew. I knew if I said anything there was a good chance I'd end up in the grave next to William."

"You're right." I backed off. Who was I to question the decision of a traumatized ten-year-old in the segregated South?

I tried to shift this new information into place. "There wasn't a lynching. The whole thing was made up to cover up for Ava's hit-and-run." I walked a few steps away and sat down on a rickety wrought-iron garden bench. "Did you tell Jodi this?"

"No. I've never told anyone."

I looked up at him. "But Coleman knows."

We stared at each other for a few seconds; then I looked at the house, the house where Nash lived with his mother, that was now part of Crooner's junk market.

He said, "I'm not proud of what I done. I only done it to take care of my family. I need this place and Kate needed that house for her bed-and-breakfast." He climbed the steps to the porch at his slow pace.

"You realize that the sheriff's department isn't going to take my word for this. You have to tell them what you saw," I said. "Things have changed. You've heard about the Emmett Till case being reopened, right? Lots of civil rights cases are being reinvestigated. People will listen to you now."

"I'm not repeating what I told you. Anyone comes asking questions, I'll say I don't know what that crazy lady is talking about." He slammed the screen door and latched it.

I pulled a Hershey's Kiss out of my purse and popped it in my mouth. My brain processes definitely needed chocolate to work out this mess. No matter what I said to Waraday, he was going to have to talk to Crooner.

I shook my head, thinking you really never knew what people had seen. I was in the process of unwrapping another chocolate Kiss. I stopped. *You never knew what people had seen.* Hadn't I thought that exact same thing after talking to Dorthea at Nathan's birthday party? Images formed one after another in my mind: a pickup nose-diving into the lake and the picture of the bridge fund-raiser in the paper almost crowding out the story about Nash's disappearance. The shiny new Bel Air Dorthea described.

I jumped up. I had to get to the lake. I realized I was holding another chocolate and it was melting, soft against my fingers. I ate it as I pulled out my keys with my other hand, wondering how long it took to search a lake bed.

I didn't have any trouble figuring out where to park. Instead of parking and walking across the field, I'd come down Elliott Road, which ran alongside the lake. Satellite news trucks, cars from the sheriff's department, and regular old cars with no logo on their doors or light bar on top filled the shoulders on both sides of the road. As I crossed the field to the stand of trees, I spotted Nita's gold Taurus and breathed a sigh of relief. I wasn't sure if I could get Waraday to listen to me, but I was sure he'd listen to Nita.

She stood on the outskirts of a group of people, looking pale and tense. Dorthea was there with her and spotted me. She waved. Nita never moved. Her focus was on the lake. The water was almost smooth. A few ripples from the gentle breeze chased across the surface.

I hurried up to Dorthea and said, "Have they found anything?"

"Hello, Ellie," Dorthea said. "Yes, a pickup, a car, and a rowboat. And a lot of trash, from what I can tell."

"What kind of car did Coleman have before he bought that fancy one, the Bel Air?"

Dorthea tilted her head and even Nita tore her gaze away from the lake to look at me. Both of them had concerned expressions on their faces.

"I don't really know. I just remembered the Bel Air because it was new and caused such a sensation. Ellie, are you feeling all right?" Dorthea asked.

"Yes. I'm feeling fine. The pickup at the bottom of the lake is Cotner's, right?" I asked. "The one you saw go in."

"Well, he's not here to identify it, but I suppose it is," Dorthea said. "The divers said it was from the '30s and that would have been about right. Cotner always used everything until it fell apart."

"Or until he pushed it into the lake, apparently," Nita added. "It worked so well the first time, he decided to do it again with the car."

"No, the car isn't his. It's Coleman and Ava's car. The one she was driving when she hit Nash and killed him."

Both women stared at me for a moment; then Dorthea said, "Ellie, dear, let's get you out of the sun . . ."

"No. It all makes sense. I talked to someone today who saw the whole thing, but this person won't talk to the investigators. But if the car at the bottom of the lake belonged to them, it might have damage that could tell us what happened with Nash."

"Sherry needs to hear this," Nita said, and had Dorthea call her. "Now." Nita turned back to me and gripped my hands. "Start at the beginning."

I repeated what Crooner had told me, then described the newspaper photo of the bridge fund-raiser held the night Nash disappeared and Nita said, "Let me get Davey."

"Davey" didn't look too happy, but he was a southern boy

and he made an effort to hide his displeasure at being hauled away from the edge of the water. Or at least he did when he spoke to Nita.

When he turned to me his face looked disbelieving. "You want to know what kind of car is down there?"

"Yes. You see, I talked to someone who saw a hit-and-run car accident on the night Nash disappeared. A drunk driver hit and killed Nash as he walked home from work. The person who told me this is"—how should I put it?—"reluctant to talk to you."

"And you think that car is at the bottom of the lake?"

"Yes, I do. It all fits. Coleman's wife, Ava, was driving drunk. She'd been at the North Dawkins Women's Society Bridge Fund-raiser. I saw her picture in the paper. There was an article and photo about it below the article about Nash's disappearance. Everyone in the photo was holding a cocktail. Ava was an alcoholic. And the witness who saw the hit-and-run said Coleman and Ava returned to the scene and that Ava was obviously drunk. It would make sense to get rid of the car Ava was driving, and this is the only place deep enough to sink something that big."

There was a sharp intake of breath beside me and I looked over at Nita.

"Are you sure she was an alcoholic, dear? That's quite an accusation to make."

And accusing her of a hit-and-run wasn't a big deal? "Yes. I spoke to her daughter-in-law, Rosalee. Well, I suppose she'd be an ex-daughter-in-law since she divorced Ava's son to keep Colleen away from Ava." I turned back to Waraday. "Colleen's her daughter."

"I know Colleen."

Dorthea nodded her head. "It does explain quite a bit— Coleman doing so much for her, all of Ava's 'illnesses.' I thought she had a weak constitution. I was there that night at the bridge fund-raiser. I remember because I won. The only time I ever did. Ava was there and she always had several gin and tonics. Those were her favorite. She would have driven up the state highway past the paper factory to get home, too."

"So this individual says he saw Ava hit Nash and drive away?"

"Yes. The person went down to help, but Nash was already dead. Coleman and Ava returned. Coleman wrapped the body in a sheet or a tarp, loaded it in the trunk, and drove to the Chaunceys' family plot and buried Nash there. He must have started the rumor about the lynching as a distraction. Then he bought Ava a new car, a new Bel Air, a late Christmas present, and Ava never drove again." I looked at Dorthea with raised eyebrows and she nodded.

"She never did drive again. Anyone can tell you that."

"And you think they ditched the old car here in the lake instead of making a trade-in," Waraday said.

"Well, the car probably had damage and he couldn't fix it without someone finding out in the small town that North Dawkins was then, and if he traded it in there was always the risk that after it was repaired someone would connect the car with the hit-and-run. No, I think he got rid of it, just like Cotner got rid of his old pickup. And remember Jodi's note about Nash? She wanted to interview Rosalee, too. What if this is what she found out? What if she knew Ava killed Nash in the hit-and-run and then Coleman buried the body? He wouldn't want people to know. Look at the lengths he went to ensure that no one knew about the hit-and-run. What would he do to keep Jodi quiet?"

There was silence in our little circle; then Waraday said, "What kind of car was it?"

Shoot! Why hadn't I asked Crooner? "I don't know," I said miserably.

Waraday frowned.

Nita touched his shirtsleeve. "Please, would you check with the divers?" He visibly softened and strode back to the edge of the water.

Dorthea, Nita, and I all glanced at each other and then hurried along in his wake. The divers were on the bank, packing up their equipment. Waraday addressed the closest diver, a black woman with her hair slicked back from her forehead. "The vehicles on the bottom, what were they?"

She set down her air tank and said, "One was an old pickup. I'd say from the '30s or '40s. We didn't spend too much time around them, once we confirmed there wasn't a body there."

"And the car?"

"Russ will know. He's the car buff." She glanced back over her shoulder to the other diver. He'd pulled off the hood of his wet suit to reveal a bald head and a ruddy complexion that the cold water must have aggravated, since his cheeks were as rosy as a department store Santa's.

She shouted, "Hey, Russ! That car down at the bottom?"

"A black 1940 Ford Standard," he said promptly.

Waraday looked back at us and I glanced questioningly at Dorthea and Nita.

"One moment." Nita scanned the crowd, then hurried over to Gerald. They came back together and he looked as puzzled as the divers, but he dutifully reported, "Seems I remember Coleman May had a Ford Standard. I couldn't swear, but I think it was a '40 or '42."

Waraday turned back to the divers. "Any damage on that car?"

They exchanged glances and then the woman said, "We'd better go back in." They suited up again and disappeared under the water. The breeze had kicked up, sending waves fluttering across the lake. I shivered, glad I wasn't in that water. We waited and even the news crews who'd been packing up to leave when I arrived had stopped, sensing that something was happening.

It felt like an eternity or two, especially since Waraday's gaze kept skipping over to me, then back to the lake, then over to me again. Finally, the water heaved and the female diver made her way over to the bank. "There's damage to the grille and right headlight."

"Could that have happened from the impact with the water?"

"I don't think so. It looks more like some car-on-person damage I've seen."

A deputy broke into our circle and said, "Excuse me, Detective Waraday. We got that info you wanted on the plates. Took so long because they had to go search the paper records. The pickup was registered to George Cotner and the car to Coleman May, both of North Dawkins."

"Let's get her up, then."

An Everything In Its Place Tip for an Organized Party

Set the stage. If the party is at your home, a few simple things will help the party flow effortlessly, or at least *appear* to flow effortlessly.

- Clear out a coat closet or designate a room where guests can leave their coats and handbags.
- Put away any breakable items, preferably in a locked room.
- If children are invited, create a kid-friendly area where the kids can escape. If that area will be in one of your children's rooms, make a sweep to remove any special toys or expensive keepsake items that you want to keep out of harm's way. Also, remove Magic Markers, paints, and crayons, if the kids won't have adult supervision. Your kids may know not to mark on the walls, but your guests' kids may not be so well trained. Put the off-limit toys out of reach in another area. For older kids, set up computer games or movies.
- Unless your pets are extremely well behaved, put them in a crate or keep them in a separate part of the house away from your guests. Some of your

guests may be allergic and you won't have to worry about muddy paw prints either!

- To make your home less crowded, remove a few pieces of furniture or push certain pieces against the walls. If you're having a buffet, think about where people will sit after they have their food. Will you need to bring in extra tables and chairs or provide lap trays?

Chapter
Twenty-eight

"**M**om, my stomach feels funny."

I scratched out my signature on the Mother's Day Out sign-in form, then knelt down in front of Livvy. Her forehead wasn't warm, but she did look pale. "Do you feel like you're going to throw up?"

"A little. And swishy."

She swayed a bit. My carefully coordinated plan of finishing Scott's office while Livvy was at Mother's Day Out and Nathan was at home with the sitter was about to crumble. I gave her a hug and said, "Well, looks like we're going to have to head back home and tell Anna we don't need her." Anna was a precious find—a homeschooled teenager whose mom let her babysit during the day if she was caught up on her schoolwork. Finding an occasional daytime sitter was harder than finding Livvy's shoes, which always disappeared moments before it was time to walk out the door.

"But I want to stay."

"Well, you can't stay, if you're sick."

"All through spinning, Livvy?" asked a voice from behind me. I swiveled around and saw Miss Sandy, her teacher, leaning over the half door to the classroom. She smiled and held out her hand for Livvy's bag, which contained her lunch, jacket, and blanket—all carefully labeled with her name in waterproof marker.

"Spinning?"

"You know, twirling. One of the girls started it last week and every time I turn around the kids are spinning like tops."

I handed over the bag and kissed Livvy. "When you twirl it makes your head and tummy feel funny. You're going to be fine."

Fifteen minutes later, I had my cell phone on speaker as I pulled into STAND's office park.

"They didn't get it out until almost midnight," Nita said.

I switched my cell phone off speaker and tucked it on my shoulder, then grabbed my tote bag and bin of supplies. I looked across the field to the dark patch of woods. The only movement was the sporadic flutter of golden leaves as they floated to the ground. "Did you stay?"

"Yes. I felt I should be there with Sherry."

Mitch and I had watched the scene on one of the cable channels. They'd broadcast it live. Mostly, it was two hours of a dark night interspersed with expert interviews. Finally, the car was pulled from the lake, water streaming from it, a pretty dramatic sight, all two minutes of it.

"How's she doing?"

"As well as can be expected. It's not the answer she wanted, but when you have no answer, even the worst answer is not as bad as not knowing."

"And do you know if Waraday has talked to Coleman?"

"Yes." She sighed. "I'm afraid all that's been revealed in the last day isn't going to help us find Jodi."

"What?" How could it not help? If Jodi knew something about Coleman, he might have tried to silence her. Surely that was a lead on a possible motive.

"In all the excitement yesterday, I forgot that Coleman had a heart attack last year on New Year's Day. He was in the hospital on January eighth. In fact, he was in the hospital for the next week. So there's no way he could be involved in

Jodi's disappearance. Davey told me that when they told Coleman they'd found his car, he told him everything. Apparently, it happened almost exactly as Crooner said."

"Crooner?" How did she know he was involved?

"He showed up last night after the car was pulled out of the water. He said he'd seen the news coverage and he could help Davey with the investigation. I heard him telling Davey that he'd told you everything earlier, but he wanted to talk to Davey himself. He said when he saw the car on television, he knew he had to tell what happened, that it was all going to come out and he wasn't afraid anymore."

I hoped telling what happened helped him deal with what he'd seen. "What will happen to Coleman?" I wondered.

"The district attorney told Sherry that charges will be filed against him, concealing a death and tampering with evidence. Of course, I think the loss of respect in the community will be harder for him to take than the charges. He'll lose the very thing he tried so hard to preserve."

I stepped inside the bare hallway of the building and let the door close behind me. "I'm sorry. I wish it had helped."

"Oh, I have to go. Detective Waraday just pulled into the driveway."

I said good-bye, then paused, gathering my thoughts. Coleman wasn't involved at all in Jodi's disappearance. That meant there were precisely zero suspects. I'd been so focused on finding out what had happened in 1955 that I'd completely forgotten to wonder what Coleman had been doing on January eighth of this year.

I gave myself a mental shake and squared my shoulders. I had to focus on organizing right now. I could kick myself later.

Candy's chair was empty when I stepped inside the office. "Hello?"

"Come on in," Scott called from the back office. "Candy's at the dentist."

Scott hunched over his keyboard, the bank of muted TVs flickering beside him.

"Okay. Don't mind me. I know my way around by now."

"Great," Scott said without looking up.

I got to work in the storage room, which already looked so much better. I'd come in for a few hours on Sunday afternoon and finished up the big items on my list. Today, I only had to put the finishing touches on the storage room. The paperwork was sorted and boxed, the Christmas items had their own storage tubs, the miscellany of useless and broken items had been carted out to the trash, and the coffeepot had its own space on a small table I'd positioned behind Candy's desk.

I pulled out my cordless screwdriver to finish putting the shelves together. An hour later, I had all the boxes on shelves and a small worktable set up in the middle of the storage area, complete with a tray of office supplies. I positioned the shredder and trash can under one end of the table and looked around, hands on my hips. It looked great.

"Scott, when will Candy be back?" The volume on one of the TVs went up just as I called out, "I'd like to give you both a rundown of where everything is . . ." I trailed off when I reached the door and saw Jodi's picture on the television.

Scott stood, remote control in one hand and the other braced on the back of his chair.

The slick-looking man who'd been on my doorstep a few days ago was speaking. "Earlier today, construction workers found the body of a young female in a shallow grave in a suburban Georgia neighborhood. Sources close to the investigation told us it is the body of missing youth sports coordinator Jodi Lockworth, who disappeared over ten months ago."

Oh no. I put my hand over my mouth and walked into Scott's office.

"The Dawkins County Sheriff's Office has scheduled a press conference for later this morning and we'll bring that to you live. For now, the feelings of shock and dismay are almost palpable in this middle Georgia town that held out hope for a happier ending."

Scott hit the mute button and I sat down heavily in one of the stiff office chairs with my hand still over my mouth. All I could think of were Nita and Gerald. When I was on the phone with her earlier, Waraday must have been arriving to give them the news. I shook my head. I'd been shifting paper, building shelves, and worrying about where to put a paper shredder when their world had been falling apart. They'd be devastated.

"You don't expect it." Scott slumped down into the other visitor's chair. "Even after all this time, even though you know it's a possibility, you still don't think . . ."

I pulled my hand away from my mouth. "I know." *Should I call Nita?* Not now, I decided. What a horrible day it had to be for her and Gerald. I knew the Find Jodi network wouldn't disband now. In fact, I bet it would shift over to caring for Nita and Gerald. I decided I'd call Colleen as soon as I was finished here and ask what I could do.

I was so lost in thought that I jumped when Scott stood up slowly from his chair.

I stood up. "Why don't I come back later? I'm finished in there. I just wanted to show you and Candy the layout . . ." I trailed off. Papers and a filing system seemed so insignificant right now.

"No, go ahead and show me. I'll fill Candy in. I need to know how it works. That way you don't have to make an extra trip out here again." Scott pushed up his glasses and gazed at his desk. "It's going to be hard to get any more work done this afternoon anyway. I'll probably close down the office and get in touch with Colleen. See if there's anything I can do."

"Okay." I went into the small room. I pointed out the various storage spaces, then handed him a schematic. "Here's a drawing with all the areas marked so you'll know where everything is stored. I've also laminated this chart of guidelines on how long you need to keep various types of paperwork. Here's your tray of items that need to be filed. Take the time to file everything each day and you won't get lost in that avalanche of paperwork again. I'd recommend you have Candy do it in the late afternoon as one of her closing routines. It'll save time in the long run."

Scott studied the schematic and nodded. "Looks great. You've done an awesome job."

I smiled, thinking there was a quote for my business brochure. "No problem. I enjoy seeing the transformation. Here, I'll file these papers as an example," I said, taking the thin stack from the tray. "I found them on the floor today under the old shredder. Okay, first here's an invoice that's been paid. It would go over here in this filing cabinet." I opened the drawer and tucked it in the right folder.

"Next, you've got a couple of old receipts. Looks like business expenses, a hotel and some restaurant receipts. Since they're all on the same day, they would go in the business expenses file. They're all dated this year, January eighth, so put them over here," I said, heading over to the far corner of the storage room.

I pulled open the filing cabinet. *January eighth*. Why did that sound so familiar? I ran my fingers down the tabs and glanced at the receipts again. A Chinese restaurant in Atlanta and a Holiday Inn Express, also in Atlanta. *January eighth*. I slid them halfway into the file, then pulled them back out and looked at the signature.

January eighth was the day Jodi disappeared. You can't read most signatures, but Scott had excellent penmanship. I could even read his middle initial. I swung around, the papers gripped in my hand. "I thought you were in Washington, D.C., when Jodi disappeared."

He pushed his glasses up and smiled. "Here, let me see. The dates are probably from the year before. You know how those receipts get smudged." He reached out.

I pulled my hand back. "No. They're not from last year." I scanned the one from the restaurant and found the time stamp. Five-thirty in the evening.

He'd been smiling, but when I didn't hand him the papers, he lunged forward and I skipped back, putting the worktable between us. Atlanta wasn't that far away. He could have been back in North Dawkins in a little over an hour.

"Ellie. I need to see those papers. Hand them over."

"No." I tried to gauge the distance to the door without moving my head. I was closer, but I didn't want to turn my back on him. "Why did you say you were in D.C.?"

"I'm sure you're mistaken about those dates." His voice cracked and he cleared his throat. "Let me see them."

I was sure if I let him see them, they'd be shredded before I got out the door. We were both poised and tense. I shifted my weight from one foot to the other and saw him make a mirroring move. My heart was thundering right now. I wasn't up for this kind of cardiac workout.

A few thoughts flashed through my mind, but I discarded them as quickly as they came. I could tell from his raspy breathing that there was no way he was going to be reasonable and let me hand the receipts over to Detective Waraday.

Scott lunged one way and I skittered in the opposite direction. Now I was back on the far side of the door. I leaned forward and gripped the worktable. "Scott, please . . ."

"No. You don't understand and I can't explain it right now. I need those. If you hand them to me, you can go home, and I'll take care of it."

Right. I bet he'd take care of it. But it wasn't worth it for me to do anything stupid here. I had a husband and two kids who needed me. The credit card companies would have records of the charges. It would make more sense to hand over the papers and get out of here.

If he'd let me leave.

I swallowed and glanced at the door. I gripped the table hard. It shifted a bit and I was so hyperaware of even the tiniest movements that I picked up on it.

"Okay," I said, slowly extending the papers over the worktable. "I'll hand these to you. Then I'm walking out of here."

He lunged for them. I jerked the papers back with one hand and shoved the worktable at him with my other hand. The edge caught him in the midsection and he folded over like a piece of paper as the air went out of him.

I flew to the door, gripped the frame to help me swing toward the front door of the office, and ran into someone so hard that I went sprawling. A cascade of cold, sticky liquid rained down on me.

"What the blazes is going on here?" Candy demanded. She was still standing—she was pretty solid. Our impact had only set her dangly earrings swinging. She still gripped her Coke can, but a trail of dark liquid covered her shoulder.

I checked the papers. There were a few tiny, dark spots from the liquid, but all the relevant bits of info were still readable. I scrambled to my feet, shaking off the trail of Coke that fizzed along my arm. She glanced in the storage room where Scott was slowly standing up, but still gasping for air. "What did you do to him? Did he file something in the wrong place?" She turned around and said to someone behind her, "Well, I don't know if he'll be able to talk, but he's definitely in."

Behind her I saw Detective Waraday and a deputy. I thrust the papers in Waraday's direction. His eyebrows shot up as I said, "Here. The date—January eighth." I was still a little winded. But I managed to get the basic facts across to him. As I described what I'd found and how Scott had reacted, Waraday's eyebrows descended into a scowl. "You wait out here with Candy."

The deputy shuffled Candy and me into the small reception area, then returned to Scott's office and closed the door. "Well. That was interesting," Candy said. She tossed her almost empty Coke can in the trash and produced a container of baby wipes from one of her desk drawers.

"Why is Waraday here?" I asked.

She stopped patting her blouse and looked up. "You heard the news this morning? That they found Jodi?"

When I nodded, she said, "Her body was found on that lot Scott owns in Magnolia Estates."

I stopped scrubbing and dropped onto one of the hard plastic chairs across from her desk. "You've got to be kidding." She'd been found in my neighborhood?

"Sadly, no, I'm not kidding. I wish I was." She pulled out a pack of gum. "Want a piece?"

I shook my head. "How about some chocolate instead?" I said, digging into the pocket of my fleece vest for Hershey's Kisses. We were silent for a few seconds, munching on chocolate; then she said, "He always did act funny when that weekend came up."

"Scott?"

"Yeah. Touchy. He'd change the subject lickety-split."

"That's absurd and you know it, Dave." Despite the closed door, Scott's raised voice carried easily through the thin walls.

We could hear Waraday's calm reply, too. "You know I have to ask you."

I raised my eyebrows at Candy. "Dave?"

"They play on a basketball team."

So they were friends. How seriously would Waraday investigate him? He certainly hadn't checked out Scott's original alibi very well.

"Okay, here's the deal," Scott said. "I had a job interview at Sprinkle, the big base in Atlanta."

I decided he must be pacing, because the volume of his words fell into a pattern. They were distinct for a few seconds, then faded.

"I didn't want anyone here to know about it, so I told everyone I was going to D.C."

"Candy didn't see your itinerary? Or have a number of where to reach you?"

"No, I make my own travel arrangements and she's got my cell, if she needs me."

"Why?" Waraday's voice was faint. I could hardly hear it.

"You know how it is. These jobs don't come along very often and Sprinkle is bigger than Taylor. It would've been a good career move for me. But I didn't want to jeopardize what I had here either, in case I didn't get the job, which was exactly how it worked out."

"So take me through that weekend."

"There's nothing to take you through," Scott said. He must have been close to the door, because his impatient tone was easy to hear. "I went up to Atlanta on Friday night, met with their board Saturday morning, and drove back Saturday afternoon. I showed up to work on Monday like normal."

"So I'll be able to verify your whereabouts for part of Saturday? You have the names of the people you met with?"

"Of course."

"What about Friday night?" Waraday asked. "Can anyone verify you were in Atlanta all Friday night?"

"No! I was in my hotel room from nine until seven the next morning."

"Don't get sharp with me. I have to ask you these questions."

After a short silence, Scott's voice shifted to a subdued tone. "I know."

"So, what did you do when you got back?"

"I opened the mail and watched football. You know, normal stuff."

"Did you see Jodi?"

"No."

"Why did you lie earlier?"

There was a long pause. I had to strain to hear Scott's next words. "Because I didn't get the job in Atlanta and I couldn't let the board here know I wasn't completely up-front with them. One of the reasons they hired me was that I agreed to commit to staying here at least three years. They've had a problem keeping people in the position. I wanted to tell you, but since Jodi was missing and I'd had that disagreement with her, I couldn't."

"How'd you do it?" Waraday's voice was so soft. Candy and I exchanged looks.

"Do it? Do what? I didn't do anything to Jodi."

"Then how did you fake your alibi in D.C.?"

"Oh, that wasn't hard. I had a couple of receipts from a trip I'd taken up there the month before. A little work with the scanner and I had new dates on the receipts. Then I reported that my credit card was stolen two days before I went to Atlanta, so I could say the charges weren't mine. I figured you trusted me and that you wouldn't look into it too closely."

"My mistake." Waraday's voice was still quiet, but it had such an edge to it that I was glad I wasn't in the room with them.

"Dave, I had to do it. Surely, you can see that. STAND would find out I'd lied and then I'd be a suspect in a missing persons case on top of that."

"Well, you should have told me because it's only going to be worse. Now STAND's board is going to know you lied and you're a suspect in a murder investigation."

Chapter
Twenty-nine

I pulled into the parking lot of the church where Livvy went to Mother's Day Out. It was hard to comprehend that I'd dropped her off only a few hours ago.

I'd spent the drive thinking about Scott. When Waraday walked him out to the sheriff's car, Waraday's face had been set, but Scott had looked like many of the kids on the first day of Mother's Day Out, confused and scared. I'd looked at Candy and said, "Do you think he did it?" After all, she'd worked with him since he'd moved to North Dawkins. She probably knew him better than anyone else around here.

Her earrings slapped against her cheeks. "No. He'd never hurt anyone. He couldn't even kill the mouse that got caught half in and half out of the trap in the storage room. *I* had to take care of that."

Yuck. I wasn't sure if it was a good thing or not that I hadn't known about the mouse while I was digging around in the boxes and filing cabinets. Before I stepped out of the car, I remembered I wanted to call Colleen, so I grabbed my phone. I knew once I walked in the door at home that all those little details of taking care of the kids and the house would take over and then before I knew it, it would be ten o'clock at night. Colleen picked up and I identified myself, then said I'd seen the news. "How are you doing?"

"Okay, I guess. I'm holding myself together so I can be there for Nita and Gerald."

"Is there anything I can do for Nita or you?" I asked.

"She already has all the food she needs and there's not much else we can do now. I think she'd appreciate a call in a few days, maybe after the funeral. Just check on her and Gerald."

I closed my eyes and swallowed. "Of course, I can do that. Let me know if you need anything, anything at all."

"Sure." Her voice became slightly more animated. "I *knew* Scott was involved somehow. Detective Waraday is going to have to eat crow when I see him next time."

"Well, I don't think Waraday is arresting him yet," I said cautiously. Of course, it might not be long because the forensic team had arrived to search STAND's office as I was leaving. They were probably searching Scott's home, too.

"Yes, but Jodi was buried on his lot."

"I know, but wouldn't it be stupid for him to put her body there?" It was like an arrow pointing to him as the murderer.

"Or else he's smart enough to know that it would look like a stupid thing to do and people will assume, like you just did, that it means he wasn't involved."

It took me a second to work out Colleen's convoluted logic, but I had to admit that it made sense in a twisted sort of way. The call-waiting on my phone beeped and I said good-bye to Colleen and switched over to the other call, a number I didn't recognize.

"Hi, Ellie. This is Topaz. Just wanted to let you know I'll be there on Friday. Can I bring anything?"

Friday? Oh, right. I was hosting a party for over fifty people in four days. "Great!" I said brightly. "No, I think we've got everything covered."

I dug out my list for the promotion party. I smoothed the wrinkles out of the page and read over it. Lots to do. Time to get focused. At least concentrating on the party would give me something to do instead of dwelling on the sad news about Jodi.

I shoved the screen door to the back porch open with my hip, then backed through, carrying an ice chest. I stopped short on the patio. "What is *that*?"

Mitch stood over a silver tube perched on a stand. It looked a bit like a rocket. A cardboard box, bits of Styrofoam, and plastic littered the lawn and patio around him. "Turkey fryer."

"Why do we have a turkey fryer?"

Mitch didn't look up. He pulled a long silver pronged contraption out of the tube, mumbled a few words under his breath, and shifted it around. "So we can fry a turkey."

"Why would we want to do that?" I positioned the ice chest on the side of the patio beside the other two and walked over to Mitch. "We're already grilling burgers and dogs."

"I know, but a little more food never hurts. The guys say the turkey tastes great." He flashed a smile at me and quoted, "Crispy on the outside, juicy on the inside." He focused on the turkey fryer again as he said, "It only takes about thirty minutes to cook a turkey, as long as it's thawed."

Ah! An out. "Well, we'll have to try it another time, since we don't have time to thaw a turkey."

"Already thawed. It's in the refrigerator in the garage. I picked it up on the way home today after I got this."

"Fine. Fry a turkey. But that's all you. And it'll have to go somewhere out of the way. We're going to have kids running around here."

"I'm going to put it over there on the side of the patio," Mitch said, pointing to the alcove where we kept the grill.

"But not too close to the house. Remember that couple in base housing who set their siding on fire on the Fourth of July?"

"I'll keep it away from the kids and the house. We've got a fire extinguisher by the grill anyway."

Okay, so we were adding turkey to the menu. I could roll with the punches. I grabbed my clipboard, which I'd left on the small plastic-topped end table, and put a tick beside *ice chests*. I moved the tip of my pen down the list. "You're mowing the lawn tonight?"

"Yes, as soon as I get this set up."

"Don't we need something for entertainment? Some games?" I asked.

"No. People will just talk and eat."

"Are you sure? I could put out some board games or movies."

Mitch shrugged. "Whatever you want to do, but I'm telling you, the food and beer are the main attraction."

I went back to my list. "I weeded the flower beds this morning. I'm going to mop the kitchen floor, then start on the food."

"Food? What food? We've already got the burgers and dogs."

"I'm going to make chocolate chip cookies for dessert."

There was a clatter; then Mitch came over to me. "Ellie," he said as he wrapped his arms around me. "You're spinning out of control here. The house looks great. The yard looks spectacular. We even have plenty of chairs. You've covered it all. You don't need to make cookies. Don't get me wrong, I love your cookies, but let's pick some up at the store tomorrow."

"It's just that . . ."

Mitch rested his forehead against mine. "Ellie," he said lightly.

"Okay," I sighed. "No homemade cookies, but we get ice cream at the store, too. And some brownies."

"Fine," Mitch said.

"And I guess you don't want to hear about the appetizers we're having—mini quiches, cheese straws, and a veggie tray."

Mitch smiled and shook his head. "You're making this way harder than it has to be, but if you want to . . ."

"Well, you're the one who added the turkey."

He kissed the side of my neck and released me. "Fine, make appetizers, make cookies, just don't kill yourself."

I blew out a breath and ran my hand over the back of my neck. Maybe Mitch was right. Maybe I was getting too worked up about things that didn't really matter. Perhaps I was over-organizing? "Okay, you're right. I am freaking out a little bit. Maybe I should get out of here, go for a walk." I hadn't been on a walk in days. I'd thrown myself into preparing for the party.

"Good idea," Mitch said absently as he went back to work on the turkey fryer.

I went to get Rex's leash. Even though we hadn't had any weird or threatening incidents in the last few days—they'd felt almost normal, except for the discovery of Jodi's body— I still was extra cautious. I didn't think anyone would bother me while I had a Rottweiler by my side.

A few minutes later, I paused at the end of the street. I'd avoided the gravel path through the woods, since there had been so much activity there during the last few days, but now the cars were gone. The crime scene tape was gone, too. As I hesitated, I heard pounding footsteps behind me. I spun around and a woman jogger trotted past me with a quick wave, then continued up the gravel path.

I took a deep breath and paced up the path. I might as well get my first walk down the gravel path over with. I liked the idea of the jogger blazing the trail. At least I wouldn't be alone.

I was about halfway down the path, just hitting the gentle curve, when the runner bobbed out of sight and a flash of yellow through the trees caught my eye. I slowed. Every so often a swath of open space branched off from the gravel path. Someday there would be paved roads shooting off from this road, twisting deeper into the development. Past two huge pieces of construction equipment, a person stood at the end of one of the cut paths. It was Nita.

I pulled on the leash and walked over to her. "Hello, Nita," I said. She moved her head slightly and blinked her dark eyes. Delicate and slight, she again reminded me of a small bird as she stood there with her hands in her jacket pockets and her elbows tucked next to her body like folded wings.

I could tell she hadn't heard my noisy approach; it took her a minute to break out of her reverie. "Hello."

"I'm so sorry," I said, and the words didn't seem to be enough, so I gave her a quick hug. She wasn't a hugging-type person, but she surprised me when she gripped my shoulders in a tight, quick hug, then stepped away.

"Thank you, Ellie." It didn't look like she'd been crying. Her eyes weren't red or puffy, but her face seemed to have aged since the last time I'd seen her, as if grief had deepened the creases and wrinkles.

"Are you okay out here?" I asked.

She nodded. "This is where they found her. She was here the whole time."

I turned and saw a shallow depression in the ground, little more than a trench, really. The sun was setting and it cast everything in a golden light, a backdrop to the bright yellow leaves that still clung to the trees around us. It was so achingly beautiful that it made everything seem more surreal. There shouldn't be a grave here in this golden fall landscape. "Wasn't this area searched?"

I'd spoken more to myself than to Nita, but she answered matter-of-factly as she gazed at the field. "Yes. The whole neighborhood was searched. Twice. The areas were so immense. I've learned that it's very . . . difficult . . . to find a body that has been buried. Especially when you have no idea where to start looking. The focus of the search was the house and neighborhood immediately around it. Then attention shifted to Peter Yannis and Florida." She looked at me. "They've found him, by the way."

"Peter Yannis?" I asked.

"Yes. Apparently, he went on vacation in the Caribbean last January and liked it so much he decided to stay. He didn't even come home, just found a job and moved from the hotel to a tiny apartment in Charlotte Amalie. He's been crewing a yacht, sailing vacationers around the Virgin Islands. He arrived back in Florida a few days ago to pack and put his condo on the market."

So another suspect, however remote, was marked off the list. "What about Scott?" Party preparations had taken up all my time during the last few days, but I had watched the news and read the paper. Scott's name hadn't been mentioned. No charges had been filed, no arrest made.

"There's no physical evidence to tie him to Jodi during that weekend," Nita said with a small shrug.

I stood there not knowing what to say, but I didn't want to leave her here with the sun going down. I stood beside her. Finally, she said, "I need to come here. I've spent so long believing she was alive that I have to come here to remind myself that she's not. Gerald can't come here. He's been looking through our photograph albums and then driving around town, taking down the flyers. We're each grieving in our own way."

I swallowed. Before I could say anything, Nita went on. "She was wrapped in a blue plastic tarp with a shovel. The medical examiner says the shovel matches the injury to the back of her skull. It was over quickly."

At least Jodi's death had been instantaneous, unlike Nita's pain, which had gone on for months and was now transforming into a different type of grief. I pressed my lips together. I didn't want to know the details since I'd hoped that the end would be so different. The details made it worse somehow, but as I looked at Nita, I suspected she was reciting those details as a way to get through it. She was the type of person who faced things head-on and she was handling her grief in the same way she handled everything else in life.

Shadows were lengthening across the field. "Nita, I have to go. Is your car close to here? Can I walk you to it?" I asked doubtfully. I hadn't seen her car parked on the street or along the gravel path.

"I'm parked down at the end of the gravel," she said, nodding in the opposite direction from which I'd arrived. "You go ahead. I need to stay for a few more minutes. Thank you for listening."

"Sure." I turned and made my way back home.

Chapter
Thirty

My conversation with Nita occupied my thoughts during the rest of the walk and I arrived home and automatically stopped to get the mail before going inside. I sifted through the envelopes quickly. Most of them were bills, except for the homeowners' association newsletter and a few advertising flyers. The headline on the newsletter was a reminder to bag our leaves instead of shoving them into the street where they would clog the drains. Scintillating stuff. Other articles had pruning recommendations and reminders for the monthly HOA meeting. On the back was a small framed notice.

A Workout Designed for Moms

Are you looking for an easy way to get a quick, consistent workout but can't get to the gym? Do you have a stroller? If you answered yes to those two questions, then the Magnolia Estates Stroller Brigade is for you. You'll get a workout that combines aerobic and resistance training while making new friends.

I stuck the paper to the refrigerator door with a Bugs Bunny magnet. That sounded like a workout that might actu-

ally work for me. I was about to pitch the last piece of mail
in the trash, a glossy, oversize postcard picturing a white sand
beach and see-through turquoise water, when I noticed the
handwritten note on the back.

> *It was so nice to meet you last year. Hope you'll come
> back and see us again. December is a great time to
> visit the Gulf. Off-season is beautiful and peaceful, but
> you already know that!*

It was signed "Theresa." The postcard was addressed to
"Jodi Lockworth." The return address was the La Rue Bed-
and-Breakfast in Ocean Springs, Mississippi. I frowned at
the card.

Mississippi? Had Jodi gone to Florida *and* Mississippi in
December? Maybe I was reading too much into the few
words. I tapped the card against the counter for a second, then
picked up the phone and dialed the number listed under the
address.

A recording stated, "You've reached the La Rue Bed-and-
Breakfast. We're sorry that we can't take your call. We're taking care of our guests right now. Please leave us a message
and we'll call you back as soon as we can. Have a great day."

"Hi." I clipped the postcard to the fridge with another
magnet. "This is Ellie Avery. I got one of your postcards
today and I'd like to ask you a few questions." I figured I had
a better chance of getting a return call if Theresa thought I
was a potential customer, and who knows? We might be. That
white sand looked pretty good.

"I don't know why I bothered to clean up the rest of the
house or worried about the yard," I said to Abby as I surveyed the party. It had ended up, like most parties do, in the
kitchen. Little groups of people spilled over to the dining
room or the living room. Some people drifted onto the back

patio to get their drinks from the ice chests, but few stayed outside. Most congregated around the spread of food in the kitchen. I could have skipped planting the annuals in the flower beds.

"That's how it always is," Abby said. We were standing in the kitchen. I had Nathan perched on my hip and she had Charlie on hers. Livvy came flying through the room, dodging between the adults like she was a downhill skier clearing the gates. Five kids tailed her, trying to keep up.

I reached out a hand and stopped her, then whispered, "Why don't you show the other kids your new blocks?"

Her face, already sweaty from running, lit up. "We can build a city," she said as she sprinted down the hall.

The oven timer beeped and I asked Topaz, who'd just entered the kitchen, if she'd hold Nathan.

"Um, okay. I'm not very good with kids . . ."

"You'll do fine." She held Nathan out from her body, his legs dangling. "Just hold him close to you. Use your body to hold him up."

I pulled the cookie sheet out of the oven, transferred the mini quiches to a serving dish, and went back to get Nathan. He grabbed at Topaz's dangling metal earrings.

"Here, let me take him back."

"No, that's okay," she said as she pulled off the earrings, dropped them at the back of the countertop, then focused her attention on Nathan. "He really is a cutie."

Nathan stared, fascinated, then seized a hunk of her stripy hair. "Ouch! He's got a good grip."

"Sorry," I said, and pried his fingers off her hair, then took him back.

"Don't worry about it." She finger-combed her hair. "I don't know how you moms do it."

I'd set up some table games on the coffee table in the living room and Kyle, Nadia's husband, called out, "Hey, we need another person for our team. Who wants to play?"

I waved him off. I had too much going on being the hostess to concentrate on the game that combined four other board games into one megagame.

"Mary!" Kyle shouted to a woman standing in the entryway. Topaz's head jerked toward him.

"How about you?" Kyle called, "Come on, Mary, we need another player."

The woman in the entryway shook her head, but Topaz said, "I'll play."

Abby said, "Great party, as usual. Maybe your next business can be as a party planner."

I grimaced. "I don't think so. Too stressful for me. I keep feeling like I forgot something and worrying about every tiny detail."

Topaz's laugh rang out. She was posed with her profile turned to the group and her arms flexed out in the classic Egyptian hieroglyphic stance. Her team shouted out, "'Walk Like an Egyptian'!"

"King Tut. No, Cleopatra!"

Nadia joined us and I said, "Before I forget, I wanted to invite both of you to the Halloween Hayride. It's a big tradition for the neighborhood and it would be fun if you could come. We could order a pizza or something for dinner before."

Nadia squeezed her hands together. "Sounds wonderful! I just love hayrides, don't you? The girls will be so excited. They've never been on a hayride. I've got to tell Kyle." She hurried off.

Dorthea arrived and I went to say hello. We'd gone with the invite-the-neighbors ploy, hoping that would waylay any complaints about extra cars and noise. Nathan leaned toward her and she reached out to take him. "How's my boy?" she asked as she snuggled him close.

Above the music and chatter, I heard the phone ring and answered it.

"May I speak with Ellie Avery?"

"Speaking," I said.

"This is Theresa La Rue from La Rue Bed-and-Breakfast."

"Oh. Hold on a second." I hesitated. I didn't really want to take this call right now, but who knew how long it would be before I'd get her on the phone again? I eased into the laundry room and closed the door so I could hear better. As more people arrived, the party got louder and louder. "Thanks for calling me back."

"Sure. Did you want some specific information on the B and B?"

"Yes, that's part of the reason I called. Do you have a brochure you can send me with prices and room descriptions?"

"Of course."

I gave her my address and continued. "The other reason I called is about a postcard we received." I described it and said, "The note on the back sounded as if you'd met Jodi. Did she come to your B and B last December? She had blond hair and was a youth sports coordinator as well as a part-time reporter."

"Oh yes. The reporter doing the story on Hurricane Katrina. I remember her. She seemed like a sweet girl."

"You remember her?" I asked, surprised. There was a basket of clean towels sitting on the dryer and I pulled one out and folded it.

"Yes, she was a beautiful girl and so intelligent. She didn't stay here—that's why I can tell you about her. If she'd been a guest, I wouldn't confirm that she'd stayed here, but she just dropped in one afternoon, said she was making the rounds of the B and Bs looking for background info for a story she was writing."

"So you had a long conversation with her?"

"Well, I don't know if you'd call it a conversation. It was more like a monologue. You get me going and I can talk forever, and when the topic is Katrina, which rocked our world, let me tell you, I have plenty to say. And she wanted to hear it all."

"Was there anything in particular she was interested in?"

Theresa, who'd been so open before, shut down. "Who did you say you were, again?"

"It's kind of a long, convoluted story. Jodi lived in the house we're living in now. That's why I got your postcard. Jodi's been missing since last January. Her body was discovered a few days ago near here."

"Oh my God," Theresa breathed.

"You might have seen some news coverage about her on the cable channels."

"No, I never watch the news. Too depressing. Oh my God. I can't believe it."

"I know. It's terrible. Her family lives here and the whole town has been holding out hope that she'd turn up, but now that her body's been found, it's very bleak. I think we're all a little depressed. Of course, what we're going through is nothing like what her parents are experiencing.

"Anyway, her family knows she went to the Gulf Coast in December, to Destin. They thought she only went to Florida. And as far as I know, the investigation only checked out her activities in Florida. If she did go to your B and B . . . well, it raises some interesting questions. Like why would she go to Mississippi and why aren't there any charges on her credit cards or bank statements in Mississippi?"

"That . . . I'm shocked. She was . . ." She cleared her throat and said, "I'm speechless, which is something for me. What did you want to know?"

Before I could repeat my question, she cut me off. "You'll call the police when you hang up with me, right? Because that's exactly what I'm going to do."

"Yes, I will."

"Well, I don't remember everything, but of course, she asked about Katrina and that got me rolling. You see, we rode out the storm here. The house had been here since 1912. It survived Camille and we thought it would ride out anything. We were wrong."

"What happened?"

"The short version is that the house basically broke in half. At first, it was only rising water, and then the ocean swept through. It was a huge surge because we were so close to the beach. It ripped the house apart like it was a doll-house. You have no idea how much faith and security you put in your house. I always felt like I was safe there, but that day I saw how truly fragile everything is. I spent the rest of the storm clinging to a tree branch down the road."

"It sounds like it was awful."

"It was," she said flatly. "It was worse after the storm passed because we could see the devastation. Just founda-tions where houses had been. Clothes and blankets tossed up in trees. Scraps of people's lives scattered around like con-fetti. And that's not counting the human loss."

I flicked out another towel, folded it, and added it to my growing stack. "Were you alone?"

"Oh no. My aunt was here and we had three guests who were stranded here because of the exodus of people trying to get out of the way of Katrina. The gas stations ran out of gas or closed down and a lot of people were stuck. Vincent was a businessman on his way to Jackson and there were two women traveling to an art show. I told them they were wel-come to stay here and ride out the storm with me. Those girls were a riot. They kept us entertained in the beginning before everything went bad. We played so many games of charades and poker. They looked so much alike they could have been sisters. I kept getting them mixed up, saying the wrong name." Her tone softened. "So sad what happened."

She shifted topics and her voice picked up. "Vincent was a godsend, let me tell you. When the water destroyed the house, he caught my aunt before she was swept away. They grabbed on to a bit of wood and floated on that until they managed to climb onto the roof of a house several yards in-land. I didn't know they were alive until after the storm passed through. They had to walk back." Her tone went soft again and I almost missed what she said next. "We all made it except for one of the girls."

"The girls?" I picked up a pile of washcloths and began to fold them.

"See, there I go, trying to avoid it and it can't be avoided. I still don't like to think about it. Mary Bertram and Topaz Simoniti. I still can't believe Topaz didn't make it."

Chapter
Thirty-one

I dropped a washcloth. "But Topaz can't be . . ."

Theresa rolled on, not even aware I'd spoken. "It took three days to find her body. By then, the big refrigerated semitruck trailers had arrived to hold the bodies they'd found. That's where Mary found her. She identified the body, then left that same day on a bus taking evacuees to Georgia or Alabama, I forget which. She'd found their car a day before and was able to salvage some artwork. It was so sad. Topaz told me before the storm that she'd hired Mary to be her assistant a few weeks earlier. Apparently, she was getting so many orders that she couldn't keep up." Regret laced her tone as she went on. "I know I should have done more, but it was such a horrific time. It was like something out of a science fiction movie. We were scrounging for survival and life became basic. Where could we find water and food and stay safe?"

"What happened to Topaz?"

"It must have happened when the surge came through. She probably got knocked unconscious by a piece of debris, then drowned. It sounds awful to say this, but Mary was one of the lucky ones. At least Topaz's body was found. So many people didn't have that closure."

Questions raced through my mind. "So, did you tell Jodi about Topaz and Mary?"

"Yes. She was very interested. Took notes and everything."

I got the feeling that Theresa talked so much that most people in her life didn't pay that much attention to what she said.

I leaned against the dryer, trying to work it out. Topaz couldn't be dead. Topaz was playing a board game in my living room. But the name Mary, that was one of the names on Jodi's list.

"Are you still there?" Theresa asked.

I stood up straight. "Yes. I'm here. Just trying to process all this information. Did you keep in touch with Mary?"

"No. I haven't heard a word from her. I can't blame her. That's really all I can tell you. I told Jodi about Katrina and she left. She took down all my contact information and said she'd call if she had any follow-up questions, but I never heard from her."

"No. You wouldn't have. She disappeared a few days after arriving back here in North Dawkins. I'm going to call the sheriff's office here and give them your phone number."

I hung up and thought about everything I knew about Topaz. Not the stuff from high school, but my interactions I'd had with her here in North Dawkins. The first thing I thought of was her reaction when Kyle shouted the name "Mary."

What I knew shifted, like a kaleidoscope, and the pieces rearranged themselves into a new pattern. I realized she hadn't volunteered any information about high school. She always followed my lead when we talked about it. She hadn't remembered the Saints and Sinners quizzes or any of our classmates, like Jeremy Hoskins—that memory lapse should have tipped me off right there. No one in their right mind could forget Jeremy Hoskins. I'd never seen Topaz draw or sketch during class either.

And the name Mary. She couldn't control her instinctive reaction, turning toward the person when she heard her name called, her real name. The first time I'd seen her at the Base Exchange it had been the name Topaz Simoniti that I'd recognized, and when I saw her I'd accepted her as Topaz because that was who I was expecting to see. Her coloring and body type were close enough that I didn't question my assumption. If I'd seen her face first, would I have assumed it was her?

I glanced down, surprised to see I'd folded all the towels on autopilot. I stacked them in the basket, thinking that Jodi had written a profile about Topaz and then she'd written down the story idea about Hurricane Katrina evacuees who'd been relocated to middle Georgia. Had Topaz said something in the interview that made Jodi curious about her or her past?

I ran through what I knew and it made sense. Theresa said Topaz and Mary had a similar appearance. Everything was in disarray after Katrina. All their documentation was gone. What was there to prevent Mary from switching places with Topaz? If she identified the body as Mary and relocated with other evacuees, there was no one to question her identity. She even had some of Topaz's artwork to establish herself in a ready-made career. The "Topaz" I'd met never went to the Gulf Coast for art shows and never went back home to Texas, a smart move if you didn't want to run into anyone who'd known the real Topaz.

Jodi had to have figured this out, too. Why hadn't she exposed Topaz? Had she confronted her, giving her the option to turn herself in, and laid the groundwork for her own murder? Where were Jodi's notes of her interview with Theresa? And why did Mary want to become Topaz in the first place? There were too many questions, but I knew I couldn't figure them out standing in my laundry room.

I opened the door and pulled out the phone book, then headed back to the laundry room. It was the last place someone expected to find the hostess and I might get a few more minutes of quiet to make my call to Detective Waraday. Lord knew, I was going to need all my wits about me to attempt to explain this turn of events to him.

I ran into Dorthea in the kitchen and stopped abruptly. "Dorthea," I said, and drew her away from the crowd. "When you saw Jodi the night she disappeared, that Friday, what *exactly* did you see?"

She frowned at the abruptness of my question and shifted Nathan higher in her arms. "Well, like I said, I saw her, working at her desk."

"Did she wave or see you?"

"Oh no. Her back was to me. I could tell it was her. She still had on her baseball cap that she'd been wearing earlier."

"So you saw someone in her office. A woman in a baseball cap."

"Yes." Dorthea frowned. "Are you feeling all right?"

"I'm fine," I said. "Back in a minute." I shut the laundry room door and leaned against it.

I flipped through the pages until I found the number for the sheriff's office. I dialed and was surprised that when I asked for Detective Waraday, I was put through and he answered after one ring.

"Ah—Detective Waraday. Sorry, I didn't expect you to answer. Friday night and all."

"Paperwork."

I took a deep breath and said, "I've just talked to a woman named Theresa La Rue who lives in Ocean Springs, Mississippi. She says Jodi interviewed her in December for a story she was doing on Hurricane Katrina."

"Jodi was in Destin, Florida, not Mississippi."

"Why couldn't she have driven over to Mississippi? She got gas in Pensacola, right? I saw that charge on her credit card. Wouldn't that have been a rather circuitous way to get back to North Dawkins when she could have just driven straight north and caught I-10 in only a few miles? Why would she drive out of her way?"

"Maybe she got lost. Or maybe she simply went for a drive. Don't complicate things."

"I'm afraid this is going to get more complicated." I summarized what Theresa had told me and the discrepancies I was beginning to think weren't coincidences, including Topaz's reaction to hearing the name "Mary" called out at the party.

"So you think this Mary . . . Bertram is impersonating Topaz? That Topaz is the one who died during the hurricane?"

"Yes. It all works out. Jodi found out about Topaz and either Jodi tried to give Topaz, well, the woman we know as Topaz, a chance to come clean on her deception, or somehow Topaz found out what Jodi knew and killed her during her nightly run on the gravel path."

My stomach churned as I pictured what probably happened. "It's a fairly isolated area. She could have parked her car somewhere in the neighborhood and walked in. She would have had to bring the shovel and the tarp, but once she'd hit Jodi"—I swallowed and forced myself to go on— "she must have dragged her body down the cleared path that branched off the main one. She took Jodi's cap and went back to her house through the backyard. I know it's possible because I walked it myself not long ago. There's a back gate to our property. She could get in and out without anyone seeing her.

"She went to Jodi's office and found her notes on the interview with Theresa and then she sent the e-mail saying she was going out of town. That's when Dorthea saw Topaz and assumed it was Jodi since she had on the same hat."

"Hmmm . . . possible, but what about the purchase at the Quick Mart later that night?"

Okay. He had a point. That didn't make sense . . . unless . . . "That had to have been Topaz, too. What better way to throw everyone off? First she confused the time of Jodi's disappearance with her appearance in the house and her e-mail. Then she took a credit card—there would have been one in the house, I doubt Jodi took those on her run—and went to the Quick Mart on the other side of town, where she made the charges and then returned the credit card later that night, using the back gate again so that no one saw her.

"Then earlier this month when the search was about to shift back to Magnolia Estates, she planted the purchases she'd made in the field to draw attention away from the neighborhood. Of course, she had no way of knowing Scott was about to have his lot cleared. That was the one variable she couldn't control."

"So she saved the water bottles and the PowerBar all this time?"

"I guess so. Why not? No one suspected her at all. She only had the barest connection with Jodi. Why wouldn't she keep the purchases in case she needed them later? She's probably got the hat and map stowed away somewhere else, too."

I could barely make out Waraday's mumble, but it sounded like he said, "Along with her purse and keys, too." Then louder, "Hold on." There was a long silence and I could hear drawers slamming; then he reluctantly said, "All right, I've got Jodi's notes here. I'm going to read through them again and check out that name."

He took down Theresa's contact information and hung up. I'd done what I could. Now all I had to do was not stare at "Topaz" and get through the rest of the party.

I opened the door and it was like surfacing from underwater. Conversation, laughter, and music washed over me. Someone had turned up the music. I blinked as four kids zipped past me. More people had arrived and the room was packed. I checked on Dorthea and Nathan. They were fine. Nathan was enthralled with her long beaded necklace, which she'd given him to play with. I managed to glance at "Topaz," subtly, I hoped. She was still in the group gathered around the game board. I had a hard time thinking of her as Mary. In fact it was probably better to keep thinking of her as Topaz so I didn't give anything away.

"Come on, Nathan, let's get you some food," I said, and carried him to his high chair. I cut up food for him into bite-size portions and had a little of the turkey myself, since Mitch had been right—it really was the best turkey I'd ever had. The phone rang and I snatched it up.

"Mrs. Avery?"

I recognized Detective Waraday's voice. There was a tension in his tone that hadn't been there before.

"Is she still at your house?"

"Topaz?" I shot a quick glance at the game group. "Yes." She rolled the dice with flair.

"And there are still other people there?"

"Yes, probably between thirty and forty, right now."

"Stay put. Don't do anything. I'm on my way with backup."

"Did you find out—"

He interrupted me. "A Mary Bertram was reported among the dead after Katrina. Prior to that, she was last seen leaving the apartment she shared with her boyfriend in Lubbock, Texas. She was wanted for his murder. He was found the week after she disappeared when neighbors complained about the smell coming from the apartment. He'd died from blunt trauma to the back of the head."

"Just like Jodi," I whispered.

He went on. "Mary Bertram was arrested three years ago during a domestic dispute at the same location. She does have similar facial characteristics."

I swallowed and felt light-headed. It was Topaz. No, actually, it was Mary who'd killed Jodi. She'd been here all along, nudging the investigation just enough in one direction or another to keep it away from her. So that meant Topaz really was dead. I felt a coldness settle over me. How awful to die alone, but then it seemed worse somehow that no one knew she was dead. Not even her family.

"Mrs. Avery? Ellie!" Waraday said sharply. "Are you still there?"

"Yes," I said faintly and glanced at the group playing the game. Topaz wasn't there. "I don't see her. She was there just a minute ago."

"Don't do anything. Do you hear me? *Do not* look for her. *Don't do anything.*"

"I won't." My feet were practically bolted to the floor. I wouldn't have been able to do anything, even if I'd wanted to.

"Sit tight. It'll take me about fifteen minutes to get there." He hung up and I stood there a moment, dazed.

I replaced the phone and absentmindedly began cleaning up, clearing away a few used plates and cups that had been left on the countertop. I picked up the last plate and saw Topaz's favorite earrings. They were still there on the counter where she'd left them after she took them off to keep Nathan from pulling them out of her ears. The bits of metal, keys, were suspended on several hoops to make quirky chandelier earrings.

They looked different splayed out on the counter, each metal piece separate and distinct. There were tiny keys on the top that looked like the key I'd once had that opened a locked diary. The lower tier had heavier, larger keys. I touched one, running my finger down the rough edge. The color, faded gold, and the small three-triangle cutaway at the top were familiar. It looked like the old key to my front door.

I went over to the key rack beside the garage door and angled out the house key we'd used before we had the locks changed. It was a shinier gold, but it was the same shape. I ran my finger down the rough edge. Four small grooves, one deep, then one more small groove.

I went back into the kitchen and counted the grooves in the key on the earring. Four small, one deep, then one small.

I swallowed, feeling numb. It had been Topaz who'd cut the

gas line and keyed my car, too, then stolen it and set fire to it. And she'd probably called the reporters with the anonymous tip about Jodi coming home before Nita's birthday, too. It had kept the reporters busy and sidelined me.

Topaz appeared at my left shoulder and I jerked like I'd had an electric shock. "Ellie, can I borrow your phone? My cell phone is dead. Oh, my earrings! I can't forget these." She hooked them into her ears and the keys fell together, the other keys covering the larger house key.

I'm sure I had that deer-in-the-headlights expression, but I managed to croak out, "No, that's fine. Go ahead." I handed her the phone. She smiled a bit uncertainly at me, then dialed and put the phone to her ear. She wandered over to the refrigerator. After a few seconds, she hung up and handed the phone back. "I have to go. I'm meeting a friend in Atlanta later tonight, so I have to get on the road. Thanks for inviting me."

"Okay," I said, feeling helpless as she backed up a few steps, then turned and merged into the press of people. I caught a glimpse of the back of her head as she disappeared out the front door.

I scrolled through the list of previously called numbers and selected Waraday's number. I interrupted his greeting. "She just left."

"Stay there. Do not follow her."

"Are you kidding? I'm not going anywhere. I think she's got the old key to our front door in her earrings."

I waited for his question about that weird statement, but the line was dead. He'd hung up. I replaced the phone and realized Nathan was fussing. He'd finished with his food and wanted down. I automatically wiped his hands and face. Dorthea walked up, arms extended out to him. He strained toward his new buddy and I gratefully handed him off to Dorthea since I was so preoccupied. I chatted with various people. I have no idea what we talked about.

I ran into Mitch in the kitchen. Cradling a box of beer and a package of water bottles in his arms, he was on his way to the backyard to restock the ice chests, but he stopped short when he saw me.

"What's wrong?"

Where to start? "Too much to tell you right now."

He frowned. "Look, the party's only going to last a couple more hours and then we'll clean up everything."

Normally, I would be freaking about some minor party detail, but tonight those worries had been eclipsed.

"No, it's not the party. It's about Jodi—"

I broke off as Mitch's squadron commander appeared beside him and said, "We've got to head out. Thanks for inviting us."

"Glad you dropped in. I'll get your coats," Mitch said, glancing down at the drinks in his arms.

"Here, I'll take them," I said. I said good-bye to them and went through the screened-in porch to the back patio. The sun had set and the floodlights were the only pool of light in the blackness. It was chilly and extremely quiet outside, except for two couples huddled on the lawn furniture. I flipped open the first ice chest and dumped the beer in.

Someone in the group on the patio said, "Well, I don't know about you, but I'm going to get more of that turkey."

Another person asked, "So, who came up with the idea of frying a turkey in a vat of boiling oil? It sounds like something out of a torture chamber."

Behind me, the first person said, "Are you kidding? This is the South. We deep-fry veggies here, so anything's game. In fact, I'm surprised someone didn't think of it sooner." Their voices faded as the screen closed.

I grabbed the water bottles. As I lunged to the right to put them in the other ice chest, something whooshed past my shoulder.

I twisted around and saw Topaz. She held something in her hands, her grip cinched low on one end.

An Everything In Its Place Tip for an Organized Party

In case of disaster, have on hand
  • Paper towels.
  • Club soda.
  • Extra garbage bags.
  • Extra grill lighter.
  • Fire extinguisher.
  • Also, if your party is outdoors, have a contingency plan to move everything indoors in case of bad weather.

Chapter
Thirty-two

"Topaz . . . what are you doing?"

She positioned herself, arms bent at the elbows, like a batter getting ready to take a swing at a fastball. It was too dark to see what she held, but it was long and heavy, that much I could tell.

Then she swung.

At my head. I shifted to one side and ducked lower. There wasn't that much room to go down because I was already crouching near the ground.

She hit the open ice chest. Icy water and bottles exploded over us.

I scrambled backward and put the row of ice chests between us. "Don't pretend you don't know what's going on here. I saw the postcard on your refrigerator and the list of incoming calls on your phone. You know."

Okay, I guess playing dumb—never high on my list of things to do—was out. My gaze skittered between that heavy-duty stick that she now held over one shoulder and the brightly lit windows behind her. The party rolled on, groups of people moving from room to room. I heard a muted burst of laughter. Chances were that someone would come outside soon. After all, the beer was out here. I wished I'd opened some windows, but they were closed and the volume of the music and conversation would drown out any screams from me.

There was the back gate. I could try and make a run for it, but I nixed that plan before it was fully formed. There was no way I was turning my back on her, especially when she was pummeling things in her path.

I inched to the left, to get a better angle on the door, and said, "Waraday knows that Topaz is really dead and he knows that Jodi discovered you'd taken Topaz's identity. Even if you get rid of me, you're still busted. You'd be better off turning yourself in. Own up to your mistake and all that."

"You're almost as naïve as Topaz was." Her face looked harsher than I remembered. Her eyes were narrower and her jaw was clenched. How could I have ever thought she was Topaz? It was like a mask had been removed and I could see the anger and hate that had been just below the surface.

"You mean you killed her, too?" I asked, my voice screeching.

"No, I did not kill Topaz." She sounded almost offended. "She died in the storm. Drowned. I was going to tell them who she was . . ." Her words slowed down and even though she gazed at me, I knew she wasn't seeing me. "When I saw her lying there . . . it was hard enough to recognize her. The idea popped into my head. *Be her. Take her life.*" Her mental focus snapped back and her gaze bored into me. "It wasn't like it made a difference. She hadn't been in touch with her family for years. They probably thought she was dead anyway. And we looked alike, people had commented on it. It was like an exchange. They were so overwhelmed with bodies it wasn't like they were going to do an in-depth investigation. I gave them my name and walked out of there a new woman."

"So if you didn't kill her, why did you say she was naïve?"

Topaz laughed. "Because she *believed* me when I said my

boyfriend had beat me up and I needed to get out of Lubbock."

"But she hired you as her assistant." I'd finally figured out
what she had in her hands. It was a tire iron. She wiggled it
and made a dismissive face. "Not at first. She just told me to
hop in her car, that I could go as far as Houston with her.
That was where she was heading that day. I stuck with her.
Made myself useful. It didn't take her long to figure out she
could make more money with me than without me."

She raised her arms and sized up the distance between us.
"You really should reconsider. Turning yourself in is the
best way to go. Like I said, Waraday knows the whole story."

"Waraday's never going to see me again. You either, for
that matter. You're going to disappear, just like Jodi." She
took a step toward me and tightened her grip on the heavy
bar. "The cable channels will eat it up, won't they? Two
women disappear after living in the same house. Perhaps it's
haunted or cursed. There's a huge range of story lines there."

"That won't happen. Waraday knows about you, and I reported the cut gas line and my stolen car. He'll connect you
with those things."

She laughed. "Sorry, but you don't leave much evidence
when you hot-wire a car and then *burn* it."

"He'll find something. Can't you see it's all unraveling?"
I said, glancing at the windows. I didn't think I could keep
her talking much longer. Weren't any of those throngs of
people inside thirsty?

She lunged. I kicked one of the ice chests with all my
strength. Water gushed over the patio and Topaz, reflexively,
jumped back.

I ran for the back door, splashing through the water, and
praying I didn't slip. I glanced over my shoulder and saw
Topaz sprinting away from me, crossing the patio diagonally. She must have decided to make a run for it and was
heading for the gate on the side of the yard. I slowed down to

navigate through the lawn furniture we'd scattered around the patio and saw a movement at the far corner of the patio where Topaz had been heading. She stood, feet planted squarely, as she took a swing at the turkey fryer. The metal clanged when the tire iron made contact and oil raced across the patio.

I froze for a second. A cascade of hot oil encircled the steps to the screened-in porch and door. It was too far to jump. I knew I couldn't clear the distance from where I stood to the bottom step.

I backed up a step, then stopped. I still didn't want to turn my back on her. I didn't know if I could outrun her and I knew I'd have to slow down when I got to the fence anyway. That wasn't an option, but standing here wasn't an option either because the patio was designed to slope slightly away from the house so rainwater would run away from the foundation. The oil seeped toward me.

I jumped on one of Abby's lawn chairs and the hot oil slid beneath it. Steam hissed as it met the cold water.

I shifted my feet on the chair to make sure I was balanced. I took a deep breath and—odd as it sounds—felt myself relax a little. My heartbeat slowed down from hammering to merely thumping. The upside to being surrounded by hot oil was that Topaz wasn't coming after me here. I was safe. Sort of. "So we're just going to wait it out? This will be kind of hard to explain to Waraday when he arrives," I said as I looked at the sheet of oil covering the patio.

She smiled. "No, we're not going to wait it out." She walked over to the grill and picked up the lighter that Mitch kept there. She tightened her finger on the trigger and a golden flame appeared at the end.

My heartbeat jolted back into overdrive.

She lowered her hand and the flame hovered inches above the oil.

My breath snagged in my throat. I had to do something. I

looked around frantically. I grabbed a lawn chair beside me and threw it as hard as I could in her direction. She dodged it easily.

Stupid. My aim was terrible. I threw like a girl. I changed my strategy. I grabbed another chair and tossed it at the screened-in porch. A metallic clang rang out as it hit the screen door.

"No one will hear that over the music."

She was laughing at me. Anger threaded through my fear and I picked up the small plastic-topped end table and threw it at her. Either my aim or my luck was better. She skittered backward, then yelped as it hit her hand. She must have dropped the lighter, because she cursed and patted the grass around her feet.

I shifted my feet nervously. I was running out of ammunition. There was only one more chair within reach. I balanced over the oil, dragged it to me, then heaved it at the porch. It ripped through the screen and slammed against one of the living room windows.

Topaz stood. She'd found the lighter and I didn't know what I was going to do.

"Mary Bertram!" She flinched at the sound of the commanding male voice behind her.

The back door banged open. People from the party rushed onto the screened-in porch. A tall figure leapt down the porch steps, jumped from the bottom step over the oil, and flattened Topaz with a flying tackle.

Suddenly it seemed as if people were everywhere. "Stay clear of the concrete," a voice barked, and this time I recognized it as Waraday. "There's hot oil on it." The person who'd taken down Topaz stood up. I blinked. It was Mitch. He had a huge grass stain on his left shoulder. He gingerly flexed his arm as he looked at me with a bit of a grin on his face.

He stepped away as Waraday handcuffed Topaz. Mitch shoved the few remaining chairs together and made a sort of bridge to get to me. He gathered me into a hug, then pulled back. "Why was Topaz trying to set fire to our patio with you in the middle of it?"

"Long story. Let's get out of here," I said. I'd spent enough time on my perch. I wanted down. Mitch took my hand and as we picked our way carefully back across the chairs I said, "She's not really Topaz." I swallowed. My throat felt bristly. "Topaz is dead. That woman is Mary Bertram. She killed Jodi because Jodi found out she wasn't who she said she was."

"And I suppose you figured it out?"

I smiled. "Yes. All the pieces sort of fell together tonight. That's what I was going to tell you in the kitchen. I didn't realize she was out here. I was never so glad to see you, but you scared me to death when you did that flying tackle thing."

Mitch rotated his shoulder. "Yeah. I haven't done that since college. I think I'm going to be sore tomorrow. I'm getting old."

People on the porch were shouting questions and Waraday's deputies in the yard were shouting back. Sirens blared from the front yard. "Sorry to ruin the party. At least your squadron commander left before all this happened," I said, surveying the patio. The oil and water were swirling together, making weird patterns around the chairs and ice chests.

"Are you kidding? You were worried about hosting a good party, right?" Mitch rested his forehead against mine. "This will be the most talked about party in the history of the squadron, the one where I rescued you from the woman who wanted to burn you up. No one's ever going to top that. And you were worried about entertainment."

Abby perched on one of the bar stools. She pushed the bowl of candy away. "Keep that over there. I've already eaten enough of that tonight."

I could hear the kids outside on the front lawn. Nadia was with them, taking pictures of Halloween costumes, while Mitch, Jeff, and Kyle were positioning hay bales on the trailer for the hayride.

I stacked the pizza boxes near the trash can, then went to the sink. "Let me get these dishes out of the way before we leave," I said, rinsing sippy cups and small plastic utensils.

Abby hopped up. "Here, I'll help."

"I've got it. Almost done, in fact." I stacked the dishes in the dishwasher. "It's funny, but I haven't minded doing dishes at all, lately. It used to seem so mundane, but now I'm glad to have some normalcy, even boredom, in my life."

"I can see why, after almost being toasted by a turkey fryer." Abby sat back down and propped her chin on her hand. "You know what I don't understand? Why did Topaz—or what's her real name?"

"Mary." I closed the dishwasher and dried my hands on a towel.

"Why did Mary make Jodi's keys into earrings? That's so . . . bizarre."

"I know, but I guess she figured hiding them in plain sight was the safest thing to do. But what's even weirder is that she kept Jodi's purse and hat. I talked to Colleen after the funeral earlier this week. She said when Mary's house was searched they found those things along with the map of Florida stashed in a closet. I guess she kept them so she could plant them later like she did with the water and energy bar."

"Did you go to the funeral?" Abby asked.

I nodded. "It was sad, but it seemed like there was a feeling of relief, too. No media either, which was another reprieve for Nita and Gerald. And me. I'm so glad that Chelsea O'Mara wasn't there. I was afraid she'd be there to fire questions at me about Jodi's notebook."

"She's moved on. I saw her reporting yesterday about whether or not some movie star has a baby bump."

"Can you imagine how awful that lifestyle would be? Having the media monitor your weight and if you gained five or ten pounds, they'd think you might be pregnant?"

"Horrible," Abby said as she leaned over and plucked a chocolate Kiss out of the bowl. "There are some benefits to being a regular old nobody."

"True." I unwrapped another Kiss and popped it in my mouth.

"Where did you find Jodi's notebook?"

"Over here," I said, and I pointed to the drawers.

Abby smoothed out her square of foil. "Why did she hide just the one notebook?" she asked. "If she had all the information on Topaz and Mary, why didn't she put that in the notebook?"

I leaned on the counter and shook my head. "I don't know. Maybe she was going to, but didn't get it hidden before she was attacked? I don't think we'll ever know for sure. When Mary came back here that night, I think she did a thorough search of Jodi's office and took anything related to her and Topaz."

"It's a good thing Jodi managed to hide the one notebook, then. Otherwise . . ."

"I know."

Livvy burst in the front door. "Dad says we're almost ready."

I turned on the dishwasher and we went outside. "It's a hayride. It's a hayride. It's a hayride." Livvy, usually so reserved and thoughtful about everything, was giddy with delight, practically jumping up and down. Compared to the other kids, she was relatively calm. They were running in circles at full speed on our lawn. We had two fairy princesses, a butterfly, a cheerleader, Superman, and one Johnny Depp–inspired pirate who kept losing his dreadlocks.

"She looks so cute. So original," Abby said from beside me, her gaze on Livvy.

I smiled. "I know. I wanted her to dress up in something more . . . feminine." I'd suggested a princess, a ballerina, and a mermaid, but no. She wanted to be David, as in David and Goliath. When I'd asked why she'd picked that costume, she'd said, "Because Dad can be Goliath," like it was the most obvious thing in the world.

So Livvy was outfitted in one of Mitch's white shirts that went down to her knees. I'd wrapped a leather belt around her waist three times and she had a plastic toy slingshot in one hand and a bag of marbles in the other. "I think the slingshot was the main reason she picked that costume."

So far, Mitch had managed to put off dressing up like Goliath. I thought he was counting on candy wiping the idea out of Livvy's mind, but I knew she wouldn't forget. I was looking forward to the show.

To one side of our yard, Nadia crouched low as she photographed Nathan in his cow costume. She shifted and focused on her girls. Ribbons streamed out behind her daughters—they were the fairy princesses in shades of pink and purple.

I saw Nita at the wheel of her gold car slowly pull away from the curb in front of Dorthea's house. She saw me and waved. Dorthea stood with her hand braced on the mailbox, watching the car creep carefully around the hayride trailer, then signal at the end of the block.

I said to Abby, "Do you mind watching Livvy and Nathan for a second? I want to run over and ask Dorthea how Nita's doing."

"Sure, go ahead," Abby said, and I hurried across the street.

"You have quite a crowd over there," Dorthea said, smiling as she watched the kids.

"Yes. They're a bit hyper right now."

"Oh, they're fine. Let 'em run all they want."

"I saw Nita leaving. How's she doing?"

Dorthea gazed up the street and shook her head. "How

well can you be after burying your only daughter just a few days ago?"

I nodded. There was only one answer for that. Dorthea turned and I walked with her as she slowly crossed her lawn, climbed the steps to the porch, and took a seat on her glider. She said, "Nita drops in sometimes. I know she walks that gravel path quite a bit. Seems to help her."

"I'm glad you're there for her."

Dorthea pulled a bucket of candy into place beside her and said, "Nita and Gerald have plenty of friends. We'll keep an eye on them. Colleen checks in on them every few days."

I took a seat beside her on the glider. "That's good. Colleen is handling it okay, too?" I asked. Of everyone, she'd been the one person who'd been most adamant in refusing to even consider the possibility that Jodi might not come back.

"Seems to be. I think we all knew, deep down, that the chances of her being alive were pretty slim."

We were silent for a moment and watched the kids flitter across the lawn. Finally, Dorthea said, "Nita tells me Detective Waraday and Colleen are on the verge of being 'an item.'"

"Really?" I asked, surprised.

"Yes, seems they both go to the same Starbucks for their morning coffee. They kept running into each other and chatting. Nita says now they've added lunches to their morning coffee."

"I guess that puts Scott out of the picture."

"Yes. He's lucky to still have his job."

"STAND's board didn't fire him?" I asked, surprised.

"No. Took him to task, but told him they'd give him another opportunity since he has been a hard worker. I hope he straightens up and flies right, as my daddy used to say."

"I hope so. He seems like a nice enough guy, but he made some terrible choices."

"Okay, let's load up," Mitch shouted, and the kids scrambled onto the bales of hay. Mitch settled down beside Livvy and encircled her with his arm to make sure she stayed in the trailer. I said good-bye to Dorthea, then picked up Nathan and settled against the prickly hay beside Mitch.

There was a lurch, and then we were off, bumping along. Mitch shifted and encircled my shoulders with his other arm. Nadia snapped a picture of us at that moment.

Two days later, I wiped my hand over the glass that enclosed that photograph. Nadia had e-mailed it to me after the hayride. It was my favorite picture of us. We weren't posed, smiling stiffly for the camera like a studio portrait. We were looking at each other, relaxed and smiling, a family.

I positioned the frame on the bookshelves in the living room. Our own little circle of family—it still amazed me. Every once in a while when I managed to slow down and look past the minutiae of the everyday routine, I realized how blessed I was. I had a husband who loved me and two beautiful, healthy kids.

Mitch came in from the garage, carrying an empty box. "Ellie, do we have any more black garbage bags?" He was bagging leaves and the kids were "helping."

"There's more on the bottom shelf by the door."

He noticed the picture and said, "Nice."

"I know." I smiled. "I just have one more thing to do," I said as I pushed the chairs back under the dining room table. I put the low glass bowl filled with candy corn in the center. "Okay. That's it. We're completely finished straightening up after all the parties. Finally!" I'll be the first to admit that I get antsy after a party and want to get everything put away and back where it belongs. It had taken over a week to clean up. The backyard alone had taken several days. The concrete patio was now a shade darker, a result of the dousing with the oil, but it was very clean and Mitch had replaced the broken screen.

I walked over and wrapped my arm around his waist. "So how's it going out there?"

"Not getting a thing done, but they're having a ton of fun." He draped his arm across my shoulders as we walked back to the garage. "So, the house is back to normal? Everything's good?"

"Yep, everything's good. Now, if I could just find a couple of hours to work on the box room . . ."

An Everything In Its Place Tip for an Organized Party

Little extras.
It's those small extra touches that show your thoughtfulness and also let the party roll on without a hitch. Take the time to put fresh towels in your guest bathroom. Light some candles. If you're entertaining outdoors, make sure you have extra bug repellent and sunscreen. If you're hosting a children's birthday party, have door prizes for the winners of the games. Make place cards for a formal dinner. Don't forget to put on the music. Take pictures, then share them with your guests after the party.

Turn the page for a sneak preview
of Sara Rosett's new Ellie Avery mystery,
MINT JULEPS, MAYHEM, AND MURDER,
available in hardcover from Kensington
in April 2010!

Chapter
One

I flinched as a rifle shot fractured the air.

"Good lord, what was that?" Mitch's aunt jumped and nearly dropped the slice of peach pie she was transferring to a plate.

"Hunters," I explained, gesturing to the woods behind our backyard. "The neighborhood backs up to a state wildlife area. We hear them quite a bit, especially since deer season opened early this year." I kept my voice casual, but that shot had been awfully close, much louder than usual. I tensed, waiting for more shots, but the only sounds I heard were the low murmurings of voices punctuated with an occasional laugh from the fifty people gathered in our backyard for the annual Avery Family Reunion.

"Oh dear, I'd love a slice of that chocolate cake, too, but I really shouldn't," Mitch's aunt said as she surveyed the spread on the dessert table. Mitch's family was from a small town outside of Montgomery, Alabama, and they were a true southern family—they overflowed with charm and friendliness and they knew how to *cook*. None of the new-fangled sugar substitutes, low-calorie, or low-fat recipes for them. *The more butter and sugar, the better*, seemed to be the family motto, which I certainly couldn't argue with, since I have an affinity for sweets myself, particularly chocolate. "Here, I'll split a piece with you," I said, trying to cover for the fact that I wasn't sure if this was Aunt Christine or Aunt Claudia. Or maybe . . . Aunt Claudine? No, that wasn't right. As she cut a slice in half, I caught Mitch's gaze and mouthed the words, "Aunt Christine?"

He gave me the thumbs up, broke away from the men by the grill, and headed across the yard toward us. "Hi, Aunt Christine," Mitch said as he gave her a peck on the cheek, then ran his arm around my shoulders to give me a quick hug. "How's Grandpa Franklin doing in this humidity?" he asked her. "Would he be more comfortable inside?"

"I'm sure he would be, but he'd never admit it. He refuses to let anything slow him down. I do try to keep him hydrated," she said, holding up a bottled water dripping with condensation. "I'd better get back to him."

We watched her roly-poly figure waddle away. "She takes good care of your grandfather," I said. "She's never been married?"

"Nope, but I hear she's got a boyfriend. Aunt Nanette says the Walgreens pharmacist is a real hottie for a sixty-year-old and keeps asking Aunt Christine to dinner. They're both metal detector enthusiasts. They met at a treasure hunt."

"You have the most interesting family," I said.

Mitch glanced at me questioningly, and I said, "Don't get defensive. I've got a few quirky types in my family tree, too. I'm the one with the aunt who recycles stray paper clips and used staples. Last time I visited, she'd collected enough to fill a large coffee can. She also makes masks from dryer lint. Cake?"

He shook his head and I devoured the last bites of the rich chocolate and creamy icing. Mitch's healthy eating habits were annoying at times, but right now I was glad to finish off the cake myself. "You know, a few bites won't hurt you."

"I've learned never to come between you and chocolate," he said, the skin around his dark eyes crinkling as he smiled.

I licked the last trace of crumbs from the fork. "Wise

man. Now, since I'm fortified with chocolate, I need a re-fresher on that crash course you gave me on your relatives." The avalanche of Avery relatives had begun at breakfast this morning and I still hadn't sorted out all the names and faces. Mitch's military assignments had kept me from getting to know the whole Avery clan. I nodded to the picnic tables cov-ered with red-and-white checked cloths where the aunts had gathered at the back of the yard in the shade of the loblolly pines. "Aunt Nanette is the one with the Afghan hound at her feet, right?"

"Yes. If you run out of things to talk about, ask about her new Mini Cooper."

"Really? I saw the black one with the British flag on it in the driveway, but I figured it belonged to one of your cousins. She seems more like a Cadillac type."

"Nope. She's an Anglophile who's into sporty cars. And don't forget to pet Queen," Mitch said. "If Queen likes you, Aunt Nanette will, too."

"Oh, who's that—the man with the stubble and the phoenix tattoo on his forearm? I couldn't figure him out."

"None of us can. That's my Uncle Bud. You'd never guess that he's one of the most successful real-estate brokers in Al-abama, would you? He still lives in the double-wide he's lived in for the last twenty years. Aunt Nanette says he doesn't just pinch pennies, he makes them beg for mercy." Mitch lowered his voice and leaned closer to me. "Don't tell anyone, but I know he sponsors one of the baseball teams in Smarr. No one else in the family knows. If it got out, it would ruin his reputation as a miser."

One of the young cousins threw open the screen door from the house and galloped across the lawn toward Mitch, her pigtails flying and our ringing cordless phone clutched in her hand. The second before the door eased closed, Rex, our Rottweiler, who has a seriously scary bark but a sweet dispo-sition, slipped outside. I'd figured keeping him inside during the reunion was a good idea. It was crazy enough in the backyard without him, but he took off, running in huge, looping circles. Queen hesitated for a second, then shot after him. I glanced at Mitch and he shrugged. "We might as well let them wear themselves out. No way we're going to catch them now."

"Thanks, Madison," Mitch said as he took the phone. He listened, then his posture changed from normal and relaxed to taut. He tilted the phone away from his face. "It's Abby."

I could tell from his face that something was wrong. My heart seemed to tumble in my chest, then drop sharply. Abby was another military spouse and my best friend. My thoughts flittered from her to her husband, Jeff, then to their son Charlie. "What is it?" I asked.

Mitch put his hand on my shoulder. "She's fine. They're all fine. It's Colonel Pershall. He's at the E.R."

"Colonel Pershall? Your squadron commander?" His words didn't make sense. Colonel Lewis Pershall couldn't be more than forty. He was a towering giant of a man. He was a sturdy, broad-shouldered black man with a barrel chest and, oddly, one of the softest-spoken people I knew. Mitch said Colonel Pershall never raised his voice at the squadron. He didn't need to. Mitch enjoyed working for him more than anyone else he'd ever worked for.

"Okay, let us know if you need anything. All right. Here's Ellie." He handed me the phone.

Abby's shaky voice came over the line. "Oh, Ellie. It's so terrible and I'm sorry to call you during the reunion. I completely forgot about it."

"Don't worry about that. What's going on?" I asked.

"It's touch and go right now," Abby said. "Someone tried to strangle him, Ellie. That sounds strange to say out loud, but that's what they said happened. He'd finished a round of golf. Another golfer found him unconscious in the parking lot beside his car."

I wasn't sure if I'd heard correctly. I turned away from the chatter and laughter. "Did you say strangled?" I asked as I pressed the phone closer to my ear.

"Yes. I know, I can't take it in either, but that's what the doctors are talking about—oxygen deprivation and jugular veins and lots of other words I don't understand, but it's serious."

"How's Denise?"

"Shocked. She's not saying anything. Just sitting there. They come and talk to her and she nods, but that's about it."

"That's not like her at all," I said, thinking of the woman who hadn't been afraid to shake things up at the squadron coffees by daring to ask what the spouses wanted out of their spouse club. The thought that we didn't have to continue to meet once a month and organize fundraisers nearly caused a revolt from some spouses. Sometimes traditions die hard.

"I know," Abby said miserably. "Jeff and I were at the park and we saw the security police pull up to their house." Abby lived in base housing at Taylor Air Force Base and we'd spent several afternoons this summer at that little park situated in base housing, watching Livvy, Nathan, and Charlie clamber up and down the slides. "I went over to check on Denise. The only way I can think to describe her is shell-shocked. She was in a daze. I had to get her purse for her before she left for the hospital. It was like leading Charlie around. Jeff took Charlie home and I came up here to be with her. I'm rambling, aren't I? I think I might be in shock, too."

"No, it's okay. You're at the North Dawkins Medical Center?" I asked. North Dawkins was the city located outside Taylor's gates.

"Right, no E.R. on the base anymore, remember? I don't know if he'll be moved up to Atlanta or not. I'm going to stay until Denise's family gets here."

"We can get away for a while later tonight and come by. Do you need anything?" I asked.

"No. Denise and Lewis are the only ones who need anything. They need prayer. The outlook isn't good. They're not giving Denise much hope."

We said good-bye and I turned back to look around the yard, amazed that people still chatted, the sun still beat down. A blue jay called sharply from the trees above me, then swooped away. Nothing had changed. At least, not for us. I prayed a quick, rather incoherent prayer for Denise and Lewis and took a step toward the house, feeling like I should do something.

I stopped. There was nothing else I could do. Mitch touched my shoulder again. "Are you okay?" he asked, his face concerned.

"Yes. No. Oh, I'm okay, but poor Denise and Colonel Pershall." I couldn't even imagine what Denise was going through. "It's just . . . news like that . . . it's almost unbelievable. I mean, this is North Dawkins, Georgia. People don't get attacked and . . . and *strangled* in North Dawkins. And at a golf course? Was he on base, do you think?" There was a nice course on base.

He shrugged. "I don't know. He liked to play eighteen holes on Saturday and for the last few weeks he'd been playing there. He was determined to birdie sixteen, called it his nemesis, but I suppose he could have been at one of the other neighborhood courses around here." We didn't live in a golf course neighborhood, but there were a few of those scattered around the area.

Mitch had barely finished his sentence when someone slapped him on the shoulder, nearly knocking him over. "Uncle Kenny! How are you?" Mitch asked, and I could see him slip into host-mode, despite the worry he felt.

Uncle Kenny adjusted his University of Alabama baseball cap as he said, "What do you think about the team this year? Did you hear about the new running back? I think we've got a real shot at the SEC West."

I stood by and listened, but wasn't able to contribute much to the conversation. My thoughts were still with Denise and Colonel Pershall. I put the slim phone in my shorts pocket and pulled my thoughts back to the scene in front of me. Abby would call if anything changed. Right now, I had to concentrate on the reunion.

I tried to remember what I'd learned about Uncle Kenny and Aunt Gwen during last year's reunion. I knew they'd cornered the market on roadside boiled peanut stands. They loved the Crimson Tide and were extremely competitive. The volleyball game at the reunion last year had been as hard fought as an Olympic match with Uncle Kenny and Aunt Gwen captaining the two teams. I also remembered that Mitch said they'd wanted to paint the trim on their house crimson earlier this summer, but regulations in their subdivision had forced them to limit the crimson to their front door. I was too shaken to figure out how to work any of those topics into the conversation, so I was relieved to see Mitch's mom, Caroline, walk up with a droopy Nathan snuggled into the crook of her arm.

Caroline was an interesting mixture of reticence and southern charm. She could fold a fitted sheet so that it looked like a flat sheet and that fact alone intimidated me. She wore the same Avery Family Reunion T-shirt we were all wearing, but on her it looked stylish. She'd gathered the hem of the shirt and fastened it through a clip above her trim hip. The clip matched her heavy silver earrings, which set off her silvery white hair that swung against her jawbone as she swayed back and forth to keep Nathan dozy. Despite the heat, she looked as fresh as she did when she stepped out of the car this morning at the end of our driveway, carrying her famous peach pies and homemade rolls.

"Are you okay, Ellie? You look a little pale."

I followed Mitch's lead and said, "I'm fine. We just got a call with some bad news about a friend in the hospital." I left it at that. There was no need to trouble everyone at the reunion with the terrible news.

"That's a shame. I hope there's a quick recovery."

"Thanks, I hope so, too. Looks like Nathan is ready for a nap." There's nothing like my kids to keep me grounded and in the moment. I ran my hand down his limp, plump arm. Lately, he'd been boycotting naps, but he needed one today.

"Would you mind if I put him down?" Caroline asked, and I said not at all. Then she said, "Thank you so much for hosting the reunion this year. Everything's been lovely. With the remodel, there's no way we could have done it."

"Glad we could help out. It was nothing."

I heard what sounded like a snort from Mitch and leveled my gaze at him, but he kept his attention fixed on Uncle Kenny, who was saying, "The secret to winning at croquet is all in the order of play . . ."

"Nonsense," Caroline said. "I know how much work this is and you've pulled it off beautifully." Uncle Kenny noticed some of the guys setting up a game of horseshoes and went to join them. Mitch fell into step beside me as Caroline and I walked back to the house. One of Mitch's cousins-in-law, Felicity, nearly ran over us as she marched across the grass.

"Felicity," Caroline called, "I haven't seen Dan. Where is he?"

"Gone. He's never around anymore. I should have known better than to assume he'd skip his jog during the family reunion."

"Oh, so that was him I saw trotting down the driveway earlier? I thought it was you, Mitch," Caroline said. "You boys always have looked so much alike—same dark hair and eyes. And, you're both tall and lanky."

"I was going to run with him, but I'm not feeling one hundred percent." Mitch rubbed his hand over his stomach. "I know I couldn't keep up with him in this humidity." Unlike in so many conversations I'd had today when I had no clue about who was being discussed, I actually knew Mitch's cousin Dan. He and his wife, Felicity, had arrived yesterday and spent the night at our house. Almost everyone else, including Mitch's parents, had driven in earlier in the day.

"I knew we shouldn't have left Aunt Christine's potato salad in the sun so long," I said, but Mitch waved his hand and said, "It's nothing like that. Too much food, probably."

"Are you boys enjoying catching up with each other?" Caroline asked. Mitch said they were and Caroline turned toward me. "They got in more scrapes growing up. Have you heard about the time they hid on the roof all afternoon to avoid Summer?" Caroline asked, referring to Mitch's younger sister.

"That was the time you called the police when you couldn't find them?" I was glad Nathan was too young to pick up any details of his dad's misdeeds.

"Amazing that I can laugh about it now, isn't it, Mitch?" Caroline said.

"It's amazing I can even talk about it," Mitch countered. "Besides one heck of a sunburn, I couldn't sit down for about a week."

"Dan's not nearly as much fun now," Felicity said crossly. "Unless you're discussing the new spin class or weightlifting, forget it. You might as well be speaking a foreign language to him." With her brows lowered and jaw clenched, she reminded me of the dark thunderhead clouds I'd seen as a kid in the Texas panhandle.

Actually, comparing her to a thunderhead was a bit incongruous, since she was petite and skinny. Correction, she wasn't just thin, she was toned. There was barely an ounce of fat on her, except maybe in her cheekbones above her pert nose and pointed chin. With curly brown hair cropped short in a boyish style, she looked every inch the athlete she was. A fitness instructor at a gym in Montgomery, she taught Pilates, spinning, yoga, aerobics, and a scary-sounding class called Killer Boot Camp. Felicity continued, "Sorry he talked so much last night about his metabolism."

"Well, he is training for a triathlon," Mitch said mildly.

Felicity rolled her eyes. "I get that at work all day. Workouts and fitness are the last things I want to talk about at home."

A squeaky voice called out, "Felicity! Felicity! Watch me!" Livvy, in her pink ruffled swimsuit, waved frantically at us from the wading pool.

I said, "Sorry she's been pestering you so much." Five-year-old Livvy had taken an instant liking to Felicity. Felicity had hardly stepped through our front door before Livvy was dragging her by the hand down the hall to show off her stuffed animals. She'd practically been Felicity's shadow all day. I was glad Livvy's shyness had vanished, but I didn't want her driving Felicity crazy, either.

Mitch and his mom continued up the porch steps and into the house while Felicity and I stopped by a group of birch trees to watch Livvy. She dog-paddled around the tiny pool, then checked our reaction. "Great job," Felicity shouted as she leaned against the tree trunk. One of Livvy's cousins splashed into the pool and drew her attention away from us. Felicity said, "She's not pestering me. Actually, it's given me an excuse to get away from Jenny."

I was thankful that only one of Dan's freshly divorced parents had been able to come to the reunion. His dad was somewhere in Indiana, running a weekend seminar for corporate managers. "If Jenny says the word *green* one more time, I'm going to scream," Felicity continued. "Her whole save-the-earth thing is driving me crazy. I can't believe she gave up a great job to start a 'lifestyle cleansing' business."

Jenny's announcement that she'd quit her job as a CPA and started a business that helped companies and individuals become more ecologically friendly had caused a stir this morning. She'd even bypassed wearing the family reunion T-shirt because it wasn't made with pesticide-free cotton and nontoxic dye. Felicity said, "I've always known she was weird. I mean, she actually *likes* jigsaw puzzles. That told